ELEMENTS

VOLUME III:

BURNING HOPES

WILLIAM RICHARDS

STALKING P ART

ELEMENTS Volume 3

Copyright © 2023 William Richards

Cover art by: Stalking P

Inner book art by: Stalking P

Edited by: Tyler Marshall

For permission requests, contact:

Authorwilliamrichards@gmail.com

ISBN – 978-1-7774734-4-0

https://authorwilliamricha.wixsite.com/williamrichards

https://www.stalkingp.com/

10 9 8 7 6 5 4 3 2 1

Know that you are never truly alone in life.

CHAPTER 1
WHAT THE FUTURE HOLDS

CRISP FALL AIR SWIRLED AS THE AUTUMN SEASON rounded into form. The sun beamed down through the changing leaves of the surrounding forest.

"I've got you this time!"

A golden ball of light like the sun buried itself in the dirt covered arena. Then with a bang, the blast erupted sending dirt flying through the ripples in the air. Birds fled from the treetops of the forest as the boy landed back on his toes. He paused, letting the golden waves that swirled around his body fade.

He fought to catch his breath while sweat dripped off the tips of his dishevelled blond hair. The white and red shirt and shorts he wore were covered with patches of dirt and a multitude of rips. Through the smoke, he fixed his round emerald eyes on the silhouette standing firm in front of him.

"You're still hesitating, Minisc. Focus, remember the power you used to defeat Dusk. Draw on those emotions, let them fuel you." The man spoke in a firm but calm voice. A heroic voice. He puffed his chest out and shaped up causing the dust and smoke to evaporate instantly. Even after Minisc's massive blast, the man stood in all of his glory without a scratch on him. Of course, when training with the Hero of Light, expecting things to be easy would be foolish. Something Minisc knew all too well.

The word easy was not part of Don Premier's vocabulary. As the world's greatest champion and undisputed strongest Elementalist, the man always took the path less travelled. Which, for Minisc, meant he would be forced to do the same. Especially with the wealth of untapped potential his father still saw in him.

Three months had passed since the city of Toronto, one of the most highly populated Elementalist cities in the world, found itself in grave danger. The leader of Luminosa, Dusk, returned from the injuries dealt to him in his first fight with The Hero of Light, to fulfill his ultimate plan of revenge. Through the elimination of Humans, he would create an Elementalist kingdom where peace and unity would finally be achieved. Because of his actions, the city suffered massive damage and heavy losses, but when push came to shove, the world's champion arrived to rescue them once again. Or at least that's how the story went. For a select few, they knew the role Minisc played, standing by his father in the titanic battle. He was an integral part of putting the tyrannical leader behind bars for good.

But at the request of Minisc, the mention of his acts had been wiped from history. Not out of a noble humility, but simply to keep some peace and anonymity in his life.

The power Minisc displayed against Dusk was a rare feat from any Elementalist, but not a surprise to his father. From the first day Don started training his son, he could see the hidden potential laying dormant. For Don, knowing the city was at peace wasn't enough. He wanted to make sure Minisc continued to train to reach the full potential of his powers. He knew their fight against Luminosa was far from over.

Minisc caught his breath, holding his hands up in the sky ready to begin again, but after a second, he dropped them to his sides. "Nope, I can't... my arms are like jelly," he sheepishly laughed. Their extensive afternoon training started hours ago and Minisc was running on fumes.

"Maybe you're right, it's been over two hours. No point in continuing if you can only go at half-speed."

Minisc nodded, putting his hands on his knees. Each deep gasp filled his lungs modestly helping take away the aches from his chest. He looked up at his father, seeing the majestic glow fade from the man's body.

"Are you sure you're getting weaker? Because frankly, it doesn't feel like it. We've been at this for weeks and I still can't land a single hit on you."

Don nodded, walking up to his son and placing his large hand on the boy's shoulder, "Yeah, I'm sure."

Most people believed the Hero of Light was an infallible entity. A man whose unprecedented power would never fade from this world. And for Don, that was the way he wanted it. Society would sleep better with such hope. But unfortunately, that couldn't be further from the truth.

Each day that passed, and every time Don tried to draw on the same power that once made him invincible, his body refused the demand more and more. Perhaps Minisc struggled to notice the subtle changes, but for Don they were unmistakable. First, when protecting his son and friends in the Tournament of Elements, the skirmish pushed him well past his limits and showed his decline, but more recently when facing off with Dusk. If not for Minisc coming to the rescue, he would have faced bitter death.

Because of Don's fading power and the potential threat of Dusk's apprentice, Brooklyn still on the loose, he knew Minisc was the next chosen Hero. The one with the power to hold the peace. However, placing such a burden on his son alone would never do. So, until he had nothing left he would continue to honour his title as the Hero of Light as best he could.

The Premier household was on the outskirts of the city, not that everyone didn't know where their hero lived. The small, one-story home backed onto a large lush forest in which Minisc and his father spent most of their time training. The home was quaint, and at a glance, nobody would've thought it belonged to such an icon.

After returning home Minisc sat at the kitchen table wafting in the sweet scent of pancakes as his father cooked a few feet away from him. Breakfast was one of the few reasons Minisc endured the brutal training. As with most teenagers, he hated early mornings.

Frankly, some days the thought of having his father cook him a delicious breakfast was the only motivation to wake up to train so early.

Once the meal was prepared, Minisc took a big bite of his well-earned reward, letting the soft, fluffy texture dance on his tongue. He savoured the sweetness, feeling the aches and pains of his battered body fade to the background.

Don took a seat around the small wooden table enjoying the peaceful silence as he readied to join his son in breakfast. Unfortunately, such bliss was short lived when a familiar hymn that sounded like wind chimes began singing from the countertop behind them. Don looked at his son, expecting him to leap for the device but Minisc simply shrugged.

"Don't look at me. My phone's in my room. Must be yours," Minisc said, taking a hefty bite of his food.

"That's odd, the only one who would call me is-" Don walked over and picked up his phone, "Zale?"

"Sorry to call so early this morning but you did ask me to let you know when we were ready... well, we're ready. I can send a driver to you in an hour... but are you sure you want to do this? I mean I don't think it's exactly gonna be amicable."

"I know, but if it's only me he wants to talk to then we don't have much choice. Besides, Humans are disappearing almost every day and we haven't been able to find a trace of them. And as long as Brooklyn is still out there, Luminosa's plans continue."

Don glanced over at his son. Although Don knew his son held the power to beat Luminosa, there was still a long way for him to go. He was just a kid, after all. Added to that, Don still believed his obligation as the Hero of Light was to fight until he had nothing left.

After the battle against Dusk, Don finally sat down with his son and explained everything. His dwindling power and how soon he would lack the power to fight Luminosa. The news shocked Minisc at first, but over time he came to accept the fact. From then on, he began working harder, knowing even though his father didn't outright say it, it was now his duty to take up the man's battle against Luminosa.

Minisc, however, was far too entranced in his food to pay attention to his father.

Once the conversation finished, Don took a seat beside his son and said, "Looks like we're gonna have to skip training this afternoon. I'm going to Penatang for most of the day."

Minisc finally halted his eating and raised an eyebrow, "Penatang? Penatang Jail? Why would you be going there?"

"Zale has me doing some EC stuff. I'm sure it's nothing big." Don played off the question knowing the matter was not that simple.

"Um, okay... well that's fine I guess, Lily and Jules wanted to see Ms. Wright today about this Elemental Council-Elemental Academy collaboration program anyways. I guess while they rebuild the school, they want all the students to take on some sort of volunteer role with the EC."

Since Elemental Academy was heavily damaged in Luminosa's attacks, the school would not start for a few more months. With that and so much of the city needing help rebuilding, the governing branch for Elementalists, the Elemental Council, came up with a way to provide real-life experience even without a school to attend.

Don nodded in agreement, "That's not a bad idea. If you three are gonna be off school for the next few months, at least this will let you be productive. Plus, it might even break up the monotony of training every day."

Minisc smiled, "That's the hope."

Waves crashed up against the cliffside and rain drizzled down at a frantic pace, a far cry from the warm, sunny morning Don enjoyed a few hours ago. He stepped out of the long black vehicle before popping open an umbrella. He stared up at the looming building that touched the sky. Penatang.

On the other side of the Fairhall Bridge and in the middle of the lake stood Penatang Jail. Since most jails were not readily equipped to hold the more dangerous and powerful Elementalist criminals, a special high-security prison was built. Over time, it became a place for the scum of the earth Humans to be placed as well. The requirements to be sent to such a horrid place were nothing less than a death sentence by the justice systems, a sign the city had been cleaned up greatly since the communion between Humans and Elementalists strengthened.

For Don, many years had passed since his last visit, possibly even before Minisc was born. And for good reason. Plenty of the *patrons* would have a bone to pick with him.

Blocking his way were reinforced steel gates that stretched thirty feet high. At each corner of the rectangular building stood multiple guards, armed to the teeth and large spotlights that danced back and forth making sure all areas were visible. Not only were there Human guards with guns and ammunition at the ready, but some of the best students to come out of EA would go on to work security at Penatang as well.

Don walked up to the unmovable doors, waiting for someone to greet him. Without EC-mandated access, nobody got in, and nobody got out. Exactly the way it needed to be.

A minute later, the doors began to screech open and much to Don's surprise a tinge of nerves befell him. Of course, coming to such a gut-wrenching place could cause that reaction.

From behind the doors, a young timid voice pulled Don out of his fears. The man, who looked only a few years older than Minisc, walked down the gravel path and through the gates. He wore a long, white and red jacket with gold trim that fell past his knees. The uniform let Don know he was part of the EC. Normally, that would not be an unusual sight, but because the uniforms of everyone working in Penatang were full black, he stood out.

The man stumbled up to Don and took a deep bow letting his ash brown hair fall in front of his eyes.

"Hello, Hero of Light," the man said with the utmost respect. His voice contained a hint of excitement though. When he looked back up Don could see a glimmer in the man's cobalt eyes, which suggested he was relatively new to the job.

Don extended his hand to the young man, "Please, Don is fine, thanks."

"Oh, okay... well, hello Don. I'm Marshall Donavon." The two exchanged a handshake, but after letting go Marshall continued to admire his palm. He was fighting the internal trembling from joy, trying to remain cool.

"Good to meet you, Marshall. I take it by your uniform you're one of Zale's men?"

"Just as perceptive as one would expect from the Hero of Light." Marshall grinned. "President Osiris left me in charge of seeing you into the building while he took care of some other business."

The two stood in silence for a moment, before Don broke it. "Well, here I am... so shall we?" He hated to come off as rude to a prospective fan, but he could tell Marshall was getting distracted by the man's presence. Unfortunately, his visit came with a level of urgency that could not be excused.

Marshall started waving his hands back and forth realizing his mistake, "Right right, please follow me." He turned around and retraced his steps matching the urgency Don had. They reached the first door, and he punched an extensive code into the keypad. A small series of beeps played, and the doors slid open.

The first floor of Penatang was nothing to write home about. The walls and floors were white cement and the only way through was straight. However, getting into the main floors of Penatang required passing through another security gate, which two other workers carefully patrolled. They were in charge of the bullet tunnel, which was an advanced elevator that could travel to every section of Penatang in quick order.

Marshall approached the two other workers before taking another shorter bow. On his left, behind a small desk sat another man of similar age, and walking back and forth was a young woman. Neither of them bothered to bow back or acknowledge Marshall's greeting. But when they caught a glimpse of Don their attitudes changed in a hurry.

"You... you're the... Hero of Light," The woman gawked.

The man hopped out of his chair, pulling a thin notebook out of his jacket pocket, clearly used for noting disruptions or issues on the job. He hurried up to Don and said, "Mr. Hero, can I have your autograph, you're the reason I joined the EC in the first place. You're my idol."

"Come on guys, leave Mr. Premier alone, he's here on official business for President Osiris, he doesn't have time for autographs," Marshall said, attempting to play things cool, despite his actions a minute earlier.

"What? With you? Why would President Osiris give you that job?" The woman backed.

"Yeah, what makes you so special? He should have picked me," The man said, turning to jab a finger in Marshall's chest. The timid boy stepped back putting his hands up in mercy until Don adjusted his throat.

"Look guys, I would love to sign autographs for you, but this is a rather urgent issue and we need to get to cellblock D-27 right away." The orders were kind, but he made sure to put some emphasis on his request as well.

The man and woman both bolted upright saluting to their idol while saying, "Yes sir, Hero sir, right away." The woman walked back over to the desk and started typing away. Once she finished, the oval doors at the end of the hall opened wide.

"Thank you," Don nodded as he headed for his next destination.

Inside the elevator, Don sat on the left bench while Marshall sat on the right. They were patiently waiting for the ride to start. Because of the multiple elevators travelling all over the building at once, sometimes a five-minute wait was necessary for what would otherwise be a 30-second trip. While they were waiting Marshall kept his head down. His jovial smile and excitement of seeing the Hero of Light were distant memories. It wasn't hard to tell the words of his fellow EC members were digging at his heart.

"So..." Don started awkwardly, "Do you know those two?" Admittedly, the relationship of the three was none of his business, but as a beacon of hope, he wanted to help people, not just from tangible danger, but from mental struggles as well.

Marshall folded his hands in his lap before looking up, "Yeah, their names are Tara and Kurt. We all attended EA together. But when everyone graduated, they were number 1 and 2 in the class. They dominated everything through our 4 years, and I could never come close to keeping up. But when President Osiris came to speak to our class before graduation, he seemed to take a shine to me. Frankly, I don't know why. I didn't graduate with honours, I only participated in the Tournament of Elements once and even then, I lost in the first round, and there's nothing special about me. I'll certainly never be a hero like you." Marshall turned his head down to stare at his feet, slumping his shoulders.

"You know Marshall, I don't know about the other two, but what I do know is Zale doesn't take a shine to just anyone. I've known him longer than you've probably been alive and let me tell you, every choice he makes is deliberate and holds purpose. If he chose you to work so closely alongside him, then it means he sees something great in you that he doesn't necessarily see in others. So even if you don't feel like you've earned it, put your trust in him. I promise you're in good hands."

The words lifted Marshall's spirits and when he raised his head that jubilant smile returned once again. "Thanks, Don. That means a lot coming from you."

Shortly after, the elevator came to a screeching halt and Marshall led the way into another small waiting room. The cell D waiting hall. Much like before, they were in a long narrow hallway, but this time instead of one door at the end, there were many different branching paths to take. Each one led to a maximum security cell.

From a room to the left stepped out Zale. As per usual, his short brown hair was neatly combed and his lavish suit and tie without a crease in it. A pristine look for a man of such high authority.

"There you are," Zale said. He looked at Marshall and gave a mild smile, "Thank you for escorting Mr. Premier, Marshall. You're free to go back to your post now."

"Yes sir." Marshall saluted before turning back to Don and giving a small bow. "It was nice to meet you Don... and thanks for the advice." Taking his encouragement with him, Marshall took his leave.

With pleasantries out of the way, Don wasted no time getting down to business. "Where is he?"

"Follow me." Zale led the way down the futuristic looking hallway and around the corner.

As they walked, Zale said, "You know this is a bad idea right. He's just trying to get in your head and nothing more."

"I'm aware, but if he were to slip up, perhaps he could give us a hint as to Brooklyn's location. We find him, we probably find these missing people as well."

As they kept walking, small trepidation crept into Don's mind. Once again, he was heading in to face his greatest nemesis. At least this time, the villain would be restrained with the highest security equipment known to man. But a lingering trauma remained.

Down through an elevator they went before exiting into a dark room. Inside sat a man in front of six different screens that created a wall of videos. On his left was a large window that peered down into the cell below.

First, Don looked at the display of monitors. From all different angles, he could see a pale, frail man, his bald head filled with various scars. The black cloak he wore hung off his body, showing the loss in muscular definition from over the years. He was heavily secured to a chair, where he could not move of his own accord. He looked to be clinging to life, a sight that almost made Don feel pity. Almost.

"Have you tried talking to him at all today?" Zale asked, turning to the only other man in the room besides Don.

"We told him the Hero of Light was coming at his request. He showed no emotion from the info," The man replied.

"Alright, Don, follow me." Zale waved his hand and led Don to a small elevator carved into an alcove in the room. They dropped down a floor and after they came to a stop Don felt a palpable disgust grip him. A lingering sense of evil. It sent chills to his core.

Lights turned on in the room and Don found himself on the other side of a large pane of glass. He looked at the debilitated man who could only move what remained of his eyes, looking up.

"Dusk..." Don whispered.

"Hero of Light... it's been far too long since our last acquaintance." Dusk spoke in a soft, raspy, voice letting out a cough as he ended his sentence.

"Not long enough."

"Ahh, still bitter in your defeat I see..." The man's feeble cockiness irked Don. He gripped his fist, knowing the pane of glass would stop them from returning to blows.

"You haven't won, Dusk. We're closing in on Brooklyn, and when he's stuck in here with you, it will all be over."

"Is that so? Do you think bringing him closer to me would be wise?"

The comment took Don by surprise, unable to tell if Dusk was mocking him, or being serious.

"You're nothing but a shell of yourself... your strength can't aid him."

"Perhaps you are right, my body has grown too weak. Despite my attempt to return to my former glory, there is no going back. A fate you know all too well I am sure... and now here I sit, chained up like an animal. Even the slightest twitch and these guns placed around the room will have me killed. Such savagery only those of the Human race could pull off."

"You brought this on yourself. Now quit the games, I know you're behind the missing people around the city."

"Missing Humans? Whatever do you mean? I've been in here since our fateful battle. How could I possibly be behind such a thing?" The man's hoarse voice came off as genuine, but Don didn't bite.

"I know Luminosa is behind this. You might try to pass Brooklyn off as your apprentice, but you can't fool me, you're pulling all the strings. I might not know how you're doing it, but I know you're behind this," Don growled, about to continue with his hopeful interrogation, but Dusk spoke first.

"Tell me, Hero, was it worth it?"

"Was what worth it?"

"Accelerating the clock as the Hero of Light. We both understand the toll of using... what do you call it again, Celestial Light? We both knew using such a powerful technique would eventually lead to you losing that strength."

Don stood quietly looking down for a moment. "Yeah, it was worth it. If it meant stopping you, then I'd gladly make that sacrifice. And even so, it's clear the toll of using Mr. Howland's technique has left you frail and defeated as well. You hold no strength left in that body of yours. I know you wanted to use Dr. Jarrad's experiments in hopes of restoring your power, but that has failed all the same."

"Perhaps, but that's quite alright I assure you."

"Because of Brooklyn... even in your comatose state all those years, you've been training him. Using him to ensure that your sociopathic ideals live on even while you rot away in here."

"Perceptive aren't we, Hero? You are right, young Brooklyn possesses a power that even I could not draw upon. Stored inside him is the key to new world order."

"Not as long as I have anything to say about it he won't. I'll find where your puppet is hiding, and I'll stop him, just the way I did with you." Don looked up with a fire in his eyes. He stared down the monster who caused so much pain to the world and its people. But never again.

"Hmm, even if it means leaving such a burden to your son?" Dusk posed it as an innocent question, but his intent to needle Don was clear.

"..."

"You know it too. He carries that same latent power in him that you and I once did. No doubt he could learn to master Celestial Light just as we had... but perhaps there is still doubt in you... could it be because you know Brooklyn carries the same abilities in him... no that's not it, it's the fear of losing your only son... the worry that now you will not be able to protect him any longer. By having him learn the technique you are leading him directly into harm's way... how does it feel to know his blood will be on your hands?"

"That's enough!" Don finally barked back.

"Touched a nerve did I... too bad you can't strike me down from behind that glass. It appears once again you are at the mercy of those around you." Dusk let out a weak but mocking cough.

Don took a deep breath, letting the anger flow out of him before he spoke again. "You know the truth. The two of us lack the power to settle our differences any longer. No matter the paths that are taken, destiny will always come to fruition."

"That it will..."

Before Don could retort, a buzzer went off behind him, then Zale's voice came through the speaker.

"That's enough Don." The door behind him opened as the elevator arrived.

Don turned to glance at the elevator and then took one last look at his mortal enemy, "I won't let your plans come to fruition, Dusk. I promise you that. I'll put a stop to all of this once and for all, long before my son is involved." He stepped into the elevator given no time to think back on his brief but pointed conversation. As expected, it lacked much information on their current investigation, but perhaps it was more informative than Don realized.

Zale stood on the other side of the elevator with his arms crossed. As Don stepped out, Zale said, "Well that was strange. It almost sounded like he admitted his own defeat."

"He knows as well as I do that by using Celestial Light, it would eventually degrade our bodies over time. He's helpless." Don took one last look at the security cameras. The cold deformed body of Dusk who returned to his head down position showed a man resided to his fate. "However, that makes our need to find Brooklyn even more pressing."

CHAPTER 2
CHOICES AND DECISIONS

FROM THE BATTLES WITH LUMINOSA, ELEMENTAL Academy suffered irreversible damage. Due to those events, all students and faculty were placed on temporary leave while the school underwent construction. It would only take a few months thankfully.

However, that didn't mean the students were given free time to slack off. As the developers for the next crop of EC members, all teachers were tasked with assigning students to help different parts of the city's rebuilding efforts. Since the EC oversaw the monumental project, it gave students real life everyday experience and helped restore the city as well.

Fortunately for Minisc and his friends, they were given a few months of grace to recoup and rest after their heroism in the fight against Dusk. All of them could use it, but for Minisc in particular, the layoff refreshed him. Now his vacation was over, though, it was time to start a new adventure.

Minisc sat patiently on what remained of the shattered concrete steps of EA. He leaned back wafting in the scent of the fresh autumn flowers nearby. He continued to think about the decisions that lay in front of him. Of course, that was the reason he returned to EA in the first place. He wanted the advice of his teacher.

Ms. Wright had a reputation throughout EA as the toughest and strictest teacher around, but she was also filled with knowledge, even if her advice came with a death stare to boot. But regardless of exteriors, Minisc knew she could help point him in the right direction.

Unlike him, Jules already knew what his goals were. Since childhood, he'd dreamed of working in the EC alongside his brother Yuri. Although the once-famous Elementalist lost his powers thanks to a Luminosa virus, everyone in the EC held the man in such high respect that Zale made it a point to keep him involved. Still part of the EC, Yuri now did far more detective work investigating crime scenes rather than standing on the front lines and fighting. However, for Jules, it was enough of an opportunity to fulfill his dream that he didn't care what the work entailed.

For Lily, she wanted to help all the people who were displaced from the fighting. Many homes suffered damage from Luminosa or rogue Elementalists, and because of that, they were placed in large shelters for a few months as the rebuild continued. When it came to missing school time, Lily was the most disappointed of the three friends, but as she often did, she accepted her reality and faced it with a smile.

Each of them had some semblance of a clear path when it came to work, but for Minisc a few questions remained. Minisc was still searching.

For a student at the end of his first year, Minisc had not only demonstrated incredible power as an Elementalists but maturity and fearlessness beyond compare as he stared down the greatest evil the world had to offer. Most assumed he had nothing left to learn, but with that power he was still raw as an Elementalists. Thinking along those lines he was being tugged in two directions. The first was an offer that came from Zale Osiris himself to be on the front lines capturing the top criminals in the city, a role his father excelled at, or second, to join Lily in the rebuilding efforts of the city while helping uphold the ideals of his mother, a woman who believed with all her heart that Humans and Elementalists could live together in unity.

As much as he wanted to continue upholding that dream, he'd learned a valuable lesson when facing Dusk. Although fighting was never his first option, for him to maintain the peace his mother strived for, it meant he would have to be as strong as possible.

Defeating a severely crippled Dusk with the help of his father was one thing, but alone, against someone matching the calibre of Dusk in his prime, Minisc knew he wouldn't stand a chance.

Stuck in thought, Minisc heard his name called.

"Hey, Minisc." He looked down to see Jules waving to him as he started up the steps. The maroon-haired boy gave a cheerful smile. He wore clothes that eerily matched that of an EC uniform, but of course, it was far from official with no markings on it.

"Well look who decided to finally show up," Minisc laughed, "Took you long enough. I've been sitting here for almost twenty minutes."

"Yeah, my bad. I got caught up talking to Yuri and missed the first train..." Jules rubbed the back of his neck with a sheepish smile. He took a seat beside his friend before saying, "Where's Lily, did she get annoyed and go on without us?"

"I don't think so, but she hasn't answered me all morning. Which is weird considering this was her idea in the first place."

Jules chuckled, "Yeah, and I don't think Ms. Wright has any interest in talking to just the two of us."

Minisc joined in the chuckle. They both knew despite their teacher's crusty exterior that she only wanted and expected the best from her students. When it came to Minisc and Jules though, she had always been particularly crusty, mostly because of how often they found themselves in trouble.

Jules leaned back. "We should probably give her a few minutes, you know how mad she'd be if we left without her."

"True, I'd prefer not to catch the wrath of an angry Lily today," Minisc joked.

"And why would you be catching my wrath?" A sweet voice asked from the bottom of the steps. Minisc and Jules turned their attention to Lily. She was eying them sharply. Hands in the pockets of her new autumn dress. Her chestnut brown hair flowed slightly through the breeze.

"No reason, we were just waiting for you, that's all," Jules laughed.

"Sorry, I was just finishing some errands this morning."

"It's fine, Jules wasn't exactly early," Minisc mocked, "but now that we're here, we should probably get going, I'd rather not keep Ms. Wright waiting."

The inside of the school was far from what they were used to. It mirrored a construction zone more than a place of education. When the group walked through the cafeteria, workers were standing on tall ladders hammering away at the railing which used to belong to the second-floor balcony.

"I know I haven't been here in months but man this place looks like a dump," Jules joked.

"Yeah, Lily, you really did a number on this place. And here I was thinking Jules and I would be the ones to end up destroying the school."

Lily smacked Minisc in the arm before pursing her lips. "Don't you try to blame this on me. It was Luminosa's fault."

"I know I know," Minisc said, rubbing his now-sore arm. "Still, it does feel like it's been a long time since we've actually been here."

Minisc paused, thinking about the last three months. For him, they were mostly a blur. He'd spent much of his free time rehabbing the injuries sustained while fighting Dusk, but that was not all. Due to him becoming infected with Luminosa's element-erasing virus, and more so for taking an unproven vaccine created in haste to negate the effects, he had to undergo constant testing for side effects of the vaccine. Luckily for him, he harboured no ill effects and appeared to suffer no consequences regarding his element. Through his testing, the EC even managed to mass produce and vaccinate Elementalists rendering Luminosa's virus useless.

When all the memories came rushing back to him, and he continued to see the destruction of areas like his school, the EC and so many other places it still caused his heart to sink.

Although Minisc's time at EA started rockily, he'd created many fond memories in that year of school, from meeting Lily to watching Jules struggle with math homework, to training with his teacher. Those were simpler times, and times he wished to be in again.

"Are you coming Minisc?" Lily asked as she looked back, noticing the boy lagging.

"Oh," Minisc snapped out his funk picking up his pace, "Yeah I'm coming."

Only one part of the school had avoided significant damage, the back half of the fourth-floor classrooms. For the time being all the teacher's offices were placed in the area, although most were rarely around unless called upon. They were helping in the rebuild efforts of the school as well.

"Well, this is it," Jules said standing in front of the steel door. It had a small name plate at the top indicating the office was currently Ms. Wright's.

Minisc and Jules looked at each other, neither making a move for the handle.

Jules muttered, "So... you wanna knock...?"

"What, I'm not knocking, you knock," Minisc countered.

Lily groaned, rolling her eyes. "You two are ridiculous." She stepped between them and softly knocked on the door with the side of her knuckle.

"Yeah, easy for you to say, she actually likes you," Jules sulked.

The door flew open a second later and standing in the frame was a middle-aged woman with curled, copper hair and fancy business clothes. She wore her traditional hardened scowl but after seeing Lily her crusty exterior faded into a smile. At least as much of a smile as the woman could muster.

"Nice of you three to finally show up," the teacher said directing her comments at Minisc and Jules in particular. "Come on in. There isn't a lot of room, but we'll make do." She turned on a heel and started walking into her office, high heels clicking loudly off the tiled floor.

Lily followed without hesitation, but Minisc and Jules exchanged a look. They nodded in solidarity and headed in.

As Ms. Wright had alluded, her new office was barely big enough for all four of them. The teacher sat at her desk in the corner, while the three friends sat squished together in front of her. It wasn't as much that the room was so small, but there were boxes and boxes of papers stacked around the room shrinking it considerably. Even Ms. Wright's desk had stacks of paper on it.

"What's with all the paperwork?" Jules asked. He was having flashbacks of his summer working with Yuri. At least this time he would be of use, and not filling our reports all day.

"Every box in here is different class forms the faculty must sign to say that you students are competent and responsible enough to work with the EC while the school is under construction." Ms. Wright sighed in defeat. She grabbed the stack of papers and moved it off her desk. Then she raised an eyebrow, "However, through all these request forms there appears to be three that are still missing."

"Well, that's why we came actually," Lily started, "President Osiris gave Jules and me some time to recover from the events over the past few months, and Minisc has been rehabbing almost every day. But now we're ready to help. Only thing is that means we've got to make some decisions."

Ms. Wright looked to Jules first, the obvious of the three, "I take it you already know what your plan is, correct?" She along with everyone else knew what Jules' dreams were.

Jules hesitated, the tone of his teacher presented the question as a trap, but he was willing to take the bait regardless. "Yep, I'm going to join my brother and work in his new detective branch." He had a grin just as he always did when he talked about working with his brother.

"I figured as much." Ms. Wright grabbed a couple of forms and handed them to Jules. "Fill out these papers and bring them back to me tomorrow. You can start as soon as everything is returned."

After Jules stuffed the permission slips into his backpack the attention turned to Minisc and Lily.

Ms. Wright asked, "And what about you two?"

Lily spoke first, "I haven't decided myself yet, but I was hoping

I could help some of the people affected by Luminosa. I was doing some research and I know there are a couple of shelters run by the EC that could use volunteer support. If I could help those who were displaced from their homes because of Luminous I would like that."

"Hmm," Ms. Wright held her bony finger to her chin. She tapped it a few times before speaking. "I do know the shelters you're referring to. One in particular near the north end of the city could really use an extra pair of hands to keep it running. I think that would be a good place for you to go, your enthusiasm and kindness will be a great help to those forced to live there for the time being."

"That's wonderful, thank you."

With his two friends set on their choices, the attention turned to Minisc. Ms. Wright shot him a look but said nothing. So Minisc filled the silence himself.

"Yeah, I have no idea... I've been so busy rehabbing and being poked and prodded by doctors that I haven't given it a ton of thought. I was actually hoping maybe you could point me in the right direction."

"Well, seeing as you are relatively fresh from recovery, I would suggest for the time being that perhaps you join Lily at the shelter. The work will be far less taxing than what you've been through, and it will give you some time to let your body fully heal from your fight with Dusk."

All three of their jaws dropped to the ground.

"How do you...?" Minisc had been assured nobody outside his friends and the highest of EC officials knew of his role.

"I have a sister, you know..." Ms. Wright gave them a sly smile as Minisc exhaled a sigh of relief before getting back on track.

"Do you mind if I take the night to think about it?" Minisc asked.

"Of course, take the weekend, see how your body feels and maybe talk it over with your father. Let me know Monday what you want to do, and I'll sign off on it." As was often the case, Ms. Wright knew when to pull back her strict persona and help her students. A knack Minisc greatly appreciated.

With pleasantries done and goodbyes said, the three headed for the train station. Some decisions had been made, but Minisc still wondered about his course. Was he to help out at the shelters, where he could no doubt ease the burden of those affected by Luminosa, or did he join Jules and prepare for a role that would help him sharpen his skills and prepare for his father's eventual retirement?

As multiple trains pulled into each side of the station Lily finally asked, "What's wrong, Minisc?"

"Yeah, this is exciting news. And it's better than all the rehabbing, right?" Jules added.

"I know, it's just... a lot to think about. It feels like everything's been happening so fast. It's hard to believe it's already been three months since we beat Dusk."

Lily grabbed Minisc's arm wrapping her own around his.

"I know what you mean, time really has flown by lately. It's a lot to take in. I think Ms. Wright was right, you should run things by your father. He knows better than any of us what it's like to work with the EC after all."

"Maybe you're right..."

Later that night, Minisc leaned back on the front porch of his home. He took deep breaths letting the fresh forest scent fill his lungs. The sun began to cast a beautiful orange hue over the front yard giving it a sense of serenity that helped clear his mind. But there was one pressing issue that continued to stick in his head, but he struggled to talk about it with anyone.

Those involved in the fights against Luminosa were focused on Brooklyn, who disappeared at the orders of Dusk, and the rest of the core group had been arrested and locked up, but there was one lesser-known member who managed to escape that night. A person Minisc knew could cause as much destruction as any Elementalist around.

Ignis.

His childhood friend turned enemy never turned up on any criminal reports, and there was no word from the EC on his whereabouts, but Minisc knew better. Ignis chose his side. The side of evil, and wherever Luminosa resided, Ignis was sure to be close by.

In Minisc's heart, he still wanted to chase after the boy. To help him see the error of his ways. But that dream was so far gone, he knew the odds were minuscule.

If Minisc joined Jules, then they would no doubt be looking into Luminosa, looking into Ignis. Their paths would cross once again, and if it did a battle would commence. A fight he didn't know if he could go through with. Every time he fought against Ignis, he couldn't help but pull his punches. He couldn't bring himself to hate the boy. There was too much pity in him.

While Minisc continued his internal debate, a black SUV with tinted windows drove up. For most that would create a level of suspicion, but as the Hero of Light's son, it was a fairly common occurrence.

As expected, his father stepped out before thanking the driver. Minisc leaned back a little further, taking in a deep breath before sitting up and saying, "Hi," with a smile.

Don raised an eyebrow returning the greeting with a little more skepticism.

"Hello…?"

"What?"

"Well, whenever I find you on the front porch it usually means you have something on your mind. So what is it this time?"

"Wow, have I really become that predictable lately?" Minisc joked.

Don smiled and took a seat next to his son. He was glad to see at least whatever was on Minisc's mind, it hadn't dampened his sense of humour.

"What can I say, you're my son after all. So, what's rattling around in that predictable head of yours?"

"It's not much really, I've just been trying to figure out where I should do my volunteer work for the next little while. Jules is going to work with Yuri on the streets, and Lily plans to help in a homeless shelter for the Humans who were displaced after

Luminosa destroyed their homes. But I'm not sure what I want to do."

"Hmm." Don leaned back, mirroring his son. He thought about the question.

Minisc continued, "It's not like I really want to fight crime or be on the streets, I never did. The only reason I kept fighting was because Luminosa had it in for me. I wanted to make sure I could keep Lily and Jules safe. To make sure I could help keep any sense of peace left between Humans and Elementalists intact."

"Because of your mother?" Don asked, well aware of the answer to follow. Minisc had always valued his mother's dream more than his father's heroic legacy.

"Yeah... I just didn't want her dream to go to waste, but it seems like tension in the city is still high even with Dusk's defeat."

"I know what you mean..." Don trailed off for a second. Thoughts of his conversation with Dusk came to mind. And thoughts of the missing people in the city as well. But Minisc knew nothing of those issues though. For the time being, they were still being kept from the public. Regardless, Don wanted to continue training his son, helping tap into his incredible potential, but he wanted to do that without putting his son in the line of fire while they hunted down Luminosa.

"Do you want to know what I think?" Don asked.

"Sure, why not? You know as much as anyone about this stuff."

"That I do. If you really want to help Elementalists and Humans mend fences, and make your mother's dream come true, then I think you should volunteer with Lily at the shelter. You can help show Humans that not all Elementalists are like Dusk and his followers. At least that's what I think anyway, but whatever you choose to do I'm sure you will help people. Just do what you think is best." Don wrapped his massive arms around his son pulling him close for a moment, "Try not to stay out here too much longer though, it's getting late."

After Don went inside, Minisc sat in silence a little longer. *If I volunteer at the shelter, at the very least I could make an immediate impact on mother's dream. Right now, that seems far more important than finding Ignis. I know he'll show himself when he chooses, I just need to remain ready for when that day comes...*

CHAPTER 3
A NEW MYSTERY

NOT ALL THE DAMAGE CAUSED BY LUMINOSA COULD be repaired. Many families lost homes, and even more, were still grieving the loss of their loved ones each day. In particular, one steel-haired teen, whose life had been indelibly marked by the sinister group.

Coro placed a small glass picture frame on his bedside table. The last of his unpacked supplies. He sat on the bed sinking into it as he stared at the woman in the picture. He was alone. Shut off from the outside world.

Unfortunately, on the day of reckoning three months ago he lost the one person who mattered most to him. And worst of all, his mother's sacrifice was to save his life. To protect him and Minisc from being captured.

For weeks if not months, Coro debated his decision to return home for his safety. Of course, if he hadn't, they would never have solved the elemental virus and he, Minisc, and potentially the world would have been done in. But a world without his mother felt hollow. Now there was no one left. No siblings to stay with, no mother to care for him, and a missing father that nobody had heard from in months.

Due to those circumstances, and Coro only turning 16, President Osiris and the EC did all they could to help the young teen out. They provided him with a small apartment, where he could live rent-free, and also helped take care of selling Coro's house and much of the family's possessions. Not that Coro cared for the place that left him with so many foul memories. He had the option to stay, but without his mother living with him, he had no desire to remain in such a large, empty house. He collected the few belongings he wanted, and some pictures of him and his mother as well as some furniture to spruce up his lonely new pad, but outside of that, all the possessions were sold to pad his bank account. Luckily that did grant him plenty of money to pay his way through EA while also living on his own, and as a winner of the Tournament of Elements, he would not have to worry about competing for a job in the EC upon graduation.

Coro took one last look at the picture frame. It was an older photo and a bit weathered, but as long as it was sealed in the frame it would survive. He stood in the middle with a less than impressed look, and to his left with her arms around him, was his mother. On the right slightly off center stood his father. Normally, Coro would never keep a photo of his father, or so much as a memory if he chose, but this one was special. It was the last photo of the three together. For Coro, the hunt was not over yet.

The night Coro returned home, his mother asked him something. She asked for Coro to put aside his hatred for his father, the man who treated him like a lab rat, and find him. Find him and bring him home, that way they could be a family again. He never could comprehend how such a loving and caring woman could live with such a self-centered egotistical scientist who cared only about his work and nothing else, but she did. And for his mother, he would find his father. After that, nobody knew what would happen, but Coro would deal with those issues later.

But one big problem remained... he had no idea where to even start looking. The last time he saw his father was at the Tournament of Elements just over three months ago, and the only information on the man's whereabouts was that Luminosa captured him. His evidence for that was more than solid. The dual elements that the Luminosa member Bex showed in their fight left no doubt as to who had his father.

Coro's father, Dr. Jarrad, was best known for his power enhancing experiments, but one facet intrigued him like no other. Dual Elements. As a scientific method to enhance someone's power by giving them a second element, he became obsessed with the skill. At least until the EC outlawed such experiments. However, the man refused to give up his goals, and after seeing success on the experiments with his son, dreams of creating the perfect Elementalists soon filled his mind. His brain would create bigger, stronger, faster Elementalists and turn them into the perfect fighting machines, just as he attempted with his only son.

Coro stood up and walked over to the desk on his side wall. On it sat a piece of official EC documentation. Just like everyone else in EA he'd been requested to aid in the rebuilding projects. However, thanks to his strong scientific background, along with his role in creating the element vaccine, his choices in where to work were lacking. Not because people didn't want him, but because President Osiris placed a special request for the boy. The president knew Coro wanted to search for his father, and on top of that, finding the man was in the EC's best interest as well, so Coro would be teaming up with another exceptional Elementalist for the time being. Hesitant at first, Coro reluctantly accepted.

The Elemental Council contained all sorts of files and records on the populace of the city, but those files were not for public consumption. Which meant the only way for Coro to access them and perhaps find clues to his father was by aiding President Osiris in his request.

He grabbed the paper and folded it up sticking it in the back pocket of his jeans.

After a short bus ride, Coro stepped out into the bright morning sun. From the bus stop, he stared up at the half-built building in front of him. The EC headquarters had been obliterated the last time Coro saw it, so when compared to that state, the building was in decent condition. At least it was built enough to be reopened, but there was still plenty of work to be done. Long walkways and lifts circled the top floors of the building with men and women doing construction work. Along with that were various tall cranes that hoisted a strapped in man who must have been an earth Elementalist. He shaped the slabs of stone on the roof with his arms to make them smooth and sleek. In due time the building would look as good as new, if not even better.

Looks like they're making quick progress, at least. I wonder if they're working as hard on the rest of the city? Coro thought as he started walking up the large cement steps.

He came to a stop as the man hanging from the crane slowly began his descent. Once he hit ground level, Coro finally recognized the muscular man. His name was Dwayne, a long-time EC member, and partner to the Hero of Light. Every part of his body was large, matching the physique of The Hero himself.

"Well look who it is." The man waved before he unhooked himself from the crane.

"Hello," replied Coro, gesturing with a formal nod.

Dwayne walked up to him with a big smile. "Boy, I haven't seen you in months. Zale told me you might be helping out at the EC for a bit." His voice hushed, "So I guess that means still no luck in finding your father?"

Coro nodded, speaking in the monotone voice that would have turned most people away.

"Not yet. Hopefully working here, I can find a few more leads."

"I hope so too." Dwayne picked up his mood and his tone, shifting the subject slightly. "Why don't I take you in to see Zale? I'm sure he's expecting you any time now." Dwayne gestured for Coro to follow as he led the way into the building.

"Thank you."

Much like the outside of the building, most of the inside remained under construction. However, there were a few areas that were finished. The first floor looked like a large ballroom with granite tile flooring that shined from a new polish and white walls surrounded him everywhere he looked. In the center and to the left and right were three large sets of stairs that branched off into even more sections of the building. All of the paths were marked by the red velvet carpet running up the stairs.

"Have you ever been in the EC before? I mean, besides The Underground?" Dwayne chuckled as he asked the question.

Coro gave a less warm reply with a simple, "No."

Where most people would have been taken aback by such a dismissive answer, Dwayne was not surprised by the lack of words. He had spent enough time with Coro to realize the boy was not one for excessive talking.

"Well, I'd give you a tour but most of the inside is still nothing but construction, so there isn't much to see currently."

"That's alright, I'd just like to start working, honestly."

Dwayne nodded, accepting the boy's wish. He could only imagine the mental strain Coro suffered over the last few months.

Up the middle row of stairs, they went to the second floor. Dwayne took him left down the hall towards Zale's office. The door had elegant markings on it along with a gold nameplate that read President. Dwayne knocked casually but didn't bother to wait for any reply. Between him and Don, neither cared too much about the president's stature in society. After all, without them, the society Zale worked so hard to try and build would have crumbled long ago.

"Zale, I have a visitor for you." Dwayne's voice boomed causing the president to nearly jump from his desk. When he looked up, he shot his friend and employee an incredulous glare. Behind the bulky man, he then spotted Coro. He tried to muster up a friendly smile despite looking like he hadn't slept in weeks.

"Coro, good to see you made it alright. Thanks for bringing him up, Dwayne. I can take it from here."

"Yes sir," Dwayne laughed with a half mocking salute. He left the two returning to his job.

Zale gestured for Coro to take a seat, removing a stack of paperwork off his desk in the process.

"How're the living arrangements going?" Zale asked, "You know if you need anything please just ask me or even Dwayne or Don, and we'll be more than willing to accommodate you."

"Thank you, sir, but you've done enough already. I do appreciate it though. It's nice to have someone to rely on while I look for my father."

"Of course. Now I guess onto the topic of your father. We'll get him out of Luminosa's hands soon, you have my word." Zale reached for a small black intercom box on his desk tapping the button, "Maranda, could you please send Olivia up to my office. I have her new partner here."

He paused for a second before the woman replied, "Yes sir, she's on her way."

Zale let go of the button and turned his attention back to Coro. "Did you manage to read the briefing package we sent to you a few days ago?"

Coro nodded. "I did, ten Humans all over different parts of the city have gone missing without a trace of their whereabouts, which follows a trend of missing Humans over the past month. The total count is currently 54 and the public remains unaware of the danger so far."

"Correct, although we don't have any proof, I fully believe that Luminosa is somehow behind this. As for what they're planning, we don't know, but they must be stopped. Olivia's team has been investigating the disappearances for the last few weeks but leads are limited. I think your talents might be just what she needs to help solve this while we gather more information on Luminosa. We find a connection to Luminosa, we might find a lead to your father as well."

"Alright, I'll see what I can do."

As Zale finished his own mini briefing, they heard a much less intimidating knock on the door. Standing in the already open doorway was a tall, fit woman. She had straight platinum hair that fell shading her left eye. What Coro really took notice of was the woman's uniform though. Much like a standard dress code, she wore a white and gold jacket with matching pants, but along her arm were five golden stripes. Each stripe signified a ranking in the EC. The only other person Coro had seen with five stripes was

Dwayne. Of course, Don would have been another rank altogether, but since he did not wear an EC uniform, stripes were of little importance. One look into her hardened teal eyes and he could feel the no nonsense attitude that radiated with such prestige. She certainly did not carry the same jovial attitude towards Zale that Dwayne or Don did. She was all business.

"Hello, Sir." She took a bow, not entering until Zale gestured her to do so.

"Please come in. Olivia, this is Coro. He's a student at EA, and he'll be working with you for the next little while. I expect he will be a big help to your investigation."

"Understood." Olivia nodded before fixing her stare onto Coro. "Come with me." The woman's voice was cold but powerful. She turned on a heel and left the office. Anyone else would have flinched at such a hostile greeting, but growing up around his father, Coro simply stood up and started to head out.

"Don't worry, her bark is worse than her bite," Zale joked as Coro left the room. Even so, he had no worries that Coro could handle his new boss's cold demeanour. After all, Coro wasn't much different.

Just before Coro left the room Zale opened a drawer and pulled out a small black device in the shape of a cell phone. "Here, keep this in your back pocket. It's a new EC phone we're trying out. It might come in handy." He tossed it to Coro who caught it and stored it away.

"Um... thank you," he said before leaving the office.

Coro followed Olivia around the corner and the two started backtracking to the main floor and to the right, which was often considered the research area of the EC. Along the short trek, Olivia made no effort at small talk. She walked with purpose and refused to waste a moment of her time.

Once they reached the door she finally began to speak. "President Osiris informed me you're rather adept when it comes to the sciences, is that correct?"

"Yes... both my mother and father excelled at research involving Elementalists. I spent most of my younger years in a lab as well."

"And your father is the one who managed to give you two elements?"

Coro hesitated; he hated having to bring up his dual elements, since it was often seen as a threat to society, but he replied, "Yes, though I hate using the fire my father gave me..."

"I advise you to get used to it. Holding back power against our enemy will do nothing but cause you harm."

For a moment Coro was confused. Olivia showed no worries about his strength, being an experimented monster, or anything common society viewed him as. She appeared to see it as a necessary burden in making progress.

"You were also the one who managed to crack the code to the Element erasing virus?"

"Well, really all I did was take my father's research notes on a few similar experiments and my mother helped apply it to the virus."

"Interesting..." Olivia whipped out a key card lanyard from around her neck and pressed it against the security box. The light turned green, and she peeled off her card before entering through the sliding doors.

The two stepped into a dark room filled with different scientific equipment. Unlike most of the research rooms Coro spent time in, particularly while they were sheltered in The Underground, this one was immaculate. All the containers, vials, books, papers and everything else was organized like a library shelf. All the equipment was labelled properly and even sparkled from a fresh cleaning.

"I assume President Osiris has already informed you of the sudden disappearances of 54 Humans over the last month?"

"He did."

"Good, then I won't go over it again." Olivia walked over to one of the shelves pulling off some equipment and chemical samples.

Coro did his best to examine each chemical as they were placed in front of him, but most looked unfamiliar. Because his father worked so diligently on only one aspect of his scientific career, even with Coro's intellect, there were still plenty of gaps in his knowledge. He still believed he could figure things out with a little backwards deconstruction.

The last chemical Olivia pulled from the shelf came in a small rack of tubes. The vials were all labelled with the letter J on them, and inside was a musty gray substance like sludge. Coro picked up one of the J vials and started examining it. The smell was putrid as it hit him.

"What is this? I've never seen anything like it," Coro asked.

"That would be the substance we've been trying to recreate over the last week. We don't have a name for it yet so for the time being we have simply referred to it as the J chemical. Although most of the disappearances have little connection between them, the thing we have consistently found near and around where those missing were last sighted, is this gray goop. We have no record of it on hand but it's the best lead we have right now. If we can figure out what this goop is comprised of, then we can figure out how it plays into these disappearances. But I'm sure for someone who can create a vaccine in a matter of twenty-four hours this would be a simple enough task for you to figure out." Olivia's voice sounded skeptical if not condescending towards Coro's achievements.

Even so, Coro didn't have time to care about how Olivia or anyone else in the EC viewed his accomplishments. Finding his father remained the top priority and no one's opinion held much weight otherwise.

Coro grabbed the chemicals and said, "I take it you've already created a chart to display all the different permutations and effects that this chemical has with others you've tested alongside it?"

Olivia raised an eyebrow, attempting to hide the smirk forming on her pale pink lips. She opened a drawer from under the table and pulled out a small book flipping through the pages. "Here." She slid the knowledge over to Coro who opened it up to find far more than he bargained for. On each page was a detailed level of notes that would make even his father's head spin. He started examining the pages again but this time he was looking for something specific.

"Do you have a chart somewhere with the breakdown of this

chemical J molecularly, that way you can try and extract the chemicals that created it?"

Now Olivia began to see why Zale was so high on Coro's smarts. "No, I don't believe that's been done yet."

"Based on these notes, the best way to recreate this J chemical would be to see if we can break it down and learn what it's composed of. With that, we can probably figure out the potential effects of it and if it's dangerous as well."

Coro picked up one of the vials before taking it over to where a microscope was set up.

"We don't have many samples of the substance, so try not to waste it," Olivia warned, walking over to where Coro set up shop.

"I should only need a few drops to get me started. This is just a base test to see if I can pick up anything similar."

Coro took an eye dropper off the table and carefully dipped it into the vial. He gave it a faint squeeze sucking up less than a quarter of the J chemical before dripping three drops onto a small rectangular piece of glass. He slid that under the microscope and began his examination.

With the items in place, he turned to the computer nearby and started typing. Various windows began popping up on the monitor. Luckily for Coro, his experience of working in similar EC labs meant he could cross-reference information far easier than if he were stuck in his father's lab.

Olivia watched with intrigue as her new partner worked swiftly and efficiently in his attempt to crack their unsolvable code. She let a grin slip when the computer started to beep with more windows popping up.

The typing came to a stop and Coro's eyes darted back and forth.

"This doesn't make any sense. This chemical shows all the same chemical makeups of the Human body..." Coro said wearily.

"Only the Human body, no signs of any Elemental genes as a match."

"Nothing."

"What do you think that could mean?" Olivia asked.

Coro mulled the data over, debating any connections he could draw from his findings.

"I'm not sure, it could be part of some sort of serum used in connection to the disappearances, but without more information on it I can't make a real conclusion."

"Hmm, perhaps President Osiris didn't exaggerate your skills as much as I first thought. Good work." She pulled out a phone from her pocket, typing for a few moments before hiding it away again. "Come on, we can leave the rest of this to the research team for the time being... not that those slackers would have ever figured any of this out, but for the moment we have other info to dig up."

CHAPTER 4
LINGERING FRUSTRATION

AFTER MINISC TOOK THE WEEKEND TO MAKE HIS decision he opted to join Lily and volunteer his time at the North York Shelter.

But before they set off on their new adventure, the three were to stop by the EC at Yuri's request.

It was a beautiful, sunny morning as Minisc, Lily, and Jules stood at the entrance of the slowly reforming headquarters.

"This is so exciting, I've been waiting all my life for this day," Jules gleamed with a smile from ear to ear. Although he had donned the uniform and worked with the EC just a few months ago, this time it would be official. On top of that now he would be working right alongside his brother and not stuck in some office filling out paperwork.

Lily and Minisc stood on either side of their friend, both with equal grins.

"They've really made a lot of progress over the past few months," Minisc commented.

"Yeah, it's coming along nicely. I guess you haven't been here since it was destroyed, have you Minisc?" Lily asked.

"Nope." Minisc thought back to the last time he stood on these same steps. The earth shook below him, his heart jumped into his throat, and then everything after that was a blur. For once it would be nice to be at the EC with no threat of danger around.

Lily looked down at her watch, "Jules, I thought you said Yuri was meeting us out front?" As if waiting for an introduction, Yuri stepped out the front doors of the building. He stood a fair bit taller than the three and dressed much nicer as well.

"Good morning everyone," he said with his usual enthusiastic smile. "You guys ready to start your first official day with the Elemental Council?"

Yuri's calmness in all situations was one of the traits that people held in high regard, but even the energy in his voice displayed his excitement. Of course, after everything he and his brother had been through, seeing the jubilation on Jules' face bred even more happiness. As an older brother, he couldn't help but be proud of his little brother for taking such a large step toward his dreams.

"Of course!" Jules replied.

Yuri looked at Minisc and Lily, "And what about you two?"

"Yeah, I'm excited," Lily said.

"We're just a little calmer about it than Jules," Minisc laughed.

"Well how about I take you three to my office and we get you guys set up for the day?"

"Wow, this place is impressive," Minisc marvelled as they walked into Yuri's new office. Compared to his old working conditions he'd received a big upgrade. The desk was twice the size of his old desk and had a much sleeker design as well. The room also had a TV along the wall and cabinets for a much more organized filing system. Not to mention a full furniture set in the middle of the room.

While Jules showed off his brother's office to Minisc, Lily walked up to the coffee table in the middle of the room. Three folded up uniforms sat waiting to be dawned by their new owners. She picked up the one with a flared skirt to it.

"Yuri, did you get us new uniforms?" She asked.

"Yep, I figured the ones you had from The Underground took a pretty heavy beating, so I got some new ones made up for you."

Lily held up her uniform, examining the clothes keenly. But before she could make a comment, Yuri said, "And yes, I made sure I kept the changes you made to yours Lily." The man laughed, knowing he was one step ahead.

Eventually, Jules and Minisc joined their friend in picking up the new threads. Jules unrolled it with love struck eyes. Unlike the previous iteration of his uniform, this one had no alterations. This was the real deal, and he couldn't wait to put it on.

After the three changed into their uniforms, they were set for a day of hard but rewarding work. When they arrived back in Yuri's office, however, a girl was sitting on the couch across from his desk. Her feet were kicked up on the table as she relaxed. When she heard footsteps, she looked up from admiring the fresh polish on her nails and spoke.

"I take it you three are the new volunteers Yuri was talking about. So which one of you is The Hero of Light's son?" The girl stood up, reaching Minisc's height. Long, cherry-pink hair fell down her back with a small braid along the side, while her youthful complexion suggested she was only a few years older than the group. She carried a mischievous air about her, with a small glint in her fire stone eyes.

Minisc half raised his hand awkwardly, "That would be me..." A feeling of discomfort always followed when the first question to come up was about being his father's son.

The girl walked up to Minisc, getting unusually close to him. The smell of her strawberry perfume nearly choked him as it came in waves. Both Lily and Jules took a step back as the girl practically cuddled up to Minisc.

"I'm Bailey," she said with a seductive charm, "It's nice to meet you." She batted her long eyelashes as she smiled at Minisc.

Minisc tried to utter a word, but his voice caught in his throat. His first reaction was to back up and put some distance between himself and Bailey, but the girl grabbed a hold of his hand making sure that was not an option.

During the awkward exchange, Jules gave a glancing look to Lily. He stifled a laugh seeing the obvious look of jealousy growing on her face but before Bailey could sink her flirtatious claws into Minisc any further, Yuri popped back in the room saying, "Bailey, he's taken," without breaking stride to his desk.

"Oh you're no fun," Bailey pouted dramatically, stepping away from her prey. "So who's the girl that beat me to the punch?" She looked past Minisc towards Lily with a devious smirk on her lips, "Is it you?" She asked.

Lily's cheeks turned red, as did Minisc's but before they could make a defence, Yuri put an end to the interrogation.

"Let it go, Bailey, I'd prefer if you didn't scare people off before they even get to work for a day." Yuri took a seat at his desk spinning around to face the group. "Anyways... Minisc, Lily, Jules, this is Bailey, as I guess you've already figured out. Don't let her flirtatiousness fool you; she is one tough cookie... Bailey, these two are my younger brother Jules, and his friend Lily... and I see you've already ingratiated yourself with Minisc... so, Lily and Minisc, you guys will be going with Bailey here to the North York Shelter. Jules, you're coming with me for the day."

"Sounds good," Jules said, "But I was kind of hoping we would all get a chance to work together. Is there anywhere around North York that needs investigating?"

Yuri smirked and said, "Oh please... the way you three get into trouble, I have a hard enough time keeping my eye on one of you, let alone all three..."

"He's got a point," Minisc laughed, rubbing the back of his neck.

"Alright, so Lily, Minisc, I'll leave you two in Bailey's capable hands," Yuri said before shooting a parental look at Bailey. "No more flirting, got it?"

Bailey dropped her hands to her side pouting for a second before nodding in compliance. She would just have to find someone new to sink her claws into.

As the name implied, North York was a little way north of the main city. Despite being far from the heart of the attacks, the damage caused by those siding with Luminosa was still prevalent. But sadly, due to the small population compared to the city, media coverage of their circumstances was sparse at best.

The weather was beautiful as Minisc and Lily walked down the streets toward the shelter, but that was about the only beautiful thing currently in North York. The subdivision resembled destruction from a bomb. Homes were decimated, roads shattered, and streetlights toppled to the ground.

"This is awful. I had no idea places outside the city were left in such bad shape." Lily frowned. Even the road they currently walked on had pot holes in some spots and in others, the asphalt was sticking out like small jagged rocks. There were no worries of cars coming where they were heading, the roads would not permit it.

"North York doesn't get much attention in the way of Toronto media. I guess they have better things to talk about than us..." Bailey made no effort to hide the contempt in her voice. "Unfortunately, this is one of the most heavily populated Human areas in North York, so when Luminosa went on their little rampage some Elementalists decided to join the attacks and went after this area specifically."

"I've seen so much destruction while working with Jules over the last month... but it's sickening every time," Lily sighed, "So many innocent lives were ruined by such a monstrous group of people."

Bailey perked up, trying to keep some semblance of joy in the conversation, "I know it's rough to look at, but if it makes you feel any better, the EC has managed to put up everyone who lost their homes in these shelters for the time being. And they're working quickly to help restore the houses to a more reasonable living condition. Of course, those with family close by went to stay there rather than a shelter, and others still would rather live in their ruined homes than accept help from the EC at this point, but I promise everyone at the shelter is much more tolerant of Elementalists than what you're probably imagining. You have nothing to worry about." When Bailey talked about the shelter her tone was far more subdued compared to her flirtatious and bombastic ways back in the office. It was clear to see Bailey truly cared about her hometown and the people who lived in it.

After a few more minutes of walking the group finally came upon a massive rectangular building at the end of the street. At a glance, the building looked much like a supermarket or warehouse, with its box shape and murky yellow outer walls. There were no signs, and nothing indicated that the building was a shelter, but the clues were obvious. Several large trucks meant for moving crates of food sat at the front with a few people helping unload, while others sat on lawn chairs tanning in the morning sun. To the side of the building was a large grassy field where a dozen or so kids were kicking a soccer ball around. They had no nets, and no equipment, but were having a blast as they ran and cheered with each other. Even some of the parents joined in on the fun.

"Well, here we are," Bailey said, "the North York Shelter. Hope you like it. For the most part today I'm gonna need your help handing out supplies to all the residents. I know it's not the most exciting task, but we can't be running around saving the world all the time now, can we?" Bailey looked back at Minisc with a wink before walking ahead.

Wait a second... does she know about Dusk? Minisc thought.

Before Lily could follow their new leader Minisc grabbed her by the arm and pulled her in close.

"Did you tell Bailey about our fight with Dusk?"

"What? When on earth would I have had time to tell her that? I've been with you all morning. I'm sure it's just because she knows who your father is. I wouldn't overthink this one."

A few steps ahead, Bailey spun around and said, "What are you two lovebirds doing back there?"

Minisc and Lily promptly separated, letting the red in their faces fade away.

"It's nothing," Lily called back. She took Minisc's hand, leading him forward. "Come on, we've got a lot of people to help today."

The inside of the building looked like an old gymnasium filled with a couple hundred people talking in different cliques. Rows of beds were in parallel lines on either side with a few elderly folks still laying in them surrounded by family. Along the left wall was a series of stations for food with lineups at each one.

Inside the shelter doors, Bailey was greeted by another man

around her age. He was tall with short black hair spiked up at the front, and he wore business casual clothes. He looked like a born leader, but also had a caring demeanour about him.

"Good morning, Ben," Bailey said walking by the man before taking off her jean jacket and tossing it on a coat rack by the door. Underneath she wore a low cut pink shirt that showed off her toned stomach, while her jean shorts left little to the imagination.

As she walked by, Ben looked at her and asked, "Bailey, I thought we talked about appropriate dress wear while you're on the clock?"

"You did, and I told you I like my cute outfits," she responded as if the answer was obvious. "Besides, I don't go to the gym just to hide how good I look." She blew past Ben again with little interest in a follow up conversation. Instead, she headed over to a table with boxes piled as high as she was tall. Getting on her tippy toes she hugged her body around three of the boxes before making her way to the middle of the room.

"She's stronger than she looks," Minisc laughed.

Since Bailey all but ditched her two subordinates, Minisc and Lily were left wondering what they were supposed to do. Luckily Ben approached them holding out his hand.

"Hi, I'm Ben."

Minisc took the man's hand and shook it, "I'm Minisc, and this here is Lily."

"We're part of the EC city rebuilding program, and we're supposed to be helping Bailey out today." The three glanced over at the girl hard at work. "Although she seems to have everything under control from what I can see."

Bailey was surrounded by a large group of people - mostly older men - who were all smiling and laughing as she handed out fresh blankets and pillows. She revelled in the attention being paid to her, all while making herself cozy with the residents.

"Bailey is definitely a bit... let's call it eccentric, but the residents really do love her, and she genuinely cares about helping these people that are unfortunately stuck here. Even though her home was destroyed as well, she always makes sure to keep a smile on her face," Ben said.

"That really is incredible," Lily said.

"Yeah, which is also why I'm really glad the EC is so committed to not only helping out the Elementalists affected by Luminosa, but also the Humans who were targeted as well. I know some Humans haven't been as forgiving about the damage, but everyone here has tried to remain upbeat about the situation, and a large part of that is because of Bailey. Even if she does cause me some headaches from time to time. Without her, this place wouldn't be nearly as pleasant..." Ben turned back to his new workers, "Anyways, if you two are here to help, then allow me to set you up. We just got a new shipment of blankets and pillows that need to be handed out. If you could start with that and then come find me when all the boxes are empty, that would be a huge help."

Task assigned, Minisc and Lily smiled and walked over to where Bailey had grabbed her boxes.

"I'm glad we can finally help the people who were hurt by Luminosa's actions," Lily said, taking a few boxes from Minisc who had taken enough to tower over him.

"Yeah, and it's nice to see even though a bunch of Elementalists were the cause of this whole mess, they aren't holding it against all of us. I was really worried about the lasting damage caused by Dusk."

"I bet your mother would be proud of you, helping Humans in need like this."

"Yeah, I know she would be. Now come on, we need to get these supplies out before Bailey is swarmed to death."

"Something tells me she'd be okay with that," Lily giggled.

Various supplies were distributed throughout the morning to the patrons of the shelter. But for Minisc, walking up to groups of strangers and trying to make small talk with them as he handed out sheets and pillows didn't come easy. Despite the uncountable number of times a stranger approached him either looking for an autograph or a tidbit of information about his father, he never grew comfortable interacting with those he didn't know. Especially when he, and Elementalists, were seen as the problem by many Humans. That weary thought always remained in the back of his mind, however unjust it might have been.

On the other hand, Lily appeared to be thriving as she walked up and down the rows of beds. Everyone she talked to smiled and laughed and at one point she ended up cradling a baby while one of the mothers used her new sheets to make up a bed. She looked as happy and at peace as at any point that Minisc could recall.

"Looks like your girlfriend might give Bailey a run for the most popular worker here," Ben laughed.

"She always has been way more sociable than me. I'm not surprised she's taking to this job the way she has." Minisc had a big smile on his face. After so many struggles, it filled his heart seeing his friend glowing with excitement. So much so that he had not even taken the time to correct Ben on his assumptions.

"I take it being The Hero of Light's son, you would rather be doing something with a little more action than be here handing out blankets to a bunch of Humans?" Ben asked again.

Minisc shook his head. "No, actually, I chose to come here over the other divisions of the EC. I never set out to follow in my father's footsteps. I'd be just as happy if we never needed a hero to save this world again. I'm not much like my father in that sense, I guess. I'm just used to keeping to myself more than Lily is. She's much more of a people person, you could say."

Ben nodded, "I understand. Even so, I still appreciate all the help you two are providing, it really does mean the world to these people. I have no doubt that Humans seeing Elementalists helping them out in a time of need will bring everyone closer together as a whole."

"Agreed."

The morning flew by quickly, and once all the supplies were handed out for the day, all four of Minisc, Lily, Bailey, and Ben sat outside enjoying the sun. There were a few picnic tables set up for lunch, and it provided a great view of the kids who were still playing soccer.

"I can't believe how happy everyone is around here, I would've thought those who lost their homes would be bitter, but they're anything but," Minisc said as he watched the kids running back and forth on the open field.

"You know, there were a few growing pains early. Many Humans were furious about the situation they were put in, but they quickly grew together like a community. Most of them were neighbours and friends before having to take shelter here so once cooler heads prevailed, they managed to band together and take care of each other. It's one big family around here," Ben said as he took another bite of his sandwich.

"I'm sure they want to get back to their homes soon though," Lily said, "How long will everyone have to live here?"

"Actually, we're well over halfway to building the new subdivision for everyone. It should only be a few more months and everyone can move back into their homes," Ben answered.

While the group continued talking a ball rolled over hitting Minisc in the side of the foot.

"Can you pass the ball, mister?" A young child asked, waving his hands back and forth.

"Sure," Minisc obliged. He stood up and swung his leg giving the ball a big hoof. It sailed right back into the middle of play as the kids resumed their giggling and laughing.

"It's going to be different once everyone's back in their homes, but it's for the best. As much as I love helping everyone here, this is far from the only part of the city that needs volunteers, and we never seem to have enough people to help everyone." Bailey sighed, putting her head in her hands.

Once they finished up lunch, Lily quickly jumped at the chance to get back to work. Behind her, Minisc and Bailey trailed when Minisc noticed a young girl around the age of 8 or 9 sitting up against the side of the building. Her knees were tucked into his chest and her head was firmly hidden.

"Hey, Bailey, who is that kid? Why isn't she playing with the others?"

"Oh… that's my sister Maya. She's sort of going through a bit of a rough patch right now. She doesn't really like to play with the other kids."

Minisc looked at the girl making out what he believed to be a sad scowl on her face. In a place so full of life and joy, seeing one single girl off in the shadows made him frown. Although not great at talking to strangers, and even less skilled with children Minisc wanted to help.

"Should we try talking to her?" He asked.

"I wouldn't do that if I were you."

"Huh? Why not? She looks so sad." Minisc turned to approach the girl expecting Bailey to follow, after all this was her little sister.

But Bailey heeded her own warning. A small smirk played on her glossy lips as she knew the soon to be outcome. However, since Minisc had ignored her warning, she decided to let things play out.

Minisc approached the girl slowly, treating her like a wild animal, hoping not to frighten her off. He bent down to be eye level with the girl before extending a greeting.

"Hey Maya."

Maya tilted her head up, not letting go of her knees. On her face were scuffs and a few small marks under her cheeks. In her arms was a small stuffed rabbit that she held with a death grip. At first, Minisc thought she looked sad, but as he came up close to the girl, he could see anger more than anything. The short, dirty brown hair that covered her eyes made it hard to tell though.

"Who are you?" Maya said in a cold voice.

"My name's Minisc… I'm with the Elemental Council, it's nice to meet you." Minisc extended his hand but Maya refused.

"Elemental Council…" Maya spat back as she pushed herself up. She barely came up to Minisc's belly button as Minisc rose with her, and yet for some reason, Minisc felt a startling sense of fear in himself.

"So you're one of them…"

"One of who?" Minisc asked, confused by the vague reference.

"You're an Elementalist…"

"Uh yeah…" Before Minisc could say another word, a sharp pain ran up his leg. Maya kicked him square in the shin before running away, yelling, "Leave me alone you monster. I hate you!"

Minisc grabbed at his leg growling as the girl rounded the back of the building. For a split second, the idea of firing a blast of light crossed his mind, but he thought better of it. Instead, he turned back to look at Bailey who was stifling a gleeful laugh.

"I tried to tell you, but no… the big ol hero didn't wanna listen," she mocked.

Throughout the rest of the afternoon, Minisc could not keep Maya off his mind. He played the interaction on repeat over and over again, the disappointment refusing to leave him. Finally, as events were wrapping up and he, Bailey and Lily were throwing out some boxes behind the building he popped the question.

"Hey Bailey… it seems like everyone here is quite forgiving to their circumstances… but your sister not so much…"

Bailey froze before finishing stuffing the boxes in the large plastic bin. When she looked back at Minisc she rubbed her shoulder and looked toward the ground.

"Let's just say she's got a lot more anger than most folks around here. Not that I can really blame her." She lowered her voice to a whisper. "It's more than just losing our home; we lost our father in the attacks as well. That night an Elementalist set our house ablaze. I managed to escape, but Maya got stuck in her room, so my father went charging in after her. He managed to find Maya and get her out safely, but unfortunately, the burns he suffered caused him to pass a few days later in the hospital. Our mother was also an Elementalist, but when she gave birth to two Humans, she abandoned our family. I haven't seen her in almost ten years. I've tried to tell Maya not all Elementalists are bad, but how do you explain to an 8-year-old who has been so traumatized by actions related to Elementalists? You can't. It's impossible."

"Wow," Minisc uttered, "I'm so sorry."

"You have nothing to be sorry about, Minisc, none of this is your fault. And it's not right to blame people who had nothing to do with the situation just because they fit into the group that did it... but Maya is young. She doesn't understand that yet."

Minisc looked past Bailey towards Lily, who had a similar expression of guilt and sickness. They'd done their best to fight Luminosa within the city, but never once thought to go further out and help.

Minisc couldn't help but think, *what if I had come here instead of having to fight Ignis... maybe I could have helped, maybe I could have done something for Maya and Bailey.*

Bailey finished tossing the boxes in the trash container and smiled, "Come on you two, it's okay. She still has me after all, and I'll never leave her. She just needs some time, that's all."

Throughout the night, thoughts of Maya continued to plague Minisc's mind. He feared the girl would hate Elementalists for life. But he knew there was little he could do. It was as Bailey said, she just needed time. For now, all he could do was work to help make hers and everyone else's life in the shelter the best it could be.

Just as they had the day before, the group finished up lunch ready to head back into the shelter before a high-pitched scream caught their attention. They jumped from their seats and ran over, following the echo of the cries. Once they rounded the back of the building, they saw a group of children, all huddled by a narrow walkway that led to other streets. They all stood petrified, nobody wanting to say a word.

"Is everyone okay? What happened?" Bailey asked. She approached the kid in the middle of the group, who had tears streaming down his cheeks and was visibly shaking.

"I... I kicked the ball into the alley," he sobbed, "and Maya... she... she went to go get it."

Lily knelt, putting her hand on the boy's shoulder, "Just breathe in... and out," She said mimicking her own instructions with her hands. They continued for a few seconds until the little boy could breathe calmly again. Even so, he still looked like he had seen a ghost.

"Okay, can you tell me what happened? Where is Maya?" Lily finally asked.

"She went into the alley to get our ball back, we told her not to, that we should get one of the adults to get it, but she said she could handle it. When I followed her, I saw a monster, and it grabbed her."

"A monster... grabbed her?" Ben stepped in. "Sam, where did this monster run off to?"

"I... I don't know..." The boy named Sam said, almost bursting into tears again.

Wasting no time, Minisc jumped into action. Whether it was by nature, or the desire to help Maya and show her Elementalists were not all bad, he would not let Maya be taken.

"Ben, call the police and the EC, have them survey the area and look for anyone who may be suspicious. I'm going to search through the alleyway and see if I can track Maya down."

"I'm coming with you," Lily said, standing back to her full height.

"Bailey, get everyone back to the shelter and stay there until the police and the EC arrive. We don't know what we're dealing with, so we need to stay on our toes."

Bailey nodded, accepting her orders. "Alright, but you two better be careful yourselves." She had to admit, she was impressed with the way Minisc had taken control of the situation so quickly. Too bad she was banned from flirting thanks to Yuri.

"Okay, let's go!" Minisc said heading down the alleyway...

CHAPTER 5
LEARNING THE ROPES

FINALLY, DREAMS WERE ABOUT TO COME TRUE. IT HAD taken years of work, hours of daydreaming, and a fair bit of patience, but finally Jules' big day had arrived. He would work alongside his brother. As equals. More or less, anyways.

"So what's the first thing we're gonna do today?" Jules asked bobbing up and down. He could barely contain his eagerness, nor did he feel he should.

After fearing his dreams were ripped away when Yuri lost his element, he gained a new appreciation for his still burning desire to learn under the man.

Although Yuri was indeed without an element and therefore technically Human, Zale remained adamant he continue working for the EC. The man's kind heart, intelligence, and even keel personality made him the perfect fit for his new role. A special ops detective dealing with cases assigned to him by Zale.

"President Osiris wants us to look into the sudden disappearances of some people in the last few weeks. Ten to be exact. All Humans."

"Humans have been disappearing around the city? Does that mean someone has been kidnapping them?"

Yuri dropped a thin brown folder filled with information on his desk. "Yeah, although based on the information we've been given I don't think it's quite that simple. This has been going on for a few months now, pretty much shortly after Dusk was defeated, and it seems to be slowly ramping up as of late. But we still have no concrete leads. Outside of all the victims being Humans, there are no connections. Some are kids, some are adults, male, female. Whoever is behind this is either picking targets at random or is strategically choosing people that wouldn't connect to each other. Either way, we need to put a stop to it and find those who are missing and return them to their families."

"But if we don't have any clues how're we supposed to know where to start?"

"I have an idea, but first we need to make a little pit stop."

Jules furrowed his brow, "A pit stop? That doesn't really answer my question."

"Come on, you'll see."

The streets of Toronto were bustling with activity. Unlike most parts of the city, this area looked completely untouched by Luminosa. So much so that nobody would've been able to tell there was a climactic battle only a few months ago. Store fronts were full with merchandise, people were walking up and down the streets laughing and talking, and the usual traffic backed up in a never ending gridlock.

Jules and Yuri emerged from the underground subway into the rays of sun and merged into the oncoming crowd. As they walked Jules groaned, "Seriously, where are we going? I'm so lost."

"Come on, Jules, if you're gonna help me as part of this detective unit then you need to train your brain to start paying attention to details. Look around you, it shouldn't be hard to tell where we are."

Yuri watched his brother look back and forth trying to astutely examine every person, building, and square inch around him.

Jules is exceptionally skilled when it comes to combat since that's what he's trained for his whole life... but he's still rather green when it comes to using his senses outside of battle. He's too narrowly focused sometimes. If he's going to fully join the EC one day, then he needs to sharpen his other skills as well. Yuri knew his brother had it in him. Jules could learn whatever traits he wanted when he put his mind to it, this was just the start after all. He was young and still had plenty of time to learn.

Yuri came to a stop in front of a building that nearly kissed the sky. "Okay, you have to know where we are now." He laughed as he watched Jules squint at the looming structure in front of them.

The boy paused putting his finger to his chin for a moment before letting out a gasp. Then he closed his mouth and sighed, "I got nothing, what is this place?"

In Jules' weak defence, most of the sky scraping buildings in the city appeared the same. They were tall and looked like they were made entirely out of glass, with windows crawling up the sides for hundreds of meters. There had to be another five similar buildings on the street alone.

"You have to be kidding me..." Yuri groaned. *I'm gonna have my hands full on this one...*

Yuri proceeded to walk through the glass doors ushering Jules to follow. Once inside, the pieces started to connect for Jules. He'd been so focused on spotting the invisible he completely overlooked the plain and obvious.

Jules gasped again, "Wait... is this your old office? Awe man, how could I not have realized that."

In his mind's eye, he could picture the first floor of that building as clear as day. Seating to the left, washrooms on the right, and a reception desk with elevators behind them.

"Finally, took you long enough," Yuri chuckled. He put his hand on his brother's shoulder, "You're gonna need to be a lot more observant than that if you wanna keep up with your big brother."

Jules shook his head, still confused. "But everything looks so different, what happened to this place? I know I haven't been here in a while, but it used to be so... gray... and now it's so... colourful..."

Jules was right; the old office of Yuri's was monotone in colour at best, but now all four walls of the reception room had been painted with different more vibrant colours and with fancy if not scribbled designs. Enchanting lights hung high and even the once gloomy black reception desk had been changed out for something far more pleasant to the eye. As far as makeovers go, the building looked like it had been given a hefty one.

"Yeah, the entire building was taken over by a new-age tech company. I guess they wanted to try and spruce things up a bit." Yuri made his way to the reception desk which also had a series of computers peering over the edge. Behind the monitor, there were two people. One was a young woman and she was speaking to a man dressed in business casual wear with large round glasses. When Yuri and Jules reached the desk, the man pulled his attention from his employee before forming a friendly smile towards those in front of him.

"Hey Yuri," the man said in a somewhat nerdy voice, "What are you doing here? Did you forget something in your old office?" The man was friendly in his disposition and must have crossed paths with Yuri at some point when he moved out.

"Nope, I think we cleaned everything out pretty thoroughly, thanks, Mark."

"Good, good, then what brings you by my new area of operation? I would've thought you'd have your hands full with all the EC rebuilding going on these days?" The man named Mark pushed his glasses slightly up his thin nose.

"Yeah, it's been pretty busy lately, but I actually came by so I could talk to you."

"Oh?"

Yuri lowered his voice a few decibels, trying to keep the conversation private. "You were one of the people who called in about the disappearance of an employee last night, correct?"

The mood in the room shifted at the drop of a hat, and the cheerful smile of Mark curved into a look of worry. "Please, come to my office, I think it's better that we have this conversation in private."

Jules and Yuri took seats in what Jules swore was his brother's old office. However, the dull bleak furniture and overall design had been replaced with a much more vibrant and modern look as well.

Yuri pulled out a small notepad and pen from his pocket flipping it open. "Alright, Mark, why don't you start from the beginning and fill us in on everything."

Mark folded his hands together, "Okay, well... her name is Joy Peterson. She was a new employee and only started working here about a month ago. But everyone was really taking a shine to her. Last night a few of us stayed late trying to finish a big project. It must have been well past midnight by the time most people left. As I was leaving the building, I saw Joy. I told her I'd walk her to the train station so she didn't have to go about it alone, but only around a block from here we were approached by this... thing... I don't even know how to describe it. It was like a Human, but it just made grunting sounds. It was some kind of monster."

"A monster?" Jules asked.

"Yeah, its eyes were lifeless, and skin slimy... I'll never forget it. Unfortunately, it was dark, and I couldn't get a better view of it, but that's what stuck out to me. It must have come out from an alley or something. I tried to step in and protect Joy, but I've never been particularly strong when it came to using my element. The thing knocked me to the ground in seconds, and I guess after I hit my head I blacked out. When I finally came to my senses, Joy and the monster were gone. I called the police immediately, but it all seemed too late by then." Mark hung his head in defeat. "If only I could have protected her..."

"It's okay, Mark, we're going to find her, and all the other missing people as well. We'll put a stop to all this, but we need as much information as we can get our hands on to find out who's behind this."

Mark raised his head to see the comforting smile of Yuri. He nodded, "Whatever I can do to help, please just ask."

"Thanks, I'll try to keep you updated on progress as well."

After a couple more questions the brothers left the office with a new goal in mind. The nearby location of where the incident took place.

"Looks like this is the place," Jules said.

He stared into an obscure back street that was smothered between two more sky scraping buildings. He took the lead showing no fear as he began to check the alleyway, but as he did, his vision became dark.

"I can barely even see through here. It's broad daylight. How is this place so dark?"

"Slow down, Jules, we need to exercise caution right now. We still have no idea what we might be up against, and until we do it's impossible to formulate a strategy."

Jules nodded, slowing his pace to match his brothers. They cautiously walked down the street. Even if they were working together, Yuri was still the older brother and would play that role no matter the situation, and that meant making sure his brother did not fall into harm's way.

Yuri and Jules were both using phones that acted as flashlights, but even then, it was only a straight line source of light. But it was better than nothing.

Along the way Jules asked, "You don't think it was actually some sort of monster, do you?"

"I highly doubt it... but as for who's behind this, it's hard to say. If the incident did happen after midnight, then it's been less than twelve hours since Ms. Peterson went missing. So, we might be able to find something left over, something that the police might've missed."

Eventually, as they moved forward, Jules kicked his foot off something heavy and metal before falling to the ground in a thud. He dropped his light source and grabbed for his left foot letting out a groan.

Yuri flashed the light towards his brother on the ground and asked, "Are you alright?"

"Ugh, yeah I'm fine, but it feels like I kicked a boulder." Jules picked up his phone and shined it in the direction of his attacker.

Yuri did the same and they saw the culprit, "Not quite a boulder, but looks like you kicked a manhole cover," he said. Then he bent down, examining his brother's foot pressing in various places to see if any pain arose. Jules winced but pushed himself up, shaking off any residual aching.

"Well, it looks like you didn't break anything at least."

"I'm fine," Jules said dusting his uniform off, "But what's a manhole cover doing in the middle of an alleyway anyways? It's dangerous." Jules bent down to pick up the iron slab, before realizing how it tripped him so easily. "What the... this thing weighs a ton. Manhole covers are not this heavy." He groaned through gritted teeth.

"That's odd." Yuri bent down next to Jules and tried to help his brother but with little results. They were both left gasping for air after only a few seconds of trying.

"Wow you weren't kidding; there's no way that could be picked up by a normal person."

Jules said, "Here, let me try something," and Yuri stepped back as the wind began to swirl around Jules' body. It was like he had been cloaked in a controlled tornado.

"Arghhh," Jules roared as he dug his fingers under the lid and began to prop it up. Thanks to his wind, he managed to alleviate some of the weight, to the point that he could finally move the cover. He slid it back one inch at a time until finally, it created enough room for someone - albeit a thin someone - to fit.

Yuri flashed the light down into the black abyss. "I think it leads to the sewers, but I wouldn't say this was any city made entrance."

"Do we go down?" Jules asked. He appeared less than thrilled at the prospect of Yuri's answer.

"I think we should, but be on your guard. We must be prepared for anything."

"Okay."

Yuri climbed down first, checking the stability of the rusty ladder. The bars creaked from the slightest pressure and looked like they could snap like twigs. Once the steps were deemed safe, Jules followed close behind, the both of them trying to maximize the amount of light their phones could produce but with little success. They could see next to nothing for their efforts. It would've been almost impossible to tell they were in the city's underground sewer system without the smell of rancid water washing up against the concrete and filling their nostrils as a reminder. And if not that, then the rats that scurried along the metal piping certainly did.

Jules, for all of his bravery and ambition, couldn't help but feel unnerved at where he found himself. His vision was impaired, the smell made him want to vomit and things scurrying around unseen would put anyone on edge.

Yuri sensed his brother's distress and said, "Stay close, we're only here to take a quick look." He understood the circumstances, but unfortunately, sometimes this was part of the job and even if Jules was technically a volunteer this was his dream, just the dirty underbelly of said dream.

"How can you even see down here... ahh!" Jules let a small squeal as he felt a wet, slushy texture seep into his shoe.

"What is it?" Yuri asked, swinging around, his light temporarily blinding his brother. He looked down at Jules' foot and said, "Jules, it's just a puddle of water, don't scare me like that."

"Hey! I would know if I stepped in water," Jules argued. He bent down to get a better look at the substance covering his shoe. Just like he claimed, it was not water, but a gray, oozing goop. "Well, that's gross..." Jules muttered.

Yuri bent down beside him and slid his finger feeling the thick texture of the syrup-like substance between his fingers. "You're right, it's definitely not water. I've never seen anything like it before..." Yuri tapped his pockets feeling for something. He looked at his brother, "Do you have anything to scoop this up with? I think we should take it back to the labs. There have been some reports of an ooze like liquid at the scene of other crimes. This might be a match."

"Um yeah, here," Jules fuddled around in his pocket for a moment before pulling out a small plastic bag from his lunch. He then took a pencil out of his pocket and began scooping up the substance with his utensil before concealing the bag and handing it to Yuri.

Yuri stood up and said, "I have a feeling whatever is producing this ooze might be what kidnapped Ms. Peterson. Come on, let's get back to the EC. If we want to explore further down here, I think we're gonna need to call in some backup."

CHAPTER 6
AN UNWANTED RETURN

LITTLE LIGHT BREACHED THE ALLEYWAY DESPITE THE sun hanging high in mid-day. An eerie chill followed as Minisc and Lily cautiously walked ahead. A small ball of light hung in front illuminating their way as they checked every inch of their surroundings. There were no clues to be found, no disturbances, and nothing out of place.

"Do you have any idea where we're going?" Lily asked.

"Not really, but there has to be something around here to tell us where Maya went, right? I mean it's an alleyway; there aren't a whole lot of places to go."

"You don't think whatever it was got away, do you?" As soon as the words left Lily's mouth, they heard another high-pitched scream bounce through the alley.

"That sounded like Maya! It came from that direction," Lily pointed left where the alley split off into two different paths. They took off chasing the sounds.

"This is bringing back bad memories," Minisc muttered as he trailed behind Lily. He was reminded of running through alleyways only to find Jules trapped.

When the exit came into view they were on a new street. Lily came to a screeching halt, making Minisc put on the brakes in a hurry.

"Whoa, Lily," he whined as he did his best not to run his friend over. "Why'd you stop?"

"Do you feel that? It feels like the temperature just got really hot..." Lily's eyes scanned the surroundings, looking for a hint. The two were now surrounded by the remains of homes on a shattered street, but because of that they knew there weren't many places to hide. And the scream had been too clear for the kidnapper to have gone far.

"You're right..." Minisc instinctively stepped in front of Lily, a small ball of light forming in his left hand. "Be on your guard; we're definitely not alone," he whispered.

The two gradually made their way to the middle of the barren street, each one looking in a different direction to cover their bases. That's when Minisc noticed a faint trail of what looked like gray goop starting from the street and leading into the forest nearby.

Lily bent down and ran her finger through the goop letting the substance ooze onto her finger. "What is this stuff?"

"I don't know, but if I had to guess, I'd say it came from whoever or whatever took Maya." Minisc stood back up and looked through the dense forest. There were hundreds of different ways to go even if a trail of goop could guide them. He turned to Lily and said, "Go back to the shelter and direct the police and any EC this way. I'm gonna follow the trail, but in a forest this large, we need as big of a search party as we can get."

"Are you crazy? It's way too dangerous. We don't even know who's out there!" Lily argued back.

"Lily... we go through this every time. I'll be fine, I promise."

He hugged her tight for good measure and once they separated Lily said, "Fine, but don't do anything stupid or I swear I'll kill you, got it?" And with that Lily began retracing her steps leaving Minisc to begin his search alone.

The forest itself was lush and untainted by the events that plagued North York. But even so, there was still a lingering smell throughout, a faint stench that overpowered the sweet scents of nature.

Every step deeper into the forest caused the light to fade, and the thick weaving ceiling of branches above him grew. Minisc did his best to follow any traces of the goop, but everywhere he looked his surroundings appeared the same.

This is ridiculous, Maya could be anywhere in here he thought. Then he heard ruffling footsteps through the bushes. He turned to his left and raised his arms to defend himself, but much to his shock, out of the bushes burst Maya, running and panting as if her life depended on it.

"Maya!" He yelled, but before they could celebrate any sort of reunion, a ball of fire ripped through the trees and hit Maya square in the back of her right shoulder. She dropped to the ground in a heap as she cried out in agony. Minisc ran over to her and tossed his jacket on the girl's shoulder smothering the flames. He looked to where the attack came from and fired a Lum Bomb out of instinct. The attack collided with another burst of flames and exploded.

Maya got on her hands and knees with eyes full of painful tears as she saw Minisc stand up in front of her.

"What are you doing here?" She tried to growl through the sobs.

"Don't worry, it's going to be okay now. I've got you." Minisc whispered back before placing himself in front of Maya as a shield. He stared in the direction of where Maya had appeared from and yelled, "Show yourself, you coward!"

Minisc would soon come to regret that demand though, as stomping out from the shadows of the trees came a strange figure. It was far from Human, or even an Elementalist, but whatever it was, Minisc already knew it had Elementalist powers.

The *thing* stood a towering seven feet tall at least, and although it carried the same general body shape of a Human, its skin oozed a disgusting grey syrup that dripped from all over its limbs. Where eyes should have been were two sockets of blackness and a small slit for a mouth. More than anything it looked like a living corpse made out of goo.

"What the hell is that..." Minisc stared at the grotesque monster, not sure how to react. What he did know was that Maya remained priority number one, and getting her back to the shelter safely was all that mattered.

Minisc stepped back as the monster stepped forward. He raised his fist ready to defend himself as sparks popped off his body. His fists started glowing, but then the monster opened its thin mouth.

"You blasted child, I said to come nicely and you wouldn't get hurt..." The monster stopped and locked eyes with Minisc. "You... Minisc Premier..."

Minisc froze, his heart shooting through his chest as the monster spoke. How did this thing know his name? Was he hallucinating? Moreover, the voice sounded familiar in some sense. He'd heard it before, but he couldn't place it. Then it hit him.

"No... It couldn't be..."

The creature's body began to ripple like waves in the ocean, and before Minisc could react, a frightening fist collided with him at a speed he wasn't prepared for. He crashed into a tree nearly blasting right through it.

"Argh," Minisc groaned as he crumpled to the ground. He got to one knee, whipping the corner of his mouth.

"You have no idea how long I've been waiting for this day... ever since you left me for dead in that blasted lab," the voice growled. "Now get up, I know you can take more punishment than that." The monster mocked finishing it off with a cackle. The voice, there was no mistaking it. That same laugh that had him dead to rights in Dr. Jarrad's lab. The tone of a woman who'd lost her sanity.

"Pascale, but how? I thought the police arrested you the day you tried to kill us."

"Oh, I wasn't arrested by anyone, I assure you. After you and that Normandy kid left me in that rubble, I was returned to Luminosa. I can't say I remember much after that, but soon I was given this body. It was the only way for my consciousness to live on. You didn't think I would let you slip through my grasp forever, did you? I told you, traitors always die, and now it's my turn to teach you that lesson."

Minisc got up, taking a peek behind him. He saw Maya quivering and unable to run. Then he looked back at Pascale, trying to solve the question of her new body. *Is that goo somehow hiding muscles underneath, or is it all one big exoskeleton? And how am I supposed to protect Maya while trying to fight? Lily should be back soon, but even then it could take too long for her to find us. Either way I don't have time to think. I need to keep Maya safe. Just rely on my instincts, I have the strength. Just like against Dusk.*

Behind Minisc, Maya started to crawl backwards not even noticing the scorching burn mark on her shoulder. She kept going till she hit a tree wincing from the pain of the collision.

Minisc heard the whimper but refused to take his eyes off Pascale. "Don't worry Maya, I won't let this traitor hurt you."

"Again with the traitor talk... look at you, still defending Humans. Guess I'll have to teach you a lesson. And this time there's no one to back you up, kid. I'll burn your corpse so badly once I'm done with you, they won't even be able to find the ashes of your remains." Pascale growled again, still not satisfied. "But no, even that's not good enough for you. I want to rip the screams from your mouth. I'll make you feel every ounce of agony you left me in."

Pascale's fist turned to fire, the grey goop around her turning a copper colour. She swung at Minisc without fear of burning down anything in her path.

Forced to defend, Minisc raised his arms creating a small barrier to avoid the burns. Even so, as his shield absorbed the blow, the force slid him backwards. Pascale remained relentless, refusing to let Minisc act. He leapt a foot into the air as one punch slammed into the ground, shaking the forest for miles. But with Minisc stuck in mid-air, he was vulnerable. He absorbed a kick into the gut, sending him flying further through the air again. He hit the ground hard coughing up blood as he did.

"So you still think you're gonna protect this kid? You might want to think about saving yourself while you have the chance. If you don't, I'll kill you!" Pascale started walking towards Maya, who was paralyzed with fear. "Did you learn nothing from before? This world is kill or be killed. It doesn't matter who you are, those that show kindness always end up dead."

Pascale snarled and shot off another ball of fire at Maya. The girl's eyes grew wide as she tried to lift her arm in defence, but before it could strike a blast of light intercepted the attack.

Minisc lay on the ground with his arm stretched out and glowing from the attack. "You're right, Pascale, I do think I'm gonna protect Maya…" He got to one knee, "But that's about the only thing you're right about. And I'll prove it."

Minisc tried to think of a plan. *I can't focus on Maya right now. If I do, I'll never stop Pascale. If I can just find a way to beat her, I can solve the rest later.*

Minisc sprang up with his fist shining gold as he slammed it into Pascale's chest. A blinding ray of light filled the forest. He held the punch, but not by choice. A slimy goopy sensation like tar began crawling up his forearm.

"That's it, that's your heroic last stand? You might be fast, but that won't be enough to save you this time."

Minisc gritted his teeth, using all his strength to pull his arm free, but as he did, Pascale landed another punch sending him sprawling backwards.

"Let me explain something to you, kid. In this body, you can't touch me. The ooze around me absorbs all impacts, meaning you can't deal me any damage. No matter how strong you think you are, like this I'm invincible."

Minisc fired blast after blast of light, but just as Pascale boasted, she took the attacks in stride before getting close. Minisc tried to defend himself, but she grabbed him, slamming him to the ground. The forest cracked, leaving a small crater behind as Minisc lay in it.

"You and your father go on talking about Humans being equal to Elementalists and sharing this world. You love to spout off your ideals and virtues, but when it comes to backing it up, you're all talk. Now get up and fight me like you mean it."

Pascale growled letting her temper fuel her strength. She loomed over Minisc who remained motionless in agony.

I need to get up, but every muscle in my body feels broken…

Finally, ready to cement her killing blow, a flash filled her eyes and out from behind the tree Maya came jumping out with a sharp stick. She stabbed Pascale in the leg, jamming it as deep into the ooze as possible.

"Stop it," she cried with streaks of tears running down her cheeks. She continued to poke away at the monster as if the skinny branch she held was a sword and she was the knight. "Stop it! Stop killing people. It's because of monsters like you that my daddy is dead. You guys ruined everything."

"Maya..." Minisc muttered from the ground.

"Oh, your dear old daddy is dead? And killed by Elementalists, no doubt..."

Maya shook her head sniffling as the tears continued to run.

"Well guess what, kid, here's a little secret for you: my father was killed by monsters known as the Human race. People just like you that took him in cold blood. This world you live in, doesn't care about you, nor does it care if your dear old daddy is killed. He was just another meaningless life sacrificed in this war. But I wouldn't worry about that for too much longer, because you'll be joining your old pops soon enough."

Pascale held out her hand, ready to burn Maya to ashes, but then turned around when she heard Minisc blast off towards her like a missile.

"You think you can launch a sneak attack against me? Nice try, idiot."

"How dare you tell her that her father's life was meaningless! Everyone's life is important!"

Minisc lodged his left fist into the chest of Pascale's impenetrable body, but once again the ooze trapped him.

"So you just thought if you tried the same technique again this time it would work, how stupid are you kid? Don't you get it; you can't hurt me!"

However, spurred on by the mounting frustration of his opponent's words, Minisc's free left hand began to glow a majestic gold. "It doesn't matter if I can't hurt you, at least I'll die trying!" He growled. Like a shotgun, Minisc's blast exploded in the left breast of Pascale's shell, sending everyone flying back. But as Minisc sailed through the air, he noticed something in Pascale's open chest hole.

He squinted through the smoke, *is that a crystal...* He only caught a faint glimpse of a diamond-shaped object glowing red, but somehow, he knew that was the target.

When the dust from the explosion settled, Minisc found himself face-down in the grass next to Maya. He looked up to see the girl sprawled out, but her chest was still rising and falling heavily. He looked to see if Pascale was around, but all that remained was a series of tumbled trees and shattered branches where he had sent her flying.

Minisc sucked in deep breaths while trying to get to his feet, before leaning over to help Maya up. "Sorry about that, but it's okay now, you're safe."

Maya looked up, seeing Minisc's body trembling. His knees were about to give way and his body was covered in streaks of blood. Maya gave a faint smile and whispered, "Uh, thank you."

Why, why would he sacrifice himself to help me... I'm just a Human and he's an Elementalists. He's supposed to hate me. Maya thought.

"Come on, we can get back to the shelter, it's not too far from here. I'm sure everyone is worried sick about you." Minisc smiled keeping a brave face. He wanted to collapse in the middle of the forest and sleep, but he needed to get Maya home first.

But before they could take a step, the ground began to rumble.

"She can't be... that was everything I had left," Minisc said in a low whisper.

The thunderous stomps and frustrated growls coming from the depth of the forest froze Maya with terror. A feeling Minisc could sense. He stepped in front of the girl again, despite every nerve and bone in his body begging him not to.

Out from the forest returned Pascale, her lifeless demeanour and once wounded body in full tact. She looked no different than when the fight started.

"I told you, you can't hurt me..."

"Stay away, you monster," Minisc shouted.

"Not gonna happen. You've been a pain in Luminosa's side for too long... once I kill you I can come back for the brat any time."

Damn it. She can't be telling the truth. There's no way she's invincible

Minisc thought, racing through ways to slow down Pascale. He finally settled on the one that seemed most obvious.

"What does Luminosa want with Maya? Why are you after her?" But his hopes of buying time were quickly dashed.

"Like I would ever tell you. Now get ready. Before, I was just playing around. This time I'm gonna show you the meaning of true pain."

With the monster lurking and ready to strike, Minisc grabbed Maya's arm, "Hurry come on."

He leapt through the air narrowly missing a punch that shook the ground. A second later and the girl would have been killed without hesitation.

Minisc landed, tumbling over and tossing Maya as he did. He got to his knee panting with the unrelenting pain coursing through his muscles.

If only I knew which way the streets were, I could send Maya on her own and fight alone. But even then, I don't think I could buy her enough time. That last attack drained most of my energy. If I turn my back for even a second, she'll kill me. So I can't grab Maya and run either. I just have to find the will to fight. I have to win.

Minisc raised his arms again, trying to let the power flow through him. The surge of his element was fading, but he had to keep fighting. He refused to give up.

"Get back, Maya, and when I say run... you get as far away from here as you can and hide. Whatever you do, don't turn around. Your sister and others will be coming to get you soon. I promise."

"You're gonna fight that thing again? But... you saw how strong it was... we both need to run. She's gonna kill you." Maya had the naïve cry of hope in her voice. She really believed running would be the best option for both of them, not that Minisc had much confidence in his own strategy. Maya was right; his attacks had had next to no effect, but he needed to try.

"Don't worry about me, I'll be fine," Minisc said as his body started to glow. No matter what it took, he wouldn't let Maya get hurt. Even if such kindness did cost him his life.

The oozing body of Pascale prepared again, bursting her arms into dancing flames. The two collided with air-rippling shock waves. They were stuck together, except this time Minisc struggled ever more to fend off the flames with his light.

"That was more pathetic than the last punch," Pascale mocked.

The ground beneath Minisc's feet started to shatter as the gray goo began to consume his body. It was beginning to trap Minisc, who had tears mixed with blood streaming down his face. He felt his body being ripped apart one cell at a time as he continued to dig as far into the depths of his power as he could.

"Minisc!" Maya yelled forgetting that she was supposed to be running.

"It's okay, I'll be fine. But you need to run!" Minisc yelled in agony, "Get away from here!"

"Even in death you still want to protect some stupid human. You really are your father's son." The monster laughed as all the ooze began to overtake Minisc's body, pushing him to the ground. The pressure overwhelmed him, and no amount of strength could hold it back; he was powerless as the world began to turn dark around him. The flames from Pascale's arms were slowly engulfing him with nowhere left to go.

"Damn it, just shut up!" Minisc cried at the top of his lungs.

"There's the screams I wanted!" The ground broke further into a hole as Minisc became fully smothered by the monster. "Now you die!"

Minisc closed his eyes, letting the life fade from them as he did. The burning sensation that coated his body became overwhelming as he took his last breaths. *Lily, Jules, I couldn't win this one... Father, I let you down... I... I'm sorry.*

That's when he heard a scream, "Leave him alone!"

Minisc's eyes fluttered open for a second, his heart starting to pump rapidly from hearing Maya's voice cry out to him. A cry to protect him, something that just yesterday seemed like an impossibility.

"Maya..." Minisc whispered. .

Maya jumped through the air, jamming a stick into Pascale's eye socket this time. She held on for dear life as Pascale let out a wincing cry, "Wait your turn, kid, I'll get to-"

Then she felt her fists being pushed up but had no idea how. She smothered Minisc for good, the boy had to be dead.

"I won't let you take Maya, not now, not ever." Minisc rose from his own grave pushing back Pascale's suffocating ooze in the process. A golden glow like fire danced around his body in swirls as a flood of revitalized strength filled him. This time, he would be sure to stay true to his promise. He would not let Maya be taken, because, like his father and mother, he would do whatever it took to help someone in need. He would show Pascale his true power.

"Damn it, where do you keep getting all this power from?" Pascale roared.

Minisc's entire body shone with the passion and desire only seen when he fought Dusk. He readied himself, his palm folding over a ball of light that gleamed like the sun.

"This is your end, Pascale! Solar Impact!" Minisc cried out, punching straight through the monster's chest. He knew that despite using every ounce of strength in his body, that alone would not finish Pascale for good. This time he had a different plan, though. The explosive punch ripped a hole through his enemy's chest, where his hand currently resided. However, unlike last time, he punched with a specific target in mind. Pascale let out a deathly roar as she flew through the air, her oozed coating exploding like a bubble in the process. But this time, she left something rather important behind.

Minisc looked up to see the oozing monster he had just obliterated. It was no more than a pile of goop on the ground, and in Minisc's hand was a small red crystal emitting a burning heat to it.

He glanced at it and said, "Was this... her heart...?" While he wanted to examine things further, he still had bigger fish to fry. He turned to look at Maya who was on her hands and knees in tears.

"Why... why would you put yourself through all of that just to help me? After I hit you and called you a monster..." Maya looked like an innocent child seeing the error of her ways, and as a child, she spilled all those emotions out at once.

Minisc limped over to the girl both his arms hanging to his sides. He smiled, "It's okay, I know why you felt the way you did. There are some horrible Elementalists out there... like the one who burned down your house and caused your father to pass. But most of us aren't like that. And I want to help show people that. Whether you're different than me or not, we're all part of the same world. Nobody deserves to suffer the way you have."

Maya nodded silently sniffling as she wiped the tears out of her eyes. She got to his feet and whispered, "Thank you..."

CHAPTER 7
CHANGE IN PLANS

"I REALLY AM SORRY FOR CALLING YOU A MONSTER," Maya muttered as she and Minisc made their way through the dense forest. She rode on Minisc's back, her hands and legs wrapped around the battered and bruised body of her saviour. Once the fight ended and the adrenaline of fight or flight wore off, Maya collapsed from exhaustion. Minisc, of course, felt the same, but he knew the job was not done until Maya was back where she belonged. So, he placed her on his back and started retracing his steps.

Minisc took a big whiff of the evergreen trees, letting the scent keep his senses intact. As long as he did that, he could keep moving.

"It's okay, I understand. I'm just glad you're safe. That's what's important right now."

"Do you know how to get out of here?" Maya asked.

Minisc came to a stop and looked around. He was surrounded by large, towering trees, but in no way could he see a way out.

"... Nope..."

Eventually, after walking in circles, Minisc heard a voice that brought him great comfort.

"Minisc, where are you? Are you in here?"

"Lily!" Minisc called back, "We're over here." He bent down and let Maya off his back. They were finally home free.

Seconds later, Lily came rushing through the trees skidding to a halt as she finally found her friend. She took one look at Minisc and gasped. The streaks of blood and ripped clothing suggest Minisc had just stepped out from his own grave - likely because he had.

"Minisc!" She said, "what happened? I thought you said you could handle it!"

Minisc looked at his worried friend and then smiled as he gestured to Maya, "I got Maya back, didn't I?" Although his injuries were causing relentless pain, he had indeed succeeded, and on top of that, while using his father's famous technique Solar Impact, it had put far less strain on his body than when he fought Dusk. As far as he was concerned, that was an improvement.

Following behind Lily were two police officers as well as two EC members. They were calm and ready to investigate, but tagging along with them was a girl who showed no sense of those traits.

Bailey rushed her little sister dropping to her knees and hugging her. "Oh thank goodness you're alive. Are you hurt? It's okay, your big sister's here now." She started examining every inch of Maya's body for injuries. The younger sibling squirmed with what little strength she had left to escape her sister's clutches.

"I'm fine... thanks to Minisc," she muttered. Bailey hugged her tight again and then stood up looking at Minisc with a genuine and warm smile. "Thank you Minisc, I'm so sorry my sister caused such trouble for you, but I'm glad you were there for her. I don't know what I'd do if I lost her too..."

While Minisc and Maya were taken back to the shelter to have their injuries examined, the police and EC continued searching around the area for clues. Once again, all they could find were the oozing remains of the monster claiming to be Pascale.

After being cleared of any extensive injuries, despite Minisc's body disagreeing with the diagnosis, he, Lily and Bailey returned to the EC to wrap up the day.

"What do you mean it was Pascale? But... as some sort of oozing monster?" Lily asked. She sat on the couch in Yuri's office beside Minisc, and across from Bailey. Even though she'd never met the EC traitor, she knew the woman as the one who tried to kill her best friend, and that was enough to hate the woman.

Bailey looked at the two, and then asked, "Who's Pascale?"

Minisc groaned leaning back sinking into the couch and letting his aching body relax. "It's a long story, but regardless, I don't know if it was really her. It sounded like her, she still had her fire element, and she certainly had a conscious awareness of who I was. But her body, that goop was like an armour and none of my attacks could hurt her. Honestly, the only way I won was by ripping this out of her chest." Minisc reached into his pocket and pulled out a small, red, diamond-shaped crystal. He held it in his fingers giving it a once over for good measure before placing it on the table.

"Huh, what's that?" Lily picked up the shard, feeling its warmth through the tips of her fingers. She spun it in her hands admiring the amber shine.

"Now that's a rock, it would make one heck of a wedding ring," Bailey said.

Minisc ignored Bailey's comment and said, "I'm not sure why, but when I finally ripped it out the goop faded. It's like this was her heart or something. But who knows."

"Either way, I'm glad you're okay. But I knew I should have stayed to help." Lily smiled, rubbing Minisc's shoulder.

Bailey put her feet up on the table just as she had when they first met and said, "No kidding, if Yuri found out I let you die on the second day, he'd have my head."

"Jeez, thanks…" Minisc muttered before sitting up. "Anyways, whatever that thing was, I think we need to be prepared for it to show up again."

"If Pascale is involved then do you think Luminosa is somehow behind this?" Lily asked.

"An attack on an innocent Human child? I wouldn't put it past them, but we can't jump to those conclusions yet. Let's wait and see what Yuri has to say about all this."

"What Yuri has to say about what?" On cue, Yuri walked into his office, where Minisc, Bailey, and Lily sat, exhausted. Behind him, Jules walked in, looking every bit as fatigued as his friends. However, when he plopped down lifelessly into the chair, he took one look at Minisc and his eyes widened.

"What happened to you?"

When Yuri heard that he spun around and formed the same expression as his brother. He put his hand to his head and said, "How does this stuff always happen to you?" He sighed. "Are you at least okay?"

"We had a run-in with some sort of slime monster trying to kidnap Bailey's sister from the shelter. But that's not all…" Minisc went on to explain the possible appearance of Pascale, and then about the monster form she had taken. When they got to the part about the remaining ooze on the ground Yuri pulled out the bag he and Jules had scooped up from their afternoon venture.

"Did it look somewhat like this?" He asked, handing Minisc the bag.

Minisc leered over it with Lily taking a peek as well.

"Isn't that the same thing the police scooped up after you beat that monster?" Lily asked.

"Yeah, definitely." Minisc looked up. "Yuri, where did you find this?"

"It was in connection to another missing persons case last night."

"Wait, does that mean Minisc took down whatever was behind the missing people?" Jules asked.

Yuri put his finger to his chin for a second, "It's hard to say. For the number of people missing, I would hazard a guess that there is more than one person behind this. But perhaps Minisc took out one of them. Which is always a good thing."

Lily nodded and said, "If that truly was Pascale, then we can only assume Luminosa is involved somehow."

"This crystal on the other hand…" Yuri bent over and picked up the partially translucent red diamond. He could feel a strange power radiating from it like a heartbeat. "Minisc, do you mind if I take this to one of the labs? I think it needs to be researched as soon as possible."

"Of course. I doubt it'd be much use to me anyways. Besides, the quicker we figure out what it really is, the better."

Yuri slid the gem into his pocket. "Alright, well I think everyone has had enough excitement for one day, so head home and get some much-needed rest, Minisc if you want me to take you for some examinations, I can do that as well."

"Thanks, but I'm okay. I've been through worse," he laughed.

"Okay, then I'll see you all in my office tomorrow morning." Yuri nodded and left the room. He wanted to waste no time getting the crystal Minisc had snagged into the hands of those that could learn its properties quickest.

This time it was Don's turn to sit on the outside porch, stuck in thought. He was waiting for Minisc to return home, but rather than sitting inside, he decided to take a shot at Minisc's mind-clearing routine. After all, his wife was the one who taught it to their son.

For days, he had continued to linger on his conversation with Dusk. Just like many others in the EC, he too was trying to solve the mystery of the missing persons, but like those in the EC, he struggled to piece together the puzzle. He hoped Dusk would slip up, provide a hint through his words, but as the man always did, he remained calm, calculated and aware of every thought that passed his lips.

He had some clues. Brooklyn, the apprentice of Dusk remained on the loose, and that made Luminosa still a threat. Alongside that Coro's father was presumed to still be in the group's possession, and then Ignis, Minisc's childhood friend. However, the three of them together would not be enough to achieve Luminosa's ultimate goal of Human extermination, and Don and Dusk both knew it. Yet Dusk did not seem at all concerned. Could the reason be with Don's strength fading he believed they could finally win? Or was there another angle?

Don glanced up when he saw Minisc walking up the gravel driveway. He had changed out of his torn-up uniform, so for the most part he looked himself. But his expression and body language betrayed any such attempt to hide the anguish his body felt. He walked hunched over and somewhat gingerly till he hit the first step and locked eyes with his father.

Don smirked, and said, "I can't let you go anywhere without getting into trouble, can I?"

Minisc fought the desire to roll his eyes, opting to say, "It's not like I go looking for it... I just seem to be in the wrong place at the wrong time a lot..." Nobody seemed to understand just how close he'd come to death.

"I wouldn't look at it like that. If you hadn't been there today, then that poor child would've been added to the growing list of missing people."

"How did you...?"

"Yuri filled me in on everything. You did well, just as you always do."

"So I don't have to explain about Pascale, or the slime and the crystal and all that?"

"No, he briefed me on everything, but we do have a meeting with Zale in the morning to go over things. Sounds like Yuri thinks if Luminosa is behind this, then maybe they're using the sewers to move around undetected, so we're putting a group together to investigate."

Minisc frowned. "Does that mean I'm not going back to the shelter with Lily tomorrow?"

"Sorry, Minisc, I know you wanted to help the people affected by Dusk..."

Minisc nodded and wiped the frown away, "It's okay. Whoever's behind this, Luminosa or not, needs to be stopped. None of what Lily and I do at the shelter will mean anything if it'll all just be undone by whoever is causing this."

"I'm glad you understand. Now let's get you some food, and maybe a shower. You look like a mess," Don laughed.

Bright and early the next morning, Minisc found himself sitting in the office of the president of the EC, surrounded by his father, Jules, and Yuri. For an hour, the five batted ideas back and forth, trying to figure out a plan of attack.

Sitting on a square table were blueprints of the entire city structure. Every entrance to Toronto's sewer systems was labelled and circled in red marker. In black marker were the general locations of every Human's last sighting based on police reports.

"This is the last one from yesterday," Yuri said as he finished circling the forested area where Minisc fought Pascale.

Zale pointed to all the circles while he added, "It looks like every incident has happened in at least a half mile of sewer gates or entrances. Or at least where the police reported finding similar slime substance." ·

"The only one that doesn't mirror that is the one Minisc dealt with yesterday," Don added.

"That might be a bit of a red herring though," Minisc said. "I know Maya made a run for it and tried to escape, plus if you look at the closest sewer, Lily and I would have been right in the path before things went off the rails." Minisc pointed to the general area where he and Lily stood coming out of the alleyway.

Yuri agreed and began giving orders, "Alright, I think we should do a preliminary sweep of the sewers and see if we can find anything out of the ordinary. Minisc and Don, I'm sorry to pull you guys away from your other work but we need someone who can provide a little more light for us. On top of that, having all four of us together will help ensure safety. Outside of Minisc, none of us really know what we're up against, and by all accounts, these things are not to be reckoned with," Yuri said.

The five looked at each other and readied to head out. But before they left, Zale said, "Remember, if things look like they could become dangerous, then abort the mission. We're not looking for another city-destroying fight here. Our goal is to gather information and hopefully with any luck find the missing victims. That's all."

The group nodded and set out for the sewers.

Unlike when Jules and Yuri entered the sewers via a manhole, this time they went to the main entrance to start their search. The opening was a large crescent moon shape with concrete walkways on either side. Musty green water flowed through the mouth of the entrance while also splashing up on the sides of each path. This route was built specifically for accessibility for any small-scale machines and extra manpower, as opposed to the small grates and manholes that were used on an individual basis.

Don walked up to the gates first and slipped into the lock a small key provided by Zale. As a precaution with this entrance being so big, it had been barred by metal bars looking like the outside of a jail cell. From the outside, the pungent stench of the water attacked in waves. Don paid it no mind, nor did Yuri, but Minisc and Jules were turning green from the smell.

A glimpse of light bled into the opening of the tunnel, but it only reached a dozen steps in. After that, they were at the mercy of total darkness. That's where Minisc and Don would help most.

Don turned to address the group. "Remember, the sewers are like a giant maze, so getting lost is a simple task. We need to stick together and watch each other's backs. Be on your guard at all times." He snapped his finger to form a floating sun sphere in front of him. Minisc did the same and now they could see a good thirty to forty feet further. Although not perfect, they were miles ahead of where Yuri and Jules were the day before.

The weather outside turned dark and rain clouds started to form as the group made their way down the left side path. Waves continually crashed violently along the walls, but other than that, the sewers were eerily quiet. Two by two they walked, with Minisc and Yuri at the front while Don and Jules covered the back. They had their eyes peeled for any oddities, and especially any more remnants of ooze.

A little way in with no signs of mischief or wrongdoing, they came up to a more open part of the sewers. In the new room, they were given four pathways to select from, with a horizontal path bridging the gap over rushing water. Don's ball of light flew to the center of the room over the bridge before gradually getting brighter to illuminate all directions.

"So which way do we go?" Jules asked. With no underlying clues, they were left with a meagre guess at the correct path.

"Based on the map Zale gave us, I think it would be best if we keep moving straight. That way if we ever lose our whereabouts then we can retrace our steps," Don advised.

Nobody debated the advice, and so they started to follow the lead of Don. The deeper into the sewers they went the more intense the cool breeze from the water became. Once Jules reached what they deemed the center of the sewers, he stopped and paused.

Minisc bumped into him before groaning, "Ugh, Jules, why'd you stop?"

"Can you guys hear that?" Jules held his ear to the cool concrete wall on his left. It was faint, and thanks to the waves almost inaudible, but once he heard it, like a tracking dog, Jules refused to let the beat escape him.

Don held his finger to his lips, and everyone fell silent. Through the deadened air and deep concentration, they began to pick up on a faint noise. A sort of beeping, like machinery. Every few seconds it would sound again, but where could it have been coming from?

"What is that? It sounds like a computer or something," Minisc whispered.

Don pulled out their map of the sewers and rolled it open on the ground. He ran his finger along the path they'd taken until he came to a stop.

"That's odd," he said.

"What is?" Minisc asked.

"There shouldn't be a wall here. At least based on the map Zale gave us." Everyone leaned in to check on the map. "The center of the sewers has been cut off."

"Is this just an old map? Or did someone do some remodeling here?" Yuri asked.

"If I had to guess, I would say the latter, and I'd say it was done with a purpose. Whatever's going on down here, somebody doesn't want to be discovered, that's for sure." Don handed the map off to Minisc before walking up beside Jules. "Stand back everyone."

"Hold on, you can't just go punching in walls down here," Minisc urged. Don turned to him and smirked.

"You're really going to chastise me for breaking a wall... after you brought down an entire laboratory?"

"..."

Jules and Yuri fought off their snickers at Minisc's befuddled face while Don turned back to the wall in question. He cocked his fist, and with a majestic light beginning to shine through his fingers as if blessed by the gods he smashed through the wall, shattering it into millions of tiny pebbles. The force and momentum of the punch nearly ripped him through the wall and threw him face-first on the ground. But that wasn't it. It wasn't an excess of force, but the simplicity with which the wall had cracked. Almost like a paper mache cover-up.

As the glowing light of a vicious hit faded, Minisc stepped over the molehill of rocks left in its wake and what he saw was nothing short of astonishing.

"No way..."

"What is this place..." Jules asked.

The newly revealed room was far more open than any other section of the sewers, and on top of that better lit as well. But none of that drew the attention from the main cause for concern in front of them.

Like statues lined up in prayer, containers were stretching to the back of the room. They were in precise rows of ten by five. But even that had not shot fear into Minisc. It was what resided in those containers, or more, what lived in the containers. Floating up and down in some sort of stasis were carbon copies of the monster version of Pascale. One had been near enough to put Minisc down for the count; he hated to think of what an army could do to the city.

"Minisc... are these the same thing that attacked you...?" Jules asked, slight fear in his inflection.

"Yeah... these are definitely it..." Minisc would not soon forget the hollowed-out eye sockets and slit of a mouth.

"This is insane. There must be fifty of them here," Jules whispered.

Don walked in behind them and said, "Whoever's behind this

must be building up an army of these creatures to overrun the city. With this many, no wonder so many people are disappearing every day."

The four started a sweeping investigation of the room looking for any other stand out clues. Minisc walked up to the closest container and stared into the oversized test tube. Along the base of the panel stood a keyboard at his navel height. There were far fewer buttons than a regular keyboard and none of them were labelled. Added to that every canister had a long, large, tube-like fire hose that plugged into the top of the canister and disappeared into the ceiling. Green and red lights flashed back and forth around the connection points of the tubes.

"Who could have created all of this?" Jules asked as he walked up and down the first row. He stopped and rubbed the condensation off a container only to be met with the cold, lifeless stare of the monster. Even if it was in stasis, just looking at it sent creeps down his back.

"I don't know... but whoever it was, they didn't just set this up overnight. They had to be working in secret for months, if not longer." Don said.

"So what do we do with them?" Jules asked. "If these were released into the city, they would overrun us in minutes."

"Jules is right, but before we dispose of this place, we need to make sure we've found every piece of information available to us. If this is Luminosa's work, then perhaps we can find a clue to their true whereabouts." Yuri added.

As they continued searching Jules made his way to the back right corner of the room, but when he whipped away the layer of condensation his breath caught for a second. He turned around and said, "Guys, I think we might have a problem..."

"What is it?" Minisc asked coming over to check on his best friend. He looked at what Jules saw and muttered, "Oh that cannot be good..."

CHAPTER 8
A STICKY SITUATION

"LILY, CAN YOU BRING OVER THE REST OF THE SHEETS for me?" Bailey asked as she finished handing the last folded up black bed sheet to the gentleman in front of her. There were still a dozen other people lined up at her station all waiting their turn for supplies.

"Coming right up," Lily chimed. She popped open another box and pulled out six red and white blankets that were neatly folded in perfect squares. She passed them off to Bailey who turned back to the next in line.

"Here you go. Fresh blankets, enjoy."

While Bailey did that Lily took the other box and started handing out supplies through the line.

"There you go, Mr. Fitzgerald. Nothing better than a fresh blanket to sleep with tonight."

"Thank you, sweetie," the elder statesman of the shelter said.

The morning flew by quickly, despite Lily and Bailey being the only volunteers at the shelter. The two of them used their passion for helping people and charming personalities to bring a smile to all the patrons they served. Even with a lack of numbers, the mood stayed positive.

"You know, when Yuri told me Minisc had been reassigned for the time being, I figured you would be going with him, but I'm glad you stuck around. It really makes my life a lot easier," Bailey said. She might not have made the greatest first impression, but as her true colours bled through more, Lily could see how kind and thoughtful the girl was. Even if she did love her fair share of attention as well.

"I am too, but I'm a little surprised Minisc didn't even tell me what they were doing. I assume it must be related to that monster from yesterday, though." Lily's voice contained a hint of concern, which Bailey picked up on.

She smiled, "You care about him a lot don't you?"

Lily blushed in return. "Of course, he's my best friend. And on top of that, he does have a habit of getting into a lot of trouble."

"You're telling me, but I'm glad he was here yesterday, I don't know what I would've done if he hadn't stopped Maya from being kidnapped."

Eventually, the morning work wrapped up and as Lily and Bailey were getting ready for lunch a buzz vibrated in Lily's pocket.

Oh, that must be Minisc she thought, but when she pulled her phone out the vibration turned into a blaring horn sound. The alarm grew louder and soon it wasn't only Lily's phone that boomed out. Everyone in the shelter with a cell phone was subjected to the same deafening alert.

Bailey came rushing out with her phone in hand. Her face was a little paler, and her pace frantic, but before she could say a word Lily already knew why.

As obnoxious as it was, the alarm served a purpose. Due to the drastic increase in missing Human cases in the city, the government implemented a new security warning system. The signal acted as a cry for help in the simplest form. But that's not all it did. Sent to each person's phone was valuable information about the incident. Things such as age, height, appearance, and last known location.

Lily started reading the details out loud, "Nicole, Andover, age 21, Human, 5 foot 2 inches, short, curly black hair. Last seen on the corner of West and King Street."

"West and King? That's not far from here. Do we go?" Bailey asked. Lily knew the obvious answer, but she had a look of hesitation on her face, a look Bailey matched. They both witnessed the beating

Minisc endured from the monster, and he was stronger than Lily and Bailey combined. So how could they hope to do anything?

Only they had to. They were close and an innocent life was on the line. Lily washed the fear off her face replacing it with determination.

"We have to go, I'm not gonna sit by and let another person be taken by those monsters."

"Agreed."

Refusing to second guess their feelings Lily and Bailey sprinted for the door leaving everyone in shock. They blew past Ben, and Bailey yelled, "We'll be back soon. Make sure everyone here is safe." Before the two disappeared out of the building.

The doors slammed closed and Ben began dialling while speaking in a frantic voice, "Hello, we have two young women on their way to the abduction alert right now. Please send any backup you can right away." He hung up the phone and then muttered a prayer, "Please be careful, you two."

The corner of King and West was only about a twenty-minute walk from the shelter, but Lily and Bailey reached it in record time. Much to their surprise, when they turned the street corner they noticed a mass number of people, at least thirty, in the middle of the road in a circle.

"Well that's quite the turn out," Bailey said.

"I guess more people were around than we thought?" Lily said.

Soft mummers circulated through the group, but nobody stepped up to take control. Whatever stood in the middle of the crowd was being treated like a foreign object. They were infatuated but concerned as well.

Lily tried to find an opening that she could squeeze through and assess the situation, but nobody would grant her access. She huffed in frustration as she turned to Bailey who had other ways of making her presence known.

"Elemental Council member here!" She yelled at the top of her lungs. Everyone in the group spun around and Lily jumped from surprise, but with the group's attention now solely focused on Bailey, she could give her next orders. "Make way, let me through," she demeaned, pushing her way past the crowd.

The sea of bodies began to part down the middle, letting Bailey march through with authority. Behind her, Lily followed, trying to smile and apologize for the girl's brashness. Bailey's motives were steeped in a good heart, and they were effective without a doubt, but Lily still thought it best to show some sense of remorse.

Inside the group on the pavement lay a young woman in a heap. She remained still, but her body was covered in the same gray ooze that had appeared near all of the victim sites thus far. The woman looked about the same age as the alert suggested and indeed had curling black hair as well.

Bailey bent down and placed her fingers on the woman's neck. "She's alive; she probably just fainted." She stood up exhaling a sigh of relief. Her words caused the same palpable stress in the group to drop a few notches. Then Lily bent down and ran her fingers along the woman's thin bare leg. The goop reached her thigh and on different parts of her body.

"She's definitely the one from the alert, but how did she escape?"

"Do you think she managed to kill it like Minisc did?" Bailey asked.

Lily looked around examining the woman's hands and the immediate vicinity.

"If what Minisc thinks is true about some sort of crystal being the monster's heart, then I would say no, since I don't see anything of the sort on her. She must've managed to run."

"True, either way, I think we get her some help and clear the area before any more of those monsters return."

They agreed and Bailey called for an ambulance.

Some more time passed, and the commotion started to die down. Two other members of the EC arrived shortly after, along with an ambulance. The victim Nicole had been safely taken to a hospital for examination and the crowd dispersed back to whence they came.

But questions remained, and Lily wanted answers. She and Bailey decided to take a few minutes and look around for anything suspicious. Something had to stick out; there was no way a Human could have broken free from a monster that nearly killed Minisc.

King and West was home to several small shops near the south side of North York. Many of which were family-owned-and-operated businesses. The tight-knit community rarely had an influx of crime and even most of the south end escaped much of the damage caused in the attacks three months ago.

Outside of a few employees, a couple of shoppers, and two remaining council members, the streets were quiet.

While exploring the sidewalks in front of the stores, Lily picked up on what looked like a series of gooey blotches on the ground. "Bailey, come look at this," She said waving the girl over from across the street.

Bailey realized what had infatuated Lily and whined, "Ew, that's so gross, keep it away from me... I just bought this dress last week!"

"Yeah yeah, that's not the point. Look." Lily gestured to the faint tracks, but the further along the gooey steps went, the more the substance faded until it hit the sewers nearby.

"They go to the sewers?" Bailey asked.

"Possibly?"

Before they could discuss further the ground below them started to quiver. It sounded like rushing water, but not quite the same, it produced a thicker fuller sound than water would have. They followed the fading steps, remaining on edge and with bad feelings coursing through their bodies. But before they could get too close, the sewer began bleeding out a metallic grey substance. It continued to spread further bubbling on the surface until it formed a large puddle on the ground.

"Uh Lily... I think maybe we should go..."

"Yeah... You're probably right..."

They agreed on what they needed to do and yet neither of them moved. They were mesmerized as the puddle began to rise taking the shape of a person. But a person void of all life. Even if they hadn't seen what Minisc fought, there was not a doubt in their collective minds the creature in front of them and the one from yesterday were an identical match.

Fear crept down their spines as the thing stood there staring at the girls through its hollowed-out eyes, gunk dripping off it like sludge. It locked eyes with Bailey.

"Uh... Bailey... I think you might have a bit of an admirer..." Lily whispered. She took a step back.

"Okay no, I am way too pretty to be dealing with these things," Bailey said. She followed Lily in shuffling backward.

"We should probably run," Lily uttered in return. However, before they moved, the monster raised its hand forward and shot out a stream of fire towards Bailey. She let out a piercing scream and slammed her eyes shut.

On instinct and nothing else, Lily cast a dome of water around the two absorbing the fire and saving Bailey. "I've got you," she said, sounding rather heroic despite the fear filling her chest. Bailey opened her eyes wide seeing the marvellous shield of water repelling the flames.

"Thanks."

The intensity of the flames heated up the ground like a scorching summer day causing Lily to grit her teeth and maintain her shield while the soles of her feet grew uncomfortably warm.

"When the flames fade, we run, got it?" Lily ordered. Bailey nodded, trying to set aside her pounding heart and racing mind readying to help Lily out.

Another few seconds passed, and the monster finally ran out of steam. With lightning-quick reflexes, Lily snapped her shield shut and the two took off down the other end of the street. They hollered trying to catch the attention of the two other EC members in the vicinity but there was no need. The car that flew over their heads crashing down and tumbling along the road was more than enough to grab everyone's attention.

They came to a skidding halt as the car landed a few feet in front of them covered in flames like a falling meteor. They spun around just in time for Lily to absorb another fire blast. This time, however, she was sent back taking Bailey with her as they slid across the shattered concrete.

"You okay?" Lily asked, getting to one knee.

"Yeah, I'm fine, but this jerk just ruined my dress... it's gonna pay for that." Lily wanted to tell Bailey her dress didn't matter at the moment, but whatever fired the girl up was fine by her.

They looked up at the monster who was now stomping toward them, it was setting everything around it ablaze with no care in the world for capturing Humans. It stepped through its self-made wall of flames, like it was rising from the gates of hell ready to pass judgment.

A deep angry roar escaped through its thin lips while the black holes for eyes focused in on the girls.

In no time, police and the other EC members arrived on the scene. Except because the EC was spread so thin around the city due to watch groups and rebuilding efforts, their likelihood of gaining substantial backup was minimal. Especially after two others were already dispatched to the location. That should have been more than enough for a regular case.

"What is that thing?" One of the EC Members yelled. He and his partner were both looking on the younger side, and with that youthful lack of experience bleeding through they were horrified.

Lily glanced at them and realized they would be of little help. At least in a fight. She could make use of their other skills though.

"You two get back and make sure all of the civilians in the area are safe; we'll try to lead this thing away from here."

The members stared at the girl, and for a split second wondered why they would be taking orders from her. Except thanks to Lily they saw their chance to escape danger and saw no reason to pass it up.

"Uh Lily, don't you think we could have used their help...?" Bailey asked.

"Our priority first and foremost needs to be making sure everyone in the area is safe. We know we won't win in a fight, so I'm gonna try and lure this thing the other way and hope everyone else can escape. Also, since King Street is already on fire, I'd rather keep the damage contained here if I can." Lily articulated her plan with confidence, trying to keep her body from shaking. She took a deep breath and steadied her emotions. She thought of Minisc and Jules. Her two best friends. She wished they were here to help her out, if for nothing more than to provide real backup, but this time it was on her. She knew what she had to do.

As an Elementalist, if Lily had any advantage over her friends, it was her speed, agility, and brains. Traits she could use against an opponent she lacked any knowledge of. Knowing that, she charged ahead out running the constant waves of fire that trailed behind her.

Bailey stood in awe watching the usually sweet and easy-going girl flip such a switch. In no time Lily got in close to the monster, the sweltering heat rising from the flames around them, and in one fell swoop, she waved her hands and sent a blast of water that exploded into the monster's chest sending raindrops all around them after the impact of the attack.

As Bailey watched she groaned, "This is ridiculous... Yuri never told me these people were going to be the death of me..." She might have been Human, but she refused to sit by and do nothing while her new friend fought to protect her hometown.

Hurrying to the other side of the street, Bailey picked up a hubcap from one of the totaled cars and with all her strength she tossed it like a Frisbee. The metal disk hurtled through the air and crashed into the monster's knee, sinking into the goop. It let out a violent roar giving Lily an opening. She jumped high into the air and hit it with another attack before landing on the other side doing her best to draw the monster away.

The monster toppled over landing in the middle of the road with a rippling crash.

Lily turned around huffing and puffing, but as she stared at the gooey lump in the middle of the shattered road, she saw the body begin to bubble. Another nonsensical roar later and the monster began to rise again.

"Minisc wasn't kidding. This thing just takes hit after hit and it's like nothing happens." Lily could tell her plan was working, though. The monster was clearly turning its attention on to her and not the fleeing citizens or even the buildings that were already partially decimated.

"Come on, Bailey, let's try to keep it contained."

"Right behind you!"

The girls ran down the burning street, weaving their way through the potholes, broken cars, and gates of fire. But as they started to pull the monster away, they came to a screeching halt. Out of the corner of her eye, Lily saw something grey covering the sewer where the first monster came from. A second later another grey gooped monster formed.

"There's more of them! But… we can't even beat one," Lily fretted.

Bailey cried at the top of her lungs, "I'm too cute to die here! I haven't even been married yet!"

As the two ran, Lily tried to look behind her, but when she did, she noticed they were not the target of the new forming monster. In fact, it could care less about her or Bailey. It was heading towards the main threat. She froze and then came to a sickening realization.

"Are they joining up!?" Lily yelled. Her assumptions were spot on as the two monsters linked up forming one beast double in size. It let out a deafening battle cry.

A fortress of flames rose through the ashes of the ground creating a dead end for the two. With their hopes dashed, Lily spun around and raised her fists seeing no other option. What she had not expected was the ball of light hurling towards her like a meteor.

"Bailey, duck!" She ordered grabbing the girl and ripping her to the ground.

"What the hell was that? How can this thing have two elements?" Bailey cried. Fear was starting to grip her, and she struggled to keep her involuntary shaking from becoming problematic. Unlike her impulsive reactions the first time, now she could see the doors of death opening and inviting her in. A door she vehemently wanted no part of.

"If it has two elements... the only one who knows how to make that happen is... Dr. Jarrad... this is bad," Lily uttered with fear.

They were trapped and outclassed. Lily reached for her phone. She needed to call for help, she needed to call Minisc and right away. However, all she could feel in her pocket was the shattered glass of her phone screen jamming into her hand. *My phone is broken...* She pulled it out to small droplets of blood on her fingers.

"Now we're really in trouble..."

CHAPTER 9
UNITED

WITH BAILEY AND LILY STRANDED IN UNCERTAIN doom, Minisc's sewer exploration team remained fixated on the hidden room housing more than fifty of the so-called ooze monsters, all in stasis. Or at least, almost all of them.

"I counted fifteen empty canisters in the back rows. They must be in the city somewhere," Jules said.

"If they're out trying to capture more people, we need to warn Zale and alert the EC right away," Yuri added.

While they discussed their next steps the conversation came to an abrupt stop. A strange beeping sound started to play.

"What's that sound...?" Jules asked as he turned to look at his nearest canister. Lights that were once red began shifting to green around the top and the intermittent beeping started speeding up.

A few canisters away, Minisc said, "Guys... I think we might have a bigger problem." Everyone turned to see what Minisc was referencing, but as they did their eyes grew wider. The greenish gray water that filled the canisters began to drain into the pipes along the ground. Then like a vacuum sucking up dirt, a wind pressure began to pull the limp sludge like bodies up and into the ceiling.

"That can't be good..." Minisc muttered. "Someone must've remotely woken the monsters from their sleep."

Each creature deformed from their human body state into a more malleable pile of sludge and flew up through the pipes disappearing. But they all knew, wherever the destination was, danger would be close behind.

"Minisc," Don said catching his son's attention, "Take Jules and go warn Zale. I don't know where these monsters are heading but we need to get as many people on alert as we can. Tell him to block off all sewer entrances and manholes and make sure we have eyes and ears in all parts of the city. Yuri and I will follow these pipes and see if we can shut things down from here. If they come back with victims, maybe we can stop them."

In the past, such orders would have been protested by Minisc. He hated leaving his father in such potentially dangerous situations, even if he was the Hero of Light. But over time he learned to trust the man. Don thought with a clear and rational mind at all times and always had a plan ready. He had to trust this time would be no different. Even if he claimed his power was fading.

Minisc nodded and turned to Jules, "Come on, it should be a straight path back."

"Right!" Jules agreed. Without a second to spare, the two flew back at top speed from whence they came.

Hurry, Minisc, we might be in for more than we bargained for, Don thought.

Minisc and Jules zipped down the sewers arriving at the exits in record time. They sprinted up the stairs beside the gated entrance and Minisc pulled out his phone. He started pushing the buttons with a furious touch.

"I'll call the office number; you call his cell," he said.

Jules followed the orders and did the same, both of them trying their best to reach Zale. Minisc tapped his foot, his stress rising and hope fading with each passing ring. It felt like minutes and a dozen rings, but eventually luck came through and he heard the dial tone pick up and a man started speaking.

"Don? What did you find out?" He asked, skipping any sort of formalities.

"Mr. Osiris, it's Minisc, we went into the sewers and found an entire army of those monsters in some sort of underground facility. We think they might've been unleashed on the city. My father and Yuri are trying to shut things down from the sewers, but we need you to get all members of the EC at every sewer entrance in the city. That's how they move around, and if we can cut them off, we might be able to stop them before they strike." For a moment, Minisc sounded like his father while breaking the situation down, strong articulate and like a leader.

"They're in the streets? How many are we talking?"

"Up to 50 possibly."

"50!?" Minisc could hear the man on the other line visibly flinch at the number. "Okay, I'll notify everyone in all sectors of the city. Thank you, Minisc. Can you check out the nearby area and make sure everyone around is safe?"

"Yes sir. Jules and I will cover this sector."

"Alright, just stay safe. Your father will kill me if something happens to you," Zale said without a hint of a joke.

Minisc hung up the phone before looking at Jules, "Come on, we need to search around and see if we can find anything." But before the two could take a step, both jumped as a ball of fire rose to the sky like a mushroom cloud in the distance.

"You don't think…?" Jules asked as the aftershocks began to shake the ground. The cloud of smoke gradually rose to the sky and the sound of what had to be a massive truck falling off a high bridge followed.

Minisc fretted, "We might be too late. Come on!"

A few more booms shook the earth and smoke started to line the horizon while cries and screams echoed to the far reaches of the city. Minisc and Jules ran down the sidewalk until they stopped at an overpass. From above, the two had a far better perspective of what was transpiring in the distance. What they saw was nothing short of a horrified war zone filled to the brim with destruction. Cars were flipped over; some were even on fire and causing the small booms they continued to hear. Most of the roadway had large cracks and holes in it as well. However, none of that meant anything as long as nobody had been harmed. The far bigger issue was what stood in the distance halfway down the road.

"Jules, look over there!" Minisc pointed directly to a similar creature he once faced, only this one was growing and forming in a much different manner. It was massive, two if not three times as tall as the last one, and it was stomping and spouting off flames from hell all around it.

"Wait, that's what you faced?!" Jules cried out.

"Not quite, this one's different... it's way bigger..."

That still wasn't the main issue pressing them though. Once they peeled their eyes away from the calamity in front of them, Minisc looked down by the monster's feet. Two girls were running in their direction on the street below. Rather, they were not running towards Minisc, but away from the monster trying to stomp them out of existence. As the girls got closer and came into focus, Minisc realized who they were and his desire to help jumped tenfold.

"Down there, it's Lily and Bailey. We need to help them." As the words left his mouth, he saw the creature blow a breath of red and yellow fire sealing off any exit for the girls and any plausible entrance for the boys.

"We won't make it in time. We have no way of getting down to them," Jules argued.

"Then we jump!" Minisc bit back.

Jules' eyes shot out of his head. "Are you insane? We can't survive a fall that far." He knew as much as anyone they had to save Lily, but swan-diving off a bridge was not the way to do it.

Minisc furrowed his brow and gave that look of determination Jules so often saw. He knew the next thing out of his best friend's mouth would be something insane.

"Create a vacuum with your wind and we'll use it to cushion the fall."

Jules looked at Minisc, and then down, muttering a silent prayer. The fall was at least fifty feet, if not much further. But for Minisc it didn't matter.

Normally Jules would be considered the impulsive and risky friend of the two, but of course, the second someone was in danger, a switch in Minisc's brain flipped. Especially when it came to Lily. The boy would move heaven and earth to see her safe, so Jules knew negotiations were out of the question. Not that he would have it any other way. This was truly what being in the EC was all about for him.

Jules nodded, accepting his orders. If this is what it took for them to save Lily, so be it, he would take the plunge.

"Okay, let's do this!" The wind around Jules picked up and a lime green tinge surrounded his body. The speeds continued to increase more and more until his feet gradually left the ground. He closed his eyes and gritted his teeth in concentration. As he did, an updraft of wind soared around both him and Minisc.

"Let's go, I can't hold this forever," he groaned.

Minisc knew his plan was risky, and if Lily were here, she would chastise him for such a suicidal idea, but he didn't care. With courage in his heart and bravery coursing through his veins, he ran full-steam towards the rail of the bridge and vaulted himself over the side. Jules followed close behind, the struggle of maintaining such powerful gusts written all over his face.

As Minisc began to free fall, his breath caught in his throat. The swirling vapours around him were doing little to slow his descent and he only had at best a five second window. For one of those seconds doubt crept in, and he feared the worst. He clenched his teeth, expecting them to shatter from the force.

One look down and he squeezed his eyes shut bracing himself for impact. Then he felt his body get hit by an updraft of wind. Although the force hurt, it did more than enough to keep him from an otherwise unceremonious death. Even with the added gusts inhibiting his crash landing, he still hit the ground legs-first. Bone-crunching shocks raced from his feet to his head and back down again. When he opened his eyes and could still feel his body cursing him for such reckless abandon, he realized they had lived. Beside him, Jules' eyes snapped open as well.

"We're alive? I can't believe that worked," Jules grinned, almost laughing.

Even though they survived, their jubilation was short-lived. The scene unfolding in front of them still painted a grim picture.

Before they could act a ball of light soared over their heads and crashed into the bridge behind them. It collapsed from the impact forcing Minisc and Jules to get on their horses and run before being buried alive.

Minisc wasted no time gripping a light ball in his left hand as he ran towards the monster. He chucked it like a baseball sending it hurling through the air and into the chest of the creature. It let out a roar as the ball sunk in, causing the creature's body to fall backwards kicking up a cloud of dust and smoke in the process.

Lily turned around in shock as she saw her two friends sprint to her aid.

"Minisc, Jules, you guys are here!"

"We came as fast as we could, are you okay?" Minisc said with a look of relief. He could not put into words how glad he was to see they made it in time.

"Yeah I'm fine, but we need to get Bailey out of here, she can't get caught up fighting this thing."

Minisc looked over to the girl sitting on her knees. Her usually perfect outfit had small rips in it and drops of blood were all over her once flawless skin.

Bailey gave a half-hearted smile to Lily at the compassion, but as she stood up weakly, she said, "Thanks for the offer, but I don't think this thing is too keen on letting any of us escape right now. We really pissed it off."

The monster gave a gargled screech as it rose back to its feet once again. It stepped through its own carnage before letting out a breath of fire towards the group.

Lily and Jules used a combined power of wind and water to restrain the attack from doing any damage.

"You have to be kidding me. This thing has dual elements as well?" Minisc groaned.

"Yeah, but we can talk about that later, right now we need to figure out a way to beat this thing or it's not gonna matter how many elements it has," Lily argued.

Jules agreed as the fire dispersed around them, "Lily's right…

Minisc what did you do before, you said something about a crystal in its chest right?"

"Yeah, I ripped the crystal out of its chest and then the monster just died. If we can do that again, maybe we can win." He quickly formed a plan. "You guys try and keep it occupied, your elements are better for defence and can help contain the flames. I'll see if I can find an opening and blow a hole through its chest. If we can spot the crystal inside, then perhaps we can find a way to rip it out."

"Worth a shot," Jules shrugged.

"I don't see any other option. Let's do it, Jules," Lily agreed.

While Jules and Lily circled the monster, holding off each attack, Minisc held his hands out in front of his chest like he was saying a prayer. His fingers began to glow bright and when they were at their peak, he thrust his palms outward. Pillar of Light. The beam boomed from his hands like a golden laser and sliced through the monster's left breast like a hot knife through butter. As anticipated, Minisc could see an oddly coloured red and yellow crystal sitting in the goopy chest cavity with strands of the ooze gripping it like a spider's web.

"Go for the crystal now!" Minisc ordered.

Lily leapt forward in an attempt to grab the crystal but was batted to the ground. Jules followed up by flying through the air before latching on to the crystal tightly.

"Ahhh!" Jules cried as a searing heat emitting from the crystal burned his hand. He loosened his grip before taking a punch to the face sending him crashing into the ground next to Lily.

"Damn, we almost had it," Minisc muttered.

The monster roared but this one was different than one of rage or frustration. It sounded more like a plea for help.

"Now what's it doing?" Lily fretted, pushing herself up from the asphalt.

"I don't know, but I have a feeling we're about to find out," Jules said doing the same.

The gap in the monster's breast bubbled up before healing like metal being melted together, but that was only the beginning.

Before Minisc could prepare another strike, he felt something whiz past his ear. It was a small blob of ooze. Only it was not one blob, and it was not coming from only behind Minisc. There were thousands of blobs, and slithering puddles making their way towards the monster attaching itself to the exterior on mass.

With a much more emphatic growl, the monster started to grow. The more it absorbed, the bigger it got.

"It's getting bigger..." Bailey said before tumbling backwards falling on her butt beside Minisc.

I don't understand. This thing is way different than the monster claiming to be Pascale. This one can't talk and doesn't fight with any such logic... it's just a mindless killing machine. Was it designed this way?

With blind rage, the newly created nightmare began its path of destruction again. This time it showed no interest in Lily Jules Minisc or Bailey. In seconds, flames created an entirely new arena to fight in, and with ten-foot walls of fire, the sky turned into a black cloud of smoke.

"If this keeps up everything is going to be destroyed. We need to find a way to stop it." Minisc decided it was his time to leap into battle. He took off with Lily and Jules ready to act as well. "It might've gotten bigger, but that means it can't move as fast." He fired a ball of light into the monster's face before jumping up and landing a vicious golden punch into its chest. Lily and Jules did their best to take out the monster's tree trunk legs and hem it for even a second, but any form of attack proved useless. The extra layer of ooze monsters the leader had absorbed created an impenetrable skin.

Minisc was slammed to the ground before Lily drew attention away from her friend. She shot off a Hydro Blast into the creature's back. It failed to pierce the new armour but did enough to stagger the beast. Jules grabbed Minisc, helping him up to safety. The ground began to shake with cracks splitting up and down the roadway.

"This is impossible. Nothing we do hurts it. We'll never reach its crystal now," Lily groaned.

Jules had Minisc around his shoulder helping keep him upright. He looked to his friend and asked, "Any bright ideas Minisc?"

"We attack it all at once. I think the only way we can break through its armour is if we concentrate all our strength on one single point. We need to hit it with everything we've got."

They were all staring at the monster which continued to attack nonsensically at the buildings and any other landmarks it saw.

"There's no way it will give us enough time to channel that much power," Jules argued.

"Let me hold it off." The three spun around to see Bailey on her feet. Her look betrayed any confidence in her words, but she meant what she said. "I can buy you guys maybe a minute, if that, but promise me you'll destroy this stupid thing alright?"

"Are you insane? That thing will kill you," Lily said.

"Look… if we don't stop it here, this thing's gonna make its way to the shelter and then destroy that as well. The people of North York have suffered enough, and I won't sit by while they have the only place left they can call home ruined as well. Just because I'm Human doesn't mean I can't help." She leaned over and picked up a broken piece of a streetlamp. Holding it like a sword, she said, "Just make it quick, cause if I die, it's on your heads." She had a small smirk play on her lips.

Minisc could see the fiery passion filling Bailey's eyes. She would not take no for an answer and arguing would just waste valuable time.

"Okay, just hold out as long as you can. We'll take care of the rest."

With their plan decided, Bailey ran away from the group and towards the hell she wanted to dispose of.

"Now I'll show you… nobody gets away with ruining my perfect outfit!" She took off without the monster seaming to care only continuing its carnage. At least until she started whacking its toes with the makeshift metal weapon. No damage would be done, but it forced the monster to look down for a second as if wondering what minute ant would dare challenge it.

"Hurry, we need to muster up all the energy we can, and channel it into one blast," Minisc said.

Swirling gold waves dance through the blazes of fire that surrounded Minisc as he readied himself. Then Jules added a lime green aura and Lily a pale blue. Despite lacking stamina and feeling the unrelenting pain coursing through their bodies, they dug deep and mustered up whatever strength they could find. Would it be enough? They had no idea. But with no other options, it had to work.

The sounds of wind swirling and power radiating from their bodies came to a stop and in unison, the group nodded. They were ready. For Bailey, what was at best thirty seconds felt closer to thirty minutes because she was already running on fumes and her only ability to fight was a heavy broken metal pole. Her body cried to give up. She continued to poke and prod the monster in its ankles even if it had no success.

"We're ready. Bailey get out of there now!" Minisc yelled.

"Took you long enough!"

With one final thrust, Bailey jammed the stick into the monster's ankle leaving it in like the pedestal for her sword. Then she took off, sliding behind a car that lay crumpled on its roof. She dropped to her knees looking back at her friends through the shattered glass window. She collapsed out of exhaustion letting the cold metal of the car numb her aching body. With the last ounce of gas in her tank, she said, "… you guys better win."

Finally, ready to face the threat levied against North York the three braced for their final stand.

"Let's do this!" Minisc yelled.

"Time to blow this blob to pieces" Jules added.

"We're gonna make you pay for the damage you've done!" Lily finished.

In a unison only friends could demonstrate, the three thrust their hands towards their opponent. Three inseparable attacks burst from their palms towards their target. With a growl sounding like something of annoyance, the goopy monster turned back to the light show heading for its heart and matched with a beam of light from its mouth.

The two attacks collided with a ferocious bang, sending shock waves violent enough to cut through buildings. The ground below cracked apart as sparks of energy ricocheted out around the collision. All corners of the city could feel the devastating clash of elements.

After the initial push, the two blasts arrived at a stalemate. Minisc, Jules, and Lily's most powerful attack, against the unrelenting and seemingly never-ending energy of the generated slime monster. Both refused to budge an inch.

"It can't be..." Minisc growled. Beads of sweat dripped off his trembling arms.

"How is this thing able to hold off all of us at full strength..." Jules whined.

They could feel the tension welling up inside their bodies. The strain on their energy supply along with the demand on their muscles caused them to feel their insides unravelling at the core. A heartbeat pounded in their ears, and it was like their muscles were being stretched until they would rip apart. After a few seconds, the ground below them shattered, pushing them further into the earth.

"It's too much, Minisc, we can't keep this up," Lily cried. If the boys were feeling their bodies on the verge of giving out, they had nothing to complain about. For Lily, she'd been part of the fight far longer and expelled far more energy than either of them. Being past her breaking point would be a gross understatement.

"Come on guys, we need to dig deeper, we need to push further. We can do this!" Minisc urged his friends on. He washed away the watering tears in his eyes and replaced them with a new resolve. He knew how unfair it was to push his friends so far past what they reasonably had to give. The limits on their powers were not so easily broken. Especially when they all knew Minisc's own strength exceeded that of their own.

Yet, not for a second did Minisc believe himself to be stronger. He was no stronger than his friends; if anything he was far weaker.

But what he learned through countless fights was that limits were nothing more than an imaginary barrier. They all had more to give, but at the moment, Minisc was the only one who believed that sentiment. He hated putting his friends in such a position, but he needed them now more than ever.

The beast let out a pained howl and as it did, the beam of light intensified.

"How is it getting stronger?!" Jules bellowed in agony. They were a foot and a half into a building-sized pothole and with each passing second, they were cracking the earth below them deeper. It would only be a matter of time till they fell straight through.

Minisc refused to concede though, not as long as he could still breathe. "Just hold on! We can win this one, you have to trust me on this. We have all the power we need. Now bring it out!"

Behind the car, Bailey opened her eyes again, looking through the gates of hell that was her city. Flames burst through the building in front of her and the shaking earth below waited to split open and swallow her up. For a moment, she had to wonder if she was dead, but that belief evaporated when she heard the monsters cry again. She snapped back to reality.

However, if looking in front of her were the gates of hell, then behind her where the battle was taking place was the other side of those gates.

She could hear the cries of her new friends, and knew they needed help. Help she could provide. She gripped the side of the car, pushing herself up before peeking around her makeshift shelter. The light displays from her friend's attacks mesmerized her. It was like nothing she'd ever seen before. But then she realized they were being pushed into their own grave.

"I'm sorry I couldn't be of more help guys..." She muttered. She looked down and in front of her were the remains of her broken lamp pole. She grasped it tight, getting to her feet. Gears in her head started turning. Then she glared at the monster and said, "This... is for my outfit." Like a javelin, Bailey tossed the sharp pole at the monster. It stuck in the monster's chest, causing a horrifying cry.

For a fraction of a second, it flinched. Bailey had managed to strike right in the so-called heart of the beast.

The beast staggered, thanks to Bailey, and Minisc could see their opportunity at hand. He didn't know what the cause was, but he could feel the resisting force against them lighten.

"Now's our chance! Together!" He ordered. With a blinding light and incredible force, Lily, Jules, and Minisc infused everything they had into one final overwhelming push. The trifecta of elements finally made headway and started to stifle the beam of light counteracting them.

In a flash the triple team blast ripped through the monster's chest, absorbing the crystals within the elements as well. The beast cried out in pain as the explosion ripped its body apart. Like a grenade, the ooze exploded in every direction landing in small clumps all over the road and buildings. After it bubbled, the ooze began melting with no source of power, until it was nothing but small, lifeless residue.

The three friends collapsed to their knees, gasping for air. Their muscles throbbed to the point you could see their arms and legs moving like they had a pulse. While on their knees, they flopped backwards laying side by side, eyes shut but growing smiles on their faces. They had nothing left in the tank to get up and see, but they knew the fight was over.

"We... did... it..." Lily panted.

"That was... too close..." Jules groaned.

"We really have to stop doing this..." Minisc moaned in agony. The three tried to laugh but even that amount of effort hurt.

For the time being, though, none of that mattered. Once again Minisc, Lily, and Jules, with a little help from Bailey, managed to survive another catastrophe in the making and keep not only the North York shelter from being destroyed but saved many more lives in the process.

CHAPTER 10
BREAKTHROUGH

UNAWARE OF THE EVENTS TAKING PLACE ABOVE THEM, Don and Yuri remained behind in the sewers. The two stood in a room full of empty canisters looking for a remote way to shut down the monsters, but had no idea of the battle they were sending their loved ones into.

Aside from that, they were still hopeful of finding any remnants of the missing Humans. So far, the only obvious clue to such a question was the maze of pipes along the ceiling and floor. They zigged and zagged, crossing over each other in intertwined patterns with no logic behind them. But they all had one thing in common... they led out of the room.

Don looked up watching the mossy green sewage move from the containers into the pipes in a slow and mundane matter. "We need to follow these pipes," he said.

Yuri pulled out his map and answered, "Based on where we are, and where the pipes go, it looks like the north wall is another Elementalist made wall."

Don marched between the canisters to the north end and gave it a firm tap with his knuckle. Behind, he could hear a faint echo implying there was another room on the other side.

"You're right, this definitely leads somewhere." Don pulled back his arm and repeated the same motion he had to break down the first wall, and with one violent collision of fist on concrete the wall shattered into piles of rubble. Don paused and let his arms fall to his sides.

He examined his work while Yuri walked up with a face of concern.

"You're struggling to maintain your power, aren't you?"

Don tried to avoid giving off any signs of frustration. He simply nodded and said, "Yeah, every time I use my element, it fades a little more."

"Well then don't overdo it. We still need the Hero of Light for a little longer. The next generation isn't prepared for a post-Hero world just yet."

Although Don tried his best to keep his diminishing power a secret to most, after the fight with Dusk and the sense of his impending fate, he turned to Yuri for advice. They might not have worked together often at the EC, but since Minisc and Jules were so tight as kids they grew to know each other quite well. At one point, Don believed Yuri could be the next Hero of Light, or rather a Hero of Wind, and even went so far as to tell him such, but Yuri shunned the idea. Even the calm and composed man could not and did not want to try and live up to such a title.

Don and Yuri both knew of his plan to train Minisc to take over his role, and Yuri agreed to do his best to help in the process even while training Jules himself. But they both hoped the time for a singular icon would not be needed, and perhaps Minisc, Jules, Lily and even other Elementalists could one day be a collective beacon of hope, rather than placing the burden all on one person. However, for the time being they had to work with the hand currently dealt. This meant training Minisc and his friends, while also helping put a stop to any threats before they were ready.

This time the room they entered looked entirely different than the previous one. They were standing in a room that resembled a factory. One that was automated to work remotely, based on the lack of workers around.

Unlike the many tanks in the other room, there was one central tank, and it was gradually filling up with the ooze from the other room. That was far from the only step in the process going on, however. The canister would spit out piles of goop one at a time, before they landed on a conveyor belt. Once there, a small mechanical hand would reach for a crystal, pinching it with two pincers at the base before jamming it into the pile of ooze and watching as streaks of light like veins formed around the crystal before being sucked back into another tube presumably up into the world.

"Unbelievable, who could have done all this? The amount of time it must have taken... how did this go undetected by the EC?" Yuri asked.

"Yeah... almost like someone who disappeared a long time ago but was never found..." Don said under his breath. Yuri looked at him puzzled.

"Come on, we need to shut this thing down before it can spit out any more of these monsters," Don said.

Yuri ran up to a nearby control panel to his left. He pulled up a hologram keyboard and began attempting to type away but with no success.

"Damn, it's password-protected."

"Forget it, we'll stop this the old-fashioned way."

"Hold on Don, the more power you waste openly, the closer you'll be to drained for when it really counts."

"If we don't do something now, then when the time really counts it's gonna be too late," Don rebutted.

He raised his hand and balls of light began to boom out shattering the tank of sludge. Liquid splashed onto the floor like a waterfall creating a small river that slithered towards him.

He then aimed at the mechanical hand and the conveyer belt and did the same. He kept it up until the room fell to ruins.

Once finished he grabbed at his arm taking in a deep breath. Strange twitching sensations crawled in his muscles but it didn't matter. He did what needed to be done.

"Well, that should stop any more production at least," Yuri said before walking over to something else that caught his interest. Beside the computer sat a holster of different crystals where the robotic hand had been picking out from. They looked familiar. A carbon copy of the one Minisc showed him the day before in his office. Only these were all sorts of different colours. Some were red, others green and blue, brown, white, and so on. There had to be more than fifty crystals in the holsters but there were over a dozen empty slots as well. Curious, he reached down to pluck the item from its display, this one a pale white. It emitted a chilling air around it like an ice cube, but when Yuri picked it up, the energy intensified. A cold sensation ran through his fingers and up to his arm before he dropped it on the ground.

"Damn, that's cold."

Don spun around from where he was looking and said, "What happened? Are you okay?"

"Yeah, I'm fine, but that crystal, it'll freeze you to the bone if you're not careful."

"Hmm..." Don took a closer look, curious. The one Minisc had in his possession was still under research, but now he could see the objects for himself. He walked up to the holders and found a golden crystal. He held his left hand centimetres from the crystal and waited. Without a doubt, the same energy was radiating off it that he could feel when he used his element.

"I think these things are what gives those monsters elemental powers," Don said. "Even the colours of the crystals line up with the elements." He pointed to each colour of crystal as he counted the elements off, "Ice, fire, light, shadow, earth, electricity, water, and wind."

Yuri, wanting to confirm for himself, reached for the emerald, green crystal. The energy felt familiar and yet strange. Like a long-lost memory, he couldn't quite recall fully.

It had been almost four months since Yuri lost his element in a surprise attack by Luminosa. That day when he awoke from his coma, he could feel the difference in his body immediately. He could never describe it, but there was definitely a difference. As he held the crystal in his hand, feeling the potent energy radiate off it, if for only a moment he could feel the rekindled power he'd lost.

"You're right, which means someone's managed to encapsulate

the Elemental cell and turn it into some sort of outside force by using these crystals," Yuri said.

"Then we need to get these to the EC right away, that way we can research them more with the one Minisc brought back. Hopefully without these at our attacker's disposal no more creatures can be given life."

"Yeah, good idea..." Yuri trailed off.

Don turned to his friend and raised an eyebrow, "What is it?"

"Well, we've found where these creatures are being created, but there is still no sign of any of the abducted people. I figured for sure they would be here, but there appears to be nothing."

"That's true, which means they must be being held somewhere nearby... but if Luminosa is behind this, then my guess is they didn't want to put all their eggs in one basket so to speak," Don added.

While they looked for ways to gather up the most crystals possible, an unearthly groan came from the broken hole in the wall.

Don stopped his gathering before turning around slowly. "Looks like we have company."

Yuri did the same and said, "These must be the ones from earlier. At least they weren't sent into the city I guess." He struck a fighting pose raising his hands and bracing himself.

They were staring down three full-sized ooze monsters all of which matched Don in size and physique, if not a little bigger.

First, the middle monster stepped in front as if signalling itself to be the leader. Letting out a growl, it flung its hand forward, firing a bolt of lightning at Don. The Hero refused to fall so easily, though. He began to retaliate, punching through the blast before slamming his fist into the monster's gut. He ripped it out, leaving a large, gaping wound in the monster's stomach, but in seconds it recovered and appeared no worse for wear.

The second one came in, but Don held his hand to his left and fired off a blast of light. It absorbed into the monster's flesh before exploding and sending it flying back.

The room shook from the impact and jagged rocks from the ceiling came crashing down around them.

"I think our time here is up, Don!" Yuri said.

"I'd say so… let's dispose of these three and get out of here."

Even if they wanted to investigate further, the falling debris took care of any remnants of the factory. Don and Yuri did their best to block and dodge the incoming array of elements being fired their way. But when one fell, two more piled through their escape route, blocking off the entrance.

One thing Don noticed was their fighting tactics. They swung and blasted with reckless abandon and lacked intelligent coordination. Nothing like what Minisc described his opponent as.

"Something's different here. Minisc claimed his opponent to be as smart as a real Elementalist," Don said as he dodged another attack before slamming two of his opponents into each other.

"Maybe these ones aren't fully formed yet? Minisc also said the one he fought had the consciousness of Pascale and could talk, but these are just mindless zombies."

He blocked each blow and dodged each blast with precision and grace, allowing the brain-dead monsters to take each other out instead. But that did little to slow them down.

Even though Yuri no longer had an element of his own, his fighting senses remained at an elite level. Over the past few months, he'd spent far more time honing his combat skills with Jules as opposed to the time he would have used training his element.

"Every time one falls they just regenerate. I'm gonna exhaust what little power I have left on these stupid things," Don yelled, engulfing one monster in a golden bath of light.

"Remember what Minisc said. We need to take out the crystals in their bodies. It's the only way to stop them."

"That's right, the jewels." Don ducked underneath another blow as two monster's fists collided where his head once resided. He stuck his hands out perpendicular to his body like the shape of a cross, firing a beam of light from each hand. The blast was strong enough to not only absorb the heart of the creatures but disintegrate them as well. The monsters melted into small piles of thick grey water on the floor.

Yuri continued to stay on the defensive, acting as bait for Don. He would attempt to create an opening that would allow Don to finish the job with as little strain as possible. Once he achieved his goal and moved out of the way he yelled, "Don, now!"

Don followed along with the man's plans, swiftly targeting the weak points. Small yet potent balls of light absorbed the crystal into their light before disintegrating them forever. One by one, each creation slumped down lifelessly before melting to the ground entirely. But still they continued piling in.

"They're never-ending," Yuri panted.

"This is just turning into a waste of time." As Don said that, the ground started to rumble violently. But it didn't appear to be caused by anything in the sewers. It sounded like a stomp from above. A stomp from an ungodly monster.

Before they were forced into another fight, as the quake of the stomp dissipated the army of monsters blocking the doorway collapsed into puddles.

"Did… they just die?" Yuri asked. He and Don eyed the puddles stunned when they started to shiver and shake along the ground.

"I don't think it's gonna be that easy…" Don said. But he was wrong. Their fight had ended.

The blobs sprung forward zipping past Don's head splattering into the wall. The others began to make their way to various cracks in both rooms seeping out of sight.

"They're… they're gone…" Yuri said. He took a deep exhale before Don dismissed his positive hope.

"I doubt it. I think they're just heading to the surface. We need to hurry before the city gets overwhelmed."

It did not take long for them to retrace their steps and reach the outside. But they gasped at the horrors in front of them. Once-calm blue skies were repainted with menacing black clouds of smoke. Attempting to bleed through the horizon were streaks of yellow and orange. The reflection of the fire. They rushed up the stairs following the streaks in the sky when they heard a scathing roar.

"No way…" Yuri gawked. Far off in the horizon marching through the streets attempting to touch the sky was the same exact monster they were swarmed by, only this time it was absolutely massive.

They looked at each other communicating with a bout of telepathy. *Minisc and Jules are facing that monster*, they both thought.

Sprinting down the same path Minisc and Jules followed minutes earlier, they skidded to a halt with their breaths catching in their throat. This time they saw an angled beam of light shooting out of the ground towards the sky. It pierced the monster's chest and exploded dropping it to the ground followed by confetti like rain of different colours sprinkling from the sky.

"Let's hurry!" Don said.

They reached the same bridge that Minisc and Jules took their swan dive off of, but now it could barely be called a bridge. The more appropriate term for what remained would be a rock slide. The flames somewhat died down from the ripples of the blast and through what remained Don could see three bodies lying next to each other in a crater. The one was his son, of that he had no doubt. Which meant the two on either side of him were the others he considered like his children. He thought he could see their chests rise and fall signifying life, but that did little to stop him from leaping into action.

He slid down the rocky hill with Yuri close behind him.

Don began to slow down when he saw a playing smirk on Minisc's lips. They were groaning in agony and their body's continued to shake uncontrollably, but he could tell they were safe. He let out a long exhale as he finally reached his son.

"Minisc…" He called out softly as he stood over the boy.

Minisc attempted to open his eyes but even that level of effort overwhelmed him. Instead, he said, "Father… is that you? I guess that means we're still alive." He tried to laugh but again his body refused.

"You three can't be left alone for a second, can you?" Yuri said, bending down and rubbing his brother's arm. "Come on, let me help you up."

"I'm pretty sure I can't move my arms… I'd just like to sleep here for a while," Jules whispered.

The three kids didn't even feign an attempt to fight the exhaustion pinning them to the ground. All they could do was smile as they lay next to each other knowing the lives they saved once again.

CHAPTER 11
NEXT STEPS

REPORTS OF THE NORTH YORK DAMAGE CAME FAST AND furious. Of course, people were looking to thank their heroes, but once the smoke cleared, they were left to wonder who their heroes were. Most reports were only able to gather that there were three Elementalists of the Water, Wind, and Light variety, but no names were found. The next day, President Osiris delivered a speech breaking down the events as well as putting out a warning in regards to the slime monsters, but over the next few days, there were no more signs of the creatures. With the factory destroyed and the supply of crystals now in the EC's possession, everyone hoped the city would be given a moment of reprieve. But still, they couldn't forget about the Humans who were missing. Their desire to find them hadn't wavered, however, without other catastrophes on the rise then they could focus more resources on such a task.

Once Minisc and friends were found, they were escorted to the hospital for examination. No life-threatening injuries were suffered in the battle, but the strain placed on their bodies would put them out of commission for a few days. At best they could walk around their shared hospital room for a few minutes, but with their bodies in such unrelenting agony, even that was a chore. Not that they would've had it any other way. It indeed was a worthy sacrifice.

A day after the incident, Lily and Jules sat on the edge of Minisc's bed while Yuri and Don sat in chairs across from him. With enough strength recovered to think straight, they had some pressing questions needing to be solved. The three looked at each other in hospital gowns with befuddlement on their faces.

"You're sure that creature could use two elements like Coro?" Don asked. It wasn't that he didn't believe his son, but they needed to be concrete in all their assumptions or fear chasing more ghosts.

"Yeah, it caught us by surprise too," Lily spoke up, "But we all saw it. It was a fire light split that could burn down buildings and shoot off blasts of light."

Minisc nodded, "What I find strange is that the big one we fought was like a mindless zombie. The one claiming to be Pascale was intelligent, and adept. But it also didn't have dual elements that I know of..."

"That adds up. The ones in the sewers were the exact same. Perhaps they were test subjects?" Yuri put his hand to his chin but came up with no answers.

The room fell silent in thought until Don spoke up with a question for the room, "Well, based on the information we've learned over the past few days, we know that someone created crystals that could harbour elemental powers, and a monster with dual elements... which points in one direction... have any of you heard from Coro lately?"

Yuri answered first. "Last Mr. Osiris told me, he was doing some volunteer work in the research department. But I haven't run into him since he started."

"I haven't heard from him since his mother's funeral..." Jules sighed, hanging his head.

"Neither have I... I didn't know what to say to him..." Lily mumbled before turning to look at Minisc, "You guys had a pretty lengthy conversation at the funeral, didn't you? What was that about, did he tell you anything?"

Minisc thought back to that solemn day. Despite taking place over three months ago he still remembered the day vividly. How could he not?

After the Luminosa attacks ended, a small funeral was held for Coro's mother. Only those who were under lock down with him at

The Underground attended, as Coro knew nothing of his extended family. He remembered having grandparents for a short time as a child, but much like most people, when Coro's elemental powers began to manifest beyond comparison, any family he knew seemed to vanish from his life. Besides, he wanted everything to be private as he always did. However, once the casket had been buried and flowers placed on the grave Coro pulled Minisc aside for a brief conversation.

"I'm going to find my father. That was my mother's last wish in this world. She wanted me to make amends with the man and do our best to return to being a family. As much as I detest him and his ways, I want to be able to fulfill my mother's wishes. I owe her that much. I don't know where he might be, but just because Dusk is defeated doesn't mean Luminosa is gone. This means they most likely still have my father held captive." The reason he pulled Minisc away was that without Minisc's help, he knew he would never have the heart to find his father.

For Minisc, even just the thought of Coro made his stomach sink. Sad guilt overcame him every time. In a way, he had carried the responsibility of Coro's mother losing her life, even if it had been a sacrifice that led to their victory.

"Let us help you. With my father and everyone else, I know we can find him. We can make sure your mother's wish is fulfilled."

"Thank you Minisc, but no. This is something I need to do on my own. I realize how ungrateful that may sound, but if I'm ever able to come to grips with my old man, then I need to do this alone," Minisc recalled Coro saying.

"What do you think he meant by coming to grips with his old man?" Jules asked.

Minisc shrugged his shoulders, looking as puzzled as everyone else.

"Perhaps you should give him a call," Lily suggested, "If Coro is still looking for his father, then maybe he has some information as well. If we pool everything we know together so far, we might be able to find him and the abducted people as well."

"Lily is right. Just because Coro wants to find his father on his own doesn't mean we can't provide the information we've dug up. Coro's incredibly smart. If Luminosa is behind this and Dr. Jarrad is being forced to create these monsters against his will, and they're being used to abduct people, then ours and Coro's goal have become the same. Shared info might lead us exactly where we need to go," Yuri advised as everyone nodded in agreement. Whether Coro was trying to keep his friends out of any danger, or if he simply wanted to fulfill his mother's wish by himself, the issue was becoming far bigger than just him. He would need to accept that others were now involved in his search.

CHAPTER 12
BURNING QUESTIONS

MEANWHILE, THE DAY AFTER THE NORTH YORK ATTACK took place, Coro and Olivia sat in silence. Grinding metal squealed off the rails as the train continued chugging down the tracks across the city.

Olivia flipped through the pages of a newspaper which had the headline of *Monster Attacks North York, What's Next?* She methodically scanned through the pages trying to gather information. On the other hand, Coro kept himself busy working diligently on different formulas for the unknown chemical J. It ate away at him that the chemical makeup shared such a resemblance to the human body. He needed to know why... and maybe more importantly, how? Not even the most scientific genius in the world could create Human life from nothing. At least so he thought.

He let out a dejected sigh before looking out the window and watching the buildings whip by him. He hoped it would bring a moment of clarity. But nothing came. When he faced his notes again, he tore the front page out and crumpled it up. Then he shoved it into his backpack, which had become home to a dozen more pages meeting a similar fate.

Finally, Olivia raised an eyebrow, barely glancing above her newspaper. She caught a glimpse of the frustrated boy before looking at the pile of trash he'd built up.

"Don't bother torturing yourself," she uttered, "You lack the information needed to solve this problem."

Though her voice seemed condescending, she was actually

throwing a lifeline to Coro. Back in the lab, he already displayed how thorough and adept he was in research and analysis, but she knew none of that would matter if a few pieces of the puzzle had been taken out of the box, so to speak.

Coro leaned back and closed his notebook accepting defeat. "Where are we going anyways?" He finally asked. With his focus squarely on solving the riddles that plagued his mind, he had followed Olivia's instructions without giving their destination much consideration.

"The Toronto Library." Her flat tone suggested she'd prefer fewer questions as well.

The young dual Elementalist displayed his skills quickly to his new boss, but he still felt like she was just dragging him along out of obligation to Zale more than as a partner. She seemed like the type to work alone. Something Coro could understand well.

For the remainder of the trip, they returned to silence. Coro looked out the window again pondering the whereabouts of his father. Even after the fact, not one news outlet reported the man missing. He never appeared on any lists, and most of the references to his name on the Internet had been wiped clean. It was as if the man had been erased from the history books. But what purpose did that serve?

After a trip that felt far too long, the train came to a gradual halt as the metal rails ached from outside. Once they were off the train Olivia led them to a friendly looking building that had luckily avoided all manner of damage from Luminosa.

Coro took a quick look around the train platform, noticing almost nobody getting off at the stop. It was like a ghost town, where the only smell was of stale garbage and burning metal.

"Come on," Olivia said, leading him up the stairs back to the outside world. Once they reached the streets Coro saw a large brick building. On the outside, it looked ordinary but a long rectangular sign along the path read Toronto Library.

The inside could only be described as a bookworm's paradise. Shelves upon shelves of books that reached to the ceiling were neatly lined up in rows throughout the massive rectangular room. In different corners of the room were tall ladders with wheels that glided along the shelves to reach the higher-up texts. The fresh scent you could only get from cracking open a new book could be smelt within every inch of the room as well.

The library had two floors, but the second was far closer to a balcony with a few scattered intellects reading in peaceful bliss around it.

To their left was a long narrow desk with three ladies sitting behind it. Olivia strode over to them ignoring the first two who were nothing more than check-out clerks and went straight for the third.

Wordlessly she held up her badge to the elderly lady. The clerk nodded before standing up and heading to the room behind them. The silent exchange left Coro confused but again he didn't bother asking questions. Olivia struck him as the type of person who had a purpose behind every action she took, and despite not knowing her, Coro did not get the same suspicious vibes he did when Pascale was asked to escort him and Minisc to his father's lab. However, for good measure he kept a sharp eye on his new partner and kept his guard up.

A few seconds later, the woman returned with a golden key clutched tightly in her weathered hands. She handed it to Olivia before taking a seat again. It was attached to a thin plank of wood. Not the highest of tech security, but it kept the tiny key from being lost.

With key in hand, Olivia began walking again without a word. Coro silently followed her lead. At the back of the library, Olivia stopped in front of the only door around. She slid the key in waiting to hear the sound of success, and once she did, she quietly pushed the door open. She gestured for Coro to walk in first, before following behind him.

This room housed far fewer books but just as many shelves filled with boxes. It was also smaller, and the shelves did not crawl to the top, but other than that it looked just like the other room in the library.

As Olivia silently closed the door again a chill overcame Coro. He turned to look at his supposed partner and a sense of deja vu came over him. But before he could brace for a fight Olivia did something he never would have expected.

"I apologize for my silence earlier," she started, "Due to the uncertainty surrounding us in regard to this case, President Osiris has asked that I and all of the high-ranking EC members not refer to this place in public spaces. It could prove a huge complication if this information fell into the wrong hands."

Coro dropped his suspicion and looked at his surroundings. "Where are we? And what is with all these boxes?" He asked.

"This is the storage site for all the official records of the entire city. For some reason we're still in the process of putting it onto computers, so we had to come here to see if we could dig up any information. This place has all the historical records of every Elementalist and Human in not only the city but all the surrounding smaller towns as well. I think it's best to pull all of the records we can on everyone and everything related to this spree of disappearances and try to find out any connections between that and the chemical J."

She walked up to the closest shelf and pulled out the box, which turned out to be a massive filing cabinet alphabetized.

Both of them began walking up and down each aisle of folders with purpose. They pulled numerous boxes off the shelves looking to solve the burning question on their minds. What is the J chemical, and how does it relate to all of the missing Humans over the past month?

Olivia returned to the rounded table in the middle of the room with one final box.

"I've pulled every relevant text in this place that could help us. All historical records, all current data and every connection between Human and Elementalist research we have to date, along with every scientific paper published since Elementalists were born. If the answer isn't in here, then I'm at a loss."

Coro grabbed the top book off the stack, flipping it open. "Then it's time to get reading, this could take a while."

The next few hours were painstakingly slow, with Coro searching through files and scanning the contents of every book in his possession. All he could afford to read were the headings, bold print, and anything that stood out. It would take him weeks otherwise.

The long table they occupied had been turned into a reading war zone, with scattered books opened and closed, and copious amounts of loose papers, some crumpled and others not. A perfect reflection of two of the smartest Elementalists the EC had to offer working furiously trying to put together a mystery that had little threads to tie.

Coro slumped back in his chair slamming the book in front of him shut. "I'm completely out of ideas. I've cross-referenced every single book with my notes and nothing. There is no data whatsoever about a chemical that matches the human body perfectly. Nothing is even remotely close."

Olivia flipped over her folder at the other end of the table and a small sigh escaped her lips. For someone that could match Coro in stoic prowess, she seemed deterred for the first time. "We still need more information..."

Coro groaned as he said words he never thought would leave his mouth. "If only my father was here, he would be able to figure this out, I'm sure."

The statement caught Olivia's attention and she said, "Oh... and who's your father?"

"My father..." Coro hesitated before concluding that Zale must not have informed her of the reason he was working so hard to solve this case. "His name is Dr. Jarrad Normanday, he's a bastard of a man and I hate him with every fibre of my body, but he's probably one of the smartest scientists alive... except, just before Dusk unleashed his hell on the city, Luminosa claimed to have captured him. I didn't believe it at first but once they started using his experiments to help enhance their powers to kill the Hero of Light, I knew they were telling the truth. Even after they were defeated, though, no signs of my father ever surfaced. That's why

Mr. Osiris asked me to work with you. He believed solving this would help lead to the whereabouts of my father."

Olivia tapped her chin and contorted her mouth in thought. "Dr. Normanday... Dr. Normanday..." She started digging through the boxes of citizen documentation looking for the man's name. Five boxes later, all of which were citizens starting in the N category, she gradually stopped.

"Uh, Coro... there doesn't seem to be a record of anyone by that name in here."

"Huh, that's not possible. My father has had numerous run-ins with the EC. There's no way they wouldn't have a record of him somewhere."

"I see you in here, your mother as well, but nothing of your father."

She slid the folders over to Coro. He opened his personal file, but discreetly he pushed his mother's to the side. He knew the second he opened it the words deceased would cut too deep for him to handle. In Coro's file, there was a relatively current photo from when he started EA. Along with that his new address, and even his registered two elements. But where the name of his father should have been, it was left blank.

"He's not here, there's nothing." As he looked further into his file, an idea sprung to mind. He looked at Olivia, "Do we have the files on the members of Luminosa? The actual group, not the wannabe cultist followers that rioted in the city."

"I believe so. They should be in a special separate folder. They're relatively new as we haven't identified their previous aliases yet, but we have been collecting information on them over the past year." Olivia walked over to a small pile of boxes and started rifling through, but came to a startling stop.

"They're gone..."

"Gone?" Coro paused before the gears in his mind started turning. "You said the only people who knew about this place were high-ranking EC members?"

Olivia nodded.

One name popped into Coro's mind. He shivered at the thought, but he had a feeling he knew where the missing files were. *Is it possible Pascale got rid of all these files before she revealed herself to us, was that part of their plan? But why wipe all known records of themselves from the database, that doesn't make sense... unless...*

"Do you have a list of all those that have been reported missing over the last month?" Coro asked.

Olivia reached into the inside of her uniform pocket, "Here." She pulled out a list of names and handed it to Coro.

"It should have occurred to me sooner... we can't be sure this place hasn't been infiltrated."

"What do you mean?"

"Does the name Pascale ring a bell?"

Olivia raised her eyebrow and tapped the table. "She was an EC officer for almost a decade. I didn't know much about her, but she was always very good at her job. But then one day she just disappeared from work. Nobody was ever told why."

"Of course... guess President Osiris wanted to keep it quiet. I can tell you why. Because she was a traitor that joined Luminosa. She would've had access to this place before anyone knew, so my guess is she would've been able to pull any of the files she wanted. Including my fathers and anyone else they would have wanted to kidnap."

Olivia started to flip through different boxes and sure enough, all the people on her list had missing files.

"You're right. Every single person on my list has a missing file."

"Stolen..." Coro said.

"So, if there are stolen files, that means there must be other files that were stolen of those they've yet to capture. But I wouldn't even know where to look if that were the case. In a city with almost two million people, it will be impossible to pick out if a dozen or so files are missing..."

"You're right..." Coro said.

That night, after spending all afternoon looking through

different files and trying to gather as much data as they could, Coro returned home. He sat on his couch watching the evening news while also continuing to dig through notes he'd made on the day. He loosely paid attention to the coverage of a story involving three unknown kids who defeated a terrible monster attacking North York. Although their names were never mentioned on the newscast Coro had no doubt in his mind of who had pulled off the feat.

He sunk into his couch fighting off the drowsiness that plagued him. They were getting close; he could feel it. The more information they gathered, the more he knew Luminosa was behind it, but some important questions lingered. The missing records of Dr. Jarrad were also annoying, but Coro had more than enough information on the man he seldom called father.

He picked up a mug of tea, the calming mint smell wafting in the room. He took a sip before placing it back down beside a half-eaten sandwich and began working again.

A few minutes later, he received a surprising phone call.

Who would be calling at this hour? Coro picked up the phone reading the name Minisc Premier on the screen. The obvious thing to do would be to answer, but Coro's thumb continued to hover over the accept button. Although he considered Minisc somewhat of a friend and one of the few people he could rely on, the two had not spoken in months. It wasn't that they'd ended on bad terms, by no means, but once his mother died, Coro folded even more inward, a fact he wasn't proud of, but he had his reasons.

In the time he had wasted debating whether to accept Minisc's call, the phone went to voicemail. He let out a sigh but sucked in deep when he heard Minisc's voice in a sharp tone.

"Coro, pick up your phone already. I know you're there. We need to talk about your father."

Apparently, Minisc recognized the chances of the stoic boy picking up were slim, even though he knew he had his phone on him at all times. Coro gripped the phone as he heard Minisc's orders, and under the command, he tapped the large green button before placing his phone on the table. The mention of his father was enough reason to break his silence.

"Oh yeah, now you pick up," Minisc uttered with enough sarcasm to drip through the phone.

One would expect such contempt to put Coro on edge, but the opposite happened. He smirked. He could tell there was no true venom in Minisc's voice, as there rarely ever was. But being a bit overdramatic was not unheard of.

"Why do you want to talk about my father Minisc?" Coro asked.

"Always straight to the point with you... glad to see some things don't change... anyways yeah, we need to talk about your father."

"You said that already, so what about him, did you find any information on his whereabouts?"

"Maybe... well not exactly... honestly, I'm not sure. President Osiris told me you were looking into the slime monsters that were abducting people, right?"

"Slime monsters?"

"The grey goopy things running around the city? Jeez Coro, turn your TV on once in a while."

"I know what they are... I just figured you would have a better name for them than slime monsters... anyways, did you call just to brag about destroying that massive thing at North York or what?"

"Huh, how did you know we... whatever, not the point. The reason I called is the monster we fought... it had dual elements. There's only one person alive who would know how to make that happen, even in some mutated monster. I don't know how but I think somehow Luminosa is using your father to create crystals that can act as an element for these things. My father and Yuri managed to shut down the underground factory that was producing them, but we didn't find any of the missing people or your father around. But that's not all, one of the monsters could talk, and it claimed to be Pascale as well." Minisc unleashed a shotgun of information leaving Coro's head spinning with possibilities.

"Whoa, slow down. Let's start from the beginning. Pascale lived?" Coro's voice carried genuine shock.

"Yeah, she was trying to abduct a child, well that and she wanted to put me in an early grave... but this time I think she's finally gone for good."

"Uh... okay... and she had dual elements?"

"No, she just had her usual fire."

"Okay I'm not following here. Who had dual elements?"

"The giant slime monster that we beat. So far that was the only one who had dual elements, but even so it must be linked to your father right?"

"And these crystals? I assume you think he created such things as well?"

"Actually, that part I don't know about, but all of the monsters have had those crystals. I think, and it feels like a long shot, but your father used Pascale as a prototype for his new creation... if anybody could do it, I guess it would be him right?"

"Right... I wonder..."

"Wonder what?"

"It's nothing, you've just given me a lot to think about, is all. Thank you. I'll try to make use of this information as best I can."

"You're welcome." They both took a brief pause before Minisc asked the question Coro had been waiting for. "Now, are you gonna let us help track down your father or what? If he's still with Luminosa, then he's with Ignis, and if that's the case then we want to find the same thing."

Coro paused. He'd made it clear he would look for his father alone, it was his burden and his mission. He didn't want Minisc involved in family affairs.

"Look Minisc, I know you mean well, but this doesn't involve you. I'll find my father; you continue to protect the city and look for Ignis. If I find any information, I'll let you know, though." And with those parting words, Coro hung up, giving Minisc no time for a rebuttal.

The next morning, Coro marched into Olivia's office. He carried a stack of papers under his arms and his usually neatly pressed clothes were a wrinkled mess. His eyes looked like they hadn't blinked in hours, and his steel hair was in desperate need of a comb. Before Olivia could say a word, he dropped the papers on her desk.

She glanced at the work and in a flat voice asked, "What's this?"

"Just read it."

Olivia obliged. She started flipping through the mountain of notes, most of which were equations or scribbles. They looked like a university student's chemistry homework but far more organized. Her eyes darted back and forth from line to line at a furious pace before looking up at Coro. "Are you sure about this... did you double check everything? There's no way, it's not possible." For once, the stone-faced woman had an expression of shock, if not outright horror.

"There's always room for error, but right now it's the most logical explanation we have. I know the result is awful, but let's just look at what we know. The past few months, Humans have been being abducted and that number only continues to climb. I went back and checked all the names of the people missing and all of them have been removed from the EC's records. On top of that, there are large chunks of other Human records missing as well. Second, the chemical J that has been found around all the abduction sites came back with a near identical build of what it would take to make a Human body function. Third, we know my father has perfected dual elements, which the latest version of these monsters had through the form of a synthetic crystal which acts as a heart. And the final piece of the puzzle, Minisc said that your traitor Pascale was turned into one of those monsters trying to abduct a Human child. I wish I was wrong, but I think this is the reason why we haven't been able to find a single missing Human thus far."

Olivia rechecked the notes and started to shake her head. "If you're right, this is an appalling move by Luminosa... to capture Humans and turn them into their own personal army of Elementalist fighters... All to carry out a misguided ideal in the process."

Coro agreed, "The good news is the Hero of Light managed to

shut down what is believed to be the factory under the sewers that was creating these things. That might buy us a bit more time."

"Even so, we still have no clue where Luminosa is, or your father, for that matter."

"No… not yet…"

CHAPTER 13
A METHOD FOR ESCAPE

THE ROOM WAS DIMLY LIT AND FILLED WITH A MISTY smell of rotten wood and even more so rotten food. A teenage boy with a thin, twig-like body leaned up against the concrete wall. His skin was pale and looked like he'd never heard of sunlight, and his hair a disheveled mess. He wore a long black draping coat and ripped t-shirt and jeans underneath. Holding a magazine tight in his grip he groaned in frustration.

"These stupid kids are becoming a real pain in my ass. I knew I should have killed them when I had the chance. First, the Premier boy takes out Pascale, not that anyone will miss her, but now they've destroyed the entire army of monsters I worked so hard to create." In reality, Brooklyn, the new *de facto* leader of Luminosa with the defeat and arrest of Dusk, did nothing but give the orders on the projects taking place in the sewers. But as the leader, he felt he deserved the credit, of course.

"It's a good thing I always come prepared though... I won't be letting you win this war that easily, Hero of Light. Not you, and not your kid either."

He reached over and grabbed the butcher's knife beside him chucking it into the wall like he was throwing a dart. It pierced the wood with a thud, landing with perfect precision. The target: a poster of the Hero of Light giving a thumbs up.

"Ignis needs to hurry up, I've got better things to do than sit around waiting for him all day." He stood up walking over to the door before a pair of claws shot out from his left hand. He sliced the door that he could have easily opened and kicked it down just to blow off some steam. He was alone at the moment, stewing away in frustration. His desire to kill the Hero of Light and wipe out the wretched society he'd grown to hate so much had been put on hold. At least until he regathered some forces on his side. The slime monsters may have been set back temporarily, but he still had choices.

Meanwhile, the partners Brooklyn relied on to achieve his plans were on the move again. Except this time, it was not of their own doing.

Because of the backlog of those being placed in the high-level jail known as Penatang, a long list of inmates had been waiting to be placed in their new home. Luckily, the city had a few other options to hold them securely for the time being, but today would be moving day for the next group.

The roads were bumpy as those two loyal followers sat in the back of a highly secure military truck. They sat, their backs pressed against the side walls with handcuffs locking their hands behind their backs. Not that they had any intention of breaking out. They would be swarmed and contained in mere seconds by the men in the front of the truck. Only those with a death wish would dare attempt to make an escape while on their way to Penatang.

The tall slim man sat on the left, his legs crossed trying to sit as comfortably as he could. His silver hair was pulled back and he had a trademark cut across the left of his eyes. They were cold and filled with hatred. His name was Bronx.

His eye twitched as he heard a strange gnawing sound from across the room.

"Can you quit biting your nails? It's disgusting," he groaned. He side-eyed the girl and muttered, "I swear being stuck here with you is gonna be a fate worse than death."

"Shut it, or I'll give you that fate." The girl snapped back. She swung her head the opposite way sending her bright blue pigtails flying as she began staring at the steel black walls that contained them. Then she started nibbling on her nails again making sure it was as obnoxious as possible. Her name was Bex.

Once done she rolled over and put her hands above her head looking up at the lifeless grey ceiling. She could hear the tires squealing through the walls and other various sounds of traffic. It sounded like they were on a busy highway for the moment.

"Ugh, I don't wanna go back to one of these places again. I'm gonna go crazy in here," she bellowed dramatically.

"Can you even go crazy if you're already a psychopath?" Bronx muttered loud enough to catch the tip of Bex's hearing.

A knife made of ice flew inches above his nose and crashed into the wall with an icicle-sounding shatter. A small icy residue remained on the wall giving Bronx a cool breeze to enjoy.

He didn't flinch from the angry retaliation, instead opting to glance up at the security cameras that tracked his every movement. They were specially designed cameras embedded into the walls so they could only be spotted by a minuscule black dot. If you knew where you were looking, at least. Bronx was aware of how they worked, but he'd never planned on having to see the technology up close.

Despite his ability to shroud the room in darkness, they could not escape. The back of the truck's four walls had built-in sensors that would alert security of any such activity. Along with that, the larger security cameras had advanced weaponry as well that would likely knock him out cold before the job could be done. The EC refused to implement lethal force outside of the actual Penatang jail, but in some people's minds, that was a big mistake.

Just for fun, he created a small purple ball of darkness that danced on his index finger. He flicked it in the direction of the leftmost camera in the corner of the room but before it could land, the ball smacked into a force field fading with a whimper. He smirked.

"What the hell is taking Brooklyn so long? I swear if we actually end up in Penatang, I'll find a way to kill him myself," Bex groaned. She turned to look at Bronx, the man who had known Brooklyn the longest, and was trusted by Dusk to help lead the boy to glory.

"He'll be on his way. As long as the Hero of Light remains, he still needs us. His training isn't done yet. When it is, we'll make every Human on this blasted planet pay for creating this twisted society we have accepted now."

"When I get out of here, I am going to make these people pay!" Bex growled, but Bronx hushed her down.

As they were traveling along, they hit a large bump. The car hopped and nearly tossed Bex and Bronx around the back.

Bex hit the wall and tumbled to her stomach before growling, "Who the hell taught these people how to drive?"

Bronx tried to get to his feet before feeling the car come to a skidding halt.

"I'd say that's our guy."

"Huh?"

Before Bex could ask any further questions, she heard screams of terror and a whooshing of flames. The inside of the vehicle turned into a sauna. Suddenly the lights in the back turned a grim red before shutting off altogether.

That's when Bronx saw his chance. "Bex, freeze the room!" He yelled.

The diminutive child heard the words and smiled with uncontrollable glee. She held her hands out, scrunching up her face. A flash of white filled the inside of the truck from corner to corner transforming it into an ice palace. The gleam of the walls sparkled while the cameras all ceased their movements.

They heard more banging and turned their attention to the back door. Even though it was covered in ice, the pale white surface was turning red, with steam rising off it. Soon a hole melted its way through the door and then arms shot in ripping the weakened door off for good.

"I can't believe I have to waste my time doing this for you two." The sharp voice cut through the smoke pouring from outside.

Bex and Bronx wasted no time hurrying through the smoke and jumping down from the lip of the truck and into the night sky. Standing in front of them, with walls of flames around him, was a boy. He wore a familiar black cloak, that when they saw it a sense of power filled them.

"Took you long enough," Bronx goaded.

"Yeah well, Brooklyn's other plan wasn't working out, so here I am," Ignis snarled, showing no concern for those who were supposed to be his partners.

"Who cares?" Bex interrupted, "We're free. Let's get the hell out of here."

"She's got a point. Brooklyn wants you. Hurry up."

But right before they left Bronx took a quick look around the carnage. He wanted to at least gather his bearings.

They appeared to be on a cliffside, and through the walls of fire he could faintly see cars burned and destroyed. Even other EC military trucks. When he looked to the front of his own vehicle, he noticed six heavily burnt bodies lying limp on the ground. There wasn't much left of them. It was a full-on assault of the EC the likes of which they'd never seen coming.

Bex was prepared to start making her way down the cliff and into the forest below by use of her ice, but before she did, Bronx asked, "Did you do all of this, Ignis?" Even he had to admit he was taken aback by the brute force of his partner's iron fist.

"These idiots were nothing but a bunch of fakes. They think they're protecting people, but they couldn't even hold up against some fire... so I disposed of them."

Once they were down the cliffside and away from the copious amount of EC personnel rushing in for backup Bex sucked back a breath of nighttime air. Despite it being filled with fire and smoke, she still revelled in the glory.

"Sweet freedom."

"We don't have time to smell the flowers. More members are gonna swarm quickly," Ignis ordered as they took off in the night.

With their escape successful, Ignis led his partners to their designated hiding spot.

The room was not all that different from the cell the two had been stuck in for the past three months. Damp, dark, and surrounded by concrete walls. They were underground, that's all Bex and Bronx could gather, but they didn't care much to ask questions as long as they were free from the EC's grasp.

Ignis thrust open a steel door and marched in with authority. Brooklyn stood leaning up against the far wall, but Ignis walked right by him, taking a seat and putting his feet up.

"There you go, now what's your big plan?" Ignis asked. He folded his arms and glared at the supposed leader.

Brooklyn glared back, "Took you long enough. I was starting to think maybe you got your ass killed." Then he turned his attention to those he considered real members of Luminosa.

"And what took you so long? I was going stir crazy," Bex whined.

"What'd you want me to do? I didn't have much choice but to wait till you guys were being moved to Penatang. Besides, Dusk needed me to stay as far away from the EC as possible."

From the back of the room, Ignis decided to give his two cents. "If Dusk is just giving you all these orders, why didn't you bother to break him out? You had an army of monsters and you didn't even try to attack Penatang."

"He didn't want us to," Bronx answered instead.

Ignis raised an eyebrow, opening up his ears as well. He said, "I'm listening…"

"You see, Dusk uses a technique called Eternal Darkness, it is kin to the same power as the Hero of Light. That's how they've ascended past all our strengths. But the cost of using such power is that it erodes your body and element over time. Dusk was hopeful he could reverse this effect, but time fell short. When he fought the Hero, the last of his power was drained."

"However, through that fight, we learned something valuable," Brooklyn interrupted, "The Hero of Light's power is fading as well. He's vulnerable now. And once he's dead, nobody will be left to stop us this time."

"And what about Minisc…" Ignis chirped. His tone was mocking.

"Who's Minisc?" Brooklyn scowled before the name finally rang a bell, "You mean the Hero's kid? He doesn't stand a chance without his father around."

"Oh yeah… if you're that confident then why don't you just take the fight to them right now?" Ignis snarled standing up. "The only reason I bothered to join you three was for a chance to kill the Hero of Light. Yet for the last three months, all you've done is cower down here with that insane doctor trying to build some mutant army, and even when you finally did, they were destroyed by Minisc and his little do-gooder friends anyways."

"That's pretty cocky for a kid who came crawling to us. I'm not stopping you from killing the Hero of Light. Be my guest," Brooklyn goaded with a sinister smile. He held his hand up, stopping Bronx or Bex from speaking. He wanted Ignis to react, to which the temperamental boy did.

Ignis snorted and huffed to the back door leaving with a slam. Bronx looked at his so-called leader and said, "You think that was a wise idea? The kid's power is incredible; don't you think he would have been useful?"

"Oh, he'll be more than useful…"

CHAPTER 14
EMERGENCIES CALL FOR ACTION

THE NEXT FEW DAYS FOR MINISC AND HIS FRIENDS WERE used for rest and recovery. Their bodies were sore, but for the most part, they were in decent shape. Luckily, with all the current commotion, their volunteer duties were suspended for a few days as the dust settled.

Thanks to the combined efforts, and a little help from Bailey, they managed to keep damage to a limited area, and no Humans were seriously injured. But perhaps most importantly, since the defeat of the slime monsters, Human abductions plummeted. Three straight days and not a single report came in. Of course, thanks to Don and Yuri's efforts in shutting down the factory as well, they were given some time to regroup.

Still, unrest followed Minisc. Yes, they bought some time, but it was only a short while before the next plan would kick in. They needed to find Luminosa, and quick.

Crickets chirped in the night as faint moonlight crept through the drapes on the window. The world was silent, but Minisc sat up in his bed, staring blankly ahead. He ran his fingers through his unruly blond locks before letting out a disgruntled groan. He dropped his head back on the pillow and cuddled himself into his covers. He stared up at the ceiling, his mind flipping the pages of all his mental notes.

Since he last talked to Coro two days ago, he had continually fought insomnia. Was it that Coro still rejected any sense of help from him, or was it that he had his own search as well, and knowing now that Coro's father was involved, then for sure Ignis would be involved as well. It only made sense. Outside of Brooklyn, those two were the only ones who eluded capture, or had even been spotted since the day Dusk failed his uprising. One way or another, he knew in his heart finding one would lead to the other.

Sick of staring at his ceiling, he decided it would serve him best to attempt sleeping again. But like before that would have to wait. His ears perked up when he heard his father's voice from down the hall. It sounded serious, but Minisc couldn't make out any of the words, only a general tone.

I'm sure it's nothing, he negotiated with himself before closing his eyes and rolling over to his side. His obvious insomnia would not deter him from attempting to rest his body. But an obnoxious buzzing on his bedside table would. It buzzed once, and then a second time before going off another three times after that. Then it started to ring. Someone was calling him. His heart pumped a little faster as he sat up. He knew the ring tone, and therefore the person calling which is what made him feel so concerned. He reached over answering the phone and said, "Jules... can't this wait till morning?"

"No! President Osiris called an emergency meeting for all members of the EC. He told Yuri he wants us there as well. It's urgent."

"Wait hold on a sec... emergency meeting?" Minisc's glazed-over eyes began to focus, and the fatigue left his body. "What's going on? Is it another attack?"

"I don't know," Jules answered honestly, "Yuri just told me to call you and Lily. We're supposed to be at the debriefing in half an hour."

Down the hall, Minisc heard footsteps, and then the door crept open. In the doorway stood his father who spoke in a whisper.

"Minisc, are you awake?" Don asked.

He had just got off the phone with Zale a moment ago, being given the same information Jules was passing along currently. Unlike Jules though, Don displayed a bit more reluctance to wake his son up. He knew the rigours of being in the EC and the possibility for a crisis to be called in the dead of night. But Minisc was not actually part of the EC, and he was still only a teenager.

He understood why Zale asked for Minisc and his friends to attend. They were as vital and skilled to the EC's success as anyone, and with his own diminishing powers each passing day, they were in desperate need of capable, talented help. But that didn't mean they were ready for the life of an EC member. Maturity was just as key to the role, and there was no substitute for experience either. Even so, Don knew Minisc would have been furious if he could've helped and been held back.

"Yeah, I'm up," Minisc mumbled taking his attention away from Jules on the phone.

Don walked further into the room and flipped the light switch beside the door. Darkness vanished, leaving Minisc to groan and cover his eyes, "Okay, I wasn't awake enough for that…"

"Sorry."

Minisc held his phone back up to his ear. "I'll be there soon Jules. Call Lily." He hung up the phone and directed his full attention to his father.

Don looked at the phone in his son's hand, "I take it you already know then?"

"Not really… I just know I have to get up…"

"Fair enough." Don took a seat on his son's bed and put his hand on the boy's shoulder. "Look, Minisc, I know you're still recovering, and on top of that you're not actually part of the EC, so even though Zale wants you to go, I'm not gonna make you. That said, this decision is yours to make, not mine. This is part of the job and if you plan to join the EC one day, then sometimes these things happen."

"Well, then I'm going," Minisc said with great assurance. "I don't know what's going on, but I wanna help if I can. Lily and Jules are going and I wanna make sure I'm there with them."

"Alright," Don nodded, "Get dressed and we'll head out immediately." Don left the room and Minisc hopped out of bed.

He tossed on some clothes and in minutes they were off to the EC.

There were multiple different rooms in the new EC headquarters. There were worker offices for the president and many others who were not on the streets every day, but there was also a copious amount of research labs as well. Minisc had seen those rooms before, but the one his father led him into was entirely different.

He stood in the back of a giant auditorium where one of the three entrances to the room was. They used the back door, and then there were two doors at the front, on the left and right. The room resembled a movie theatre, with seats scaling up to the top part of the room and a dozen carpeted stairs leading to the bottom.

More and more people were piling in, none of whom Minisc recognized. "This is insane; how many people are here?" He asked as he stood beside his father at the back and highest part of the room.

"If I had to guess somewhere between 150 to 200 people. Zale did say this was of the highest priority."

Minisc sifted through all the unfamiliar faces looking for his friends but to no avail.

I wonder if we beat them here? Minisc felt a hand fall on his shoulder. He looked up at his father who said, "I have to run through some things with Zale for the debriefing. Are you gonna to be okay staying here by yourself?"

"Yeah, I'll be fine. I'll just keep looking for Jules and Lily."

Don nodded and headed down the red-carpet stairs to his left.

An audible buzz circulated through the room as different groups of people gathered to discuss why they were called. For Minisc, after his father left and with no sign of his friends he began looking around the room and twiddling his thumbs. He decided to make himself comfy and sit down but before he sat in silence for too long the door at the bottom of the room flew open.

Zale marched in, causing the chatter to hush. He, unlike most in the room, appeared wide awake, but chances were that was because he never made it to bed to be woken up so abruptly in the first place.

Everyone took their seats and as they did the magnitude of the situation began to sink in for Minisc. Up to this point, most of being woken up and arriving at the EC happened in a blur and his brain remained on autopilot. But now he could feel the butterflies in his stomach growing. Something serious had happened, and he would be required to help. Normally those circumstances did not deter him--he'd been through plenty to know what he could handle--but this time was a little different. He rolled up the cuff of his long black sleeved shirt staring at the bandages underneath. He wondered if he was in over his head once again. But it was too late to back out now. He would just have to face it as best he could. Just the way he was taught.

Zale stepped up to the podium that stood at the bottom of the room and flipped on the projector behind him.

"Thank you everyone for coming on such short notice. I apologize for the wakeup call, but I assure you we wouldn't be doing this if the matter wasn't of the utmost urgency." As he spoke the nervous energy engulfed the room. It seemed fair to say Minisc was not the only person unaware of the situation at hand. "Late tonight, we discovered a horrifying reality that we now must face. First, as I'm sure some of you have already heard, one of our trucks was attacked on the way to Penatang just a few hours ago. Two Elementalists escaped... others were seriously harmed and unfortunately a number of our men and women occupying the truck were killed. We have already upped our security measures to make sure this cannot happen again, and we are trying to assess this tragedy as we speak."

As Minisc listened to the words, his face grew paler and his hands became clammy. Then as Zale picked up the small white clicker off the podium and changed the screen to the two escapees, Minisc's breath caught in his throat.

Zale continued, "These two are Bex Labelle, and Bronx Forte. They are two of what we consider the current big three members of Luminosa. After Dusk fell to the Hero of Light, these two were also apprehended and have spent the last 100 days in Toronto District jail. But tonight, at approximately 9:47 pm, while we were finally ready to move them to Penatang, we received a distress call saying a powerful Elementalist blocked off the roads and attacked the convoy, allowing them to escape freely. Now, we're to presume the two and whoever set them free have gone into hiding somewhere in the city, but we're still investigating the situation. As for the Elementalist who broke these two out, we remain unsure, but there is no doubt the three of them together are dangerous. Many good people were killed in acts of senseless violence, so be advised."

The second round of audible whispers began circulating from one member to the next. There was clear trepidation caused by the threat at hand.

Zale kept speaking, "Bex and Bronx are considered highly dangerous, and should you run into either of them or anyone resembling them, do not engage. I cannot stress this enough, these two will not hesitate to kill you, and they can back it up with strength. Whoever broke them out is equally as dangerous. Call either myself or The Hero of Light if you suspect something or see them, but first get to a safe location. On top of that, we need to try and keep this from the public spotlight as best we can." That's when Zale paused for a second. The crowd could tell that the heavy news had yet to come. He took a deep breath before looking back at the mass sets of eyes entranced by his words. "This second piece of news is tough to share, but at this point, we have all but confirmed it. Thanks to our very own Coro Normanday and Olivia Middleton, it saddens me to inform you that the slime monsters which have been running around the city, were in fact creations of Luminosa. They used a factory walled off in the sewers where they would take those they abducted and turned them into the veil creatures you saw destroying our city."

The room fell silent.

Minisc's eyes widened, and a sickening feeling began to overcome him. And he was not the only one, the entire room felt devastated by the news. The Humans everyone spent so much time looking for were right in front of their eyes, and yet they were not who they once were. Getting a grasp on that idea would not be easy, but Minisc couldn't help but kick himself for not realizing it. He thought back to Pascale.

She must have been a test experiment of some sort. She gave up the body that sat on the brink of death so they could perfect these monsters, and she would get another crack at killing me...

After Zale gave everyone a second to let his words sink in, he began to address the room again, "I know this is tough news for everyone, especially those who knew some of those who were taken. However, based on our numbers the amount of monster containers we found would still imply that over a dozen of those abducted have not met such a horrid fate yet. We need to find out where they're being held right away, and I believe that is where Bronx and Bex will be heading also. For now, I am going to break you off into groups, and we're going to search the city in units. Also, we're going to have more members working the night shift, making sure we have every corner of the city and beyond covered. Over the next twenty-four hours, we are on a manhunt to find these two. I need all hands on deck. The fate of many lives depends on it."

Zale clicked the button again and a map of the city displayed on the screen. Red lines intersected cutting the city into 25 strange shapes. Also, within each section were small buttons with faces of each EC member on them.

Minisc, Yuri, Lily, and Jules were stationed in the northeast end near the train stations central local. The school was nearby as well so they were relatively familiar with the area.

After Zale's briefing ended, everyone started walking up and down the stairs with conviction, splitting into their assigned groups. Minisc headed down the stairs to where his father was as the man was having a small side conversation with Zale. They conveniently stopped as Minisc got within earshot and then Don looked at his son.

"Minisc... did you find Lily or Jules?"

"No, I just stayed in the back. I haven't seen them yet."

"Seen who?" Lily's drowsy voice asked as she walked up beside Minisc. Behind her were Jules and Yuri, but they looked far more awake and alert than she or even Minisc.

"Perfect," Zale said, looking at the group he purposely put together. "I need the four of you to go to the east side of the city, near Scarborough, and search high and low. As the only ones who really know the threats those two could be, I need you to be ready for anything." He looked at Yuri and then at the kids where Jules was the only one of the three that could be considered awake. He gave them a sad smile, "I apologize for all this, I know you're supposed to be given a few days off for your efforts, but this is of the utmost importance, I hope you understand. We can't allow these two to roam free. If they do, we could have more issues than just those slime monsters returning."

"We understand," Minisc said. No matter how much he begged to crawl back into bed, sleeping would be futile while he knew Bronx and Bex, two of the evilest Elementalists he'd had the misfortune of running across, plotted their new plans. Besides, he had a feeling he knew the culprit behind their escape.

CHAPTER 15
NEEDLE IN A HAYSTACK

THE EAST SIDE OF TORONTO LED TO SCARBOROUGH, which was known for being a more peaceful area in the city. It much like many of the outer areas around Toronto's core had a much higher Human to Elementalist ratio, but over the years it was gradually shifting.

Minisc and company sat on the train in the dead of night. It was almost empty, with at best a few dozen people spread out through the twelve-cabin ride. Nobody said a word as they tried their best to will themselves awake. Even Jules had begun to fade from the time he called Minisc. The urgency of the situation remained, but maintaining such energy levels to those not accustomed to night shift rigours proved challenging.

Muffled cries of steel breaks on each standard stop plus the electronic voice calling out the locations were the only sounds keeping anyone alert. Minisc continued staring out the window while Lily slumped over on his shoulder using him as a pillow. The trip would be around twenty-five minutes, so they had some time to rest. As he watched the trees whip past by the dozens, he continued to digest the information presented in the briefing. Humans were being turned into monsters, Bex and Bronx were free, and somewhere in all of that Ignis stood in the middle.

At a loss, Minisc took a deep breath and gently shifted himself trying not to wake Lily. He looked up at Yuri who continued scrolling through different articles scouring for information.

"Hey, Yuri?" He asked in a soft tone, "Do you have any more

information on what President Osiris was talking about with Humans being turned into those monsters?"

Yuri gave him a sad smile and said, "Sorry, I found out the same time you did. I don't think any of us knew."

Jules yawned, finally opening his eyes and rubbing some drool from the corner of his mouth.

"Didn't President Osiris say Coro was the one who figured it all out? When you called him, what did he tell you?"

"He really didn't say much."

"Big surprise there," Jules mocked.

"I know, I know, but when I gave him the information we had, I think something clicked for him. Whatever he's been doing while looking for his father, I guess he managed to put all the clues together and figure out what was going on. But clearly, he still hasn't been able to find the man."

"You don't suppose Dr. Jarrad had anything to do with Bex and Bronx's escape, do you?" Lily mumbled picking her head up off Minisc's shoulder.

Yuri rested his chin in his hand. "It's hard to say. All I know is several guards and even criminals following behind on their way to Penatang were killed in the process. And due to a lack of survivors, we can't gather much info. I'm sure President Osiris wants to get all his ducks in a row before spreading any potential misinformation throughout the EC group, but even more so the public. Chances are he and Minisc's father are the only two who know the full scope of information, that is if they even know."

Don did not make the trip to Scarborough with his son. Though he wished to stand by and make sure they were safe, he and Zale had come to agreements on other plans. He knew Yuri would never let harm befall his son, and along with that Minisc's strength probably matched his own, or at least what he had left. For the time being the group of four would have to rely on each other, and not the Hero of Light. A trend society would soon have to accept as well.

The rest of the train ride went smoothly with no delays, but when the group stepped onto the platform, an eerie feeling danced through the air.

"I know it's late, but this place is like a ghost town…" Jules said. He wasn't wrong in his statement though. They stood alone in the darkness with only faint lights from the building in front of them lighting the way. No people, no noise, just the soft call of the brisk night air.

They made their way off the platform and to the building as the train began rushing down the tracks and into the night. It was a small one story building with a simple design to match its mundane role. Outside of a place to stay dry during snow or rain, the building only sold train tickets and had a board for different scheduled departure times.

When they walked into the green and white painted room, there was one other person who sat in the nearby kiosk. Even that man knew his job was more than likely done as he sat behind the glass reading a book with his feet up. He glanced at the EC members and then reverted to his book with no visible interest in them. EC members taking the train by night was not as uncommon as one might expect.

Unsure what to do first, a thought popped into Minisc's head. He turned to Lily and said, "You live around here don't you? Where do you think we should start looking?"

Lily nodded. She had lived in Scarborough her whole life. Admittedly due to a sheltered upbringing she didn't know the area as well most others, and on top of that she spent a lot of her time within the city with Jules or Minisc, but she could deduce where their culprits would likely not go, and using that she could provide an answer to Minisc's question.

"I think it's safe to say they wouldn't be hiding in any of the residential areas. That's where they'd be spotted quickest. Also, it would be the most obvious spot for the EC to place members to ensure the safety of people. There's a small business plaza nearby, but most of the stores were abandoned months ago when Luminosa attacked. They couldn't afford to repair the damage and decided to look for other work. It would make for a pretty good hiding spot at this point."

"Okay, take the lead," Yuri said. He pulled out his phone and started typing away before they left.

"Yuri, what are you doing?" Jules asked.

"I'm letting everyone else who Zale assigned to Scarborough know where we're going. We don't want to get too bunched up in our search."

A half-moon bathed the desolate streets in pale blue light as Lily led her friends down the sidewalk.

"How far is it to this business plaza area?" Jules asked.

"It shouldn't be too much longer. I can't say I came here often before everyone left, it's probably been about a year, but I don't remember it being far from the train station."

Minisc took in his surroundings as they walked.

"I always pictured Scarborough more city-like than this. There are so many homes here though."

Lining up on either side of the street were homes as far as he could see. Added to that were even more streets and intersections that lead to even more houses. For someone who lived with no neighbours and spent most of his time in areas where homes were scattered alongside business's, it was a new view of the world.

"Growing up, there were far fewer houses here. It used to be a lot more wildlife and forested areas. Sort of like your house Minisc, but I guess over the years, they just continued building. Now Scarborough is sort of a split between two sections. Right now where we are would be the residential section with all of the homes and subdivisions. The other section is where schools and business are."

"I guess in a way it's not that different than the city is it?" Jules said.

"No, it's just a little less crowded, that's all."

The four continued talking about life, in a way using it to distract from any danger that might be around the corner, and soon enough Lily led them to their destination.

"Well, here we are." Lily waved her hand, presenting what most would consider a rougher-looking area. There were more than a dozen buildings in the plaza that had either been abandoned or bordered up for safety reasons. Most were small and a few were quite big, but each one looked grim and ready to fall apart.

"This place looks awful…" Jules said.

"I told you it was abandoned. Nobody comes here anymore, which is why if Bronx and Bex were around Scarborough this would be their best place to go."

Everyone nodded, accepting the girl's wisdom before Yuri took lead of the situation again.

He looked at the three in his charge and said, "Let's split up and do a preliminary search of the area. Minisc and Lily, you two take the buildings on the left and Jules and I will sweep the right looking for anything suspicious. We'll work our way around till we meet back up in the middle." The group agreed and started their investigation.

The parking lot which connected all the buildings was large and desolate with scattered streetlights throughout. Minisc and Lily followed their instructions and headed to the far-left, starting with a small rectangular building. It looked like an abandoned fast-food joint, but with all the windows bordered up and signs ripped down. However, telling one building apart from another was near impossible.

They did a quick walk around remaining on high alert. The two could feel confident with each other watching their backs, but when it involved Luminosa, hearts always tended to beat a little faster.

Once they deemed nothing out of the ordinary was taking place they headed back to regroup. Jules and Yuri did the same and after about half an hour they met up with only one place left to look. This building, although in the same condition as the others, was far bigger, climbing two stories tall. It was all black with various windows along the top and implied some sort of office.

"What is this place?" Jules asked. He walked up to the door of the building. It was the only entrance that remained intact without boards sealing it up.

"I think it used to be an old bank. But I don't know why it hasn't been boarded up like everything else," Lily said.

"Seems like it would make for a good hideout, if you ask me. I say we check it out a little further and see what we find." Jules reached for the knob but as he did a yelp escaped his lips. He sprung back shaking his hand to relieve the numbness.

"Jules, are you okay?" Minisc asked. He and the others gathered around the boy checking on any injuries, but Jules shook his head and waved them off.

"Yeah, I'm fine, but the door's wired with electricity. Clearly, someone wants to make sure we can't get in."

After ascertaining that his brother was okay, Yuri headed to the door next. He knelt and keyed in on a small almost translucent wire as thin as thread sliding down the door and into the ground.

"That's odd…" Yuri stood up and turned back to his group, "Hey Minisc, come break this wire with your light. But try not to touch it or you're gonna end up like Jules."

Minisc helped Jules to his feet and then walked to where the older of the brothers stood.

"If we break this wire, it should shut off the electric trap," Yuri said.

Minisc nodded. "Okay." He held his hand out and a small blast of light like a little switch knife formed ripping through the single strand. The bottom half of the line drooped to the ground with small sparks of electricity sparkling on the surface.

"That should take care of that," Yuri said, putting a finger to the metal handle, tapping it to make sure no more sparks jumped out. Knowing it was safe, Yuri put the weight of his whole body into the door, but it refused to move.

"Minisc, help me out here." The two of them started pushing on the steel door, but it was a futile effort at best. Even through combined strength they were not getting in.

"This is ridiculous; a bank doesn't need a reinforced steel door to keep customers out. Someone clearly doesn't want people getting in," Yuri said, taking a step back before catching his breath.

Metal doors aside, there had to be another easier entrance, so Lily suggested, "Let's go around back and see if we can find anything." She led the three behind the side of the bank.

"Look," Jules said pointing to a shattered window three quarters of the way up the sidewall.

"Yeah, that would work, but how're we supposed to get up there? It's way too high," Lily asked.

"Leave that to me. You guys go back and wait at the front door, I've got this." Jules smiled with his usual confidence as the wind picked up around him. He crouched down and readied for his big leap while the others stepped back giving him room to work his magic. He burst up like a rocket taking off, the harsh breeze from beneath blowing in everyone's faces. With careful precision, he soared through the air majestically, going headfirst through the broken window while avoiding the jagged edges of the glass. Once he disappeared from sight the group heard a loud thud, like a bowling ball crashing onto the floor.

The three winced making faces knowing Jules was the source of the sound before Minisc called out, "Jules are you okay up there? You didn't break anything did you?"

After a few seconds Jules popped his head out from the window with a toothy grin. "Could have stuck the landing a little better, but I'm good. I'll meet you at the front door."

Now that he was inside, Jules turned from the window to gather his bearings. He stood on the second floor, but the rest of his surroundings were blind to him. First, he wanted to find some sort of light source. Currently, the moon glimmered through the window but at a sparse angle giving him only a glimpse of vision. Even through the darkness, he could tell he rolled into an office, though. Or at least what used to be an office. In the corners were a few shelves with old pictures on them, and a couple feet away from the window stood a large desk covered in webs. Jules gave himself a few seconds to let his eyes adjust before he headed for the door. He tapped the light switch but the light in the center of the room flickered before dulling into nothing. He sighed and said, "Well that's just great. Oh well, I'm sure this place can't be that hard to get through."

Outside, the hallway went around the rim of the second floor in a C shape. In the middle were two sets of stairs connecting the two floors.

Jules cautiously made his way down the stairs to the first floor, ignoring the continual haunting feeling that walking through the mysterious darkness provided him.

On the first floor were several cubicles protected by large, thin walls. It looked far more like a standard business office than the second floor which must have been for executive work Jules assumed. He hopped the long kiosk desk that was just in front of the stairs and made his way to the double steel doors that continued to impede their progress. He quickly noticed his roadblock.

"Looks like you're the reason we couldn't get in," he said as if he were talking to someone else in the room. He grabbed the two steel chains that wound tightly between the doors, sealing them from the inside. He gave them a full powered yank but with no success to show for it. He pulled harder a second time feeling the rusty steel dig into his palm, but there was still no luck. Then he heard Minisc's voice on the other side of the door.

"Jules... are you there?"

"Yeah, I'm here. There're chains on the door locking it though. I can't break them open, they're too strong." He could hear the frustrated sigh of Minisc on the other side.

"Minisc, I have an idea, but it might be a bit dangerous."

"And that would be..." A steel door between them could not stop Jules from feeling the look Minisc was shooting him.

"I can loosen the chains just enough to crack the door open. Then I need you to break the chains with a Lum Bomb. I'd do it but wind doesn't have the strength and water won't do much either."

Jules thought his plan was pretty brilliant, but Minisc had other opinions.

"How on earth do you plan to hold the door and get out of the way before I hit you?"

"Oh, I'll be fine. Besides, I can take your best hit." Jules chuckled. He couldn't see Minisc, but he could visualize the boy shaking his head in defeat. But no incoming arguments meant his idea had been greenlit.

The chains rattled as Jules grabbed them with a tight grip. He gritted his teeth and dug his feet into the dirty carpet as he fought to give Minisc an opening. Then he dropped his body weight on the ground pulling back enough to crack the door open a sliver. Through the sliver of an opening, he heard his friend argue one last time.

"Jules you've had some dumb ideas over the years, but this might be the worst one yet." Minisc groaned as he charged a ball of light in his left hand. Next to him, Lily held her fingers to her mouth, while Yuri stood by looking puzzled, but neither of them said a word. Minisc had said enough for the three of them.

But it didn't matter. What other options did they have? Minisc wound up like a big-league pitcher eying his meticulous strike zone. "Here goes nothing," he muttered before throwing the ball with as much force as he could muster.

The actual task itself was not complicated, and Minisc had held back plenty so Jules' proclamation of withstanding the blow would hold up. The whole idea just seemed so insane to him.

As predicted, the blast sliced through the chains with ease, however, Jules made one small miscalculation in his foolproof plan. He focused on dodging his friend's attack, but what he should have concerned himself with were the forces of momentum after the chains snapped. He pulled with so much vigour that when the chains broke free, Jules went flying backwards tumbling into the kiosk. The blast of light soared over his head smashing into the desk made of wood, shattering the old furniture and dropping a pile of broken lumber on top of the poor boy.

A shadow loomed over him as Jules glanced up from the pile. Minisc stood in front of him with his hand extended and a mocking smirk, "So you got this right?"

Jules took his friend's hand and brushed off the excess debris. "You're in, aren't you? I'd say that went exactly as planned."

Minisc had no arguments for that. They were indeed in the building and now free to investigate further.

"This place feels a lot bigger on the inside," Lily said as she looked up to the ceiling and back down to the floor.

Yuri followed close behind, and after observing his surroundings he made a plan.

"Looks like we only have two floors to search. Minisc, Lily, you two check all the rooms on the first floor, Jules and I will look through the second floor."

"Works for me. Come on Lil, let's see what we can find."

"We should start to the left and work clockwise around." The two steered off, with Lily leading the way, which left Jules and Yuri to march up the stairs. They opted to start on the right since Jules had already broken through the first door.

"This place gives me the creeps," Lily complained, rubbing her arm as she watched Minisc rip open one of the old desks in their first room of exploration. A layer of dust puffed out causing the two to begin coughing but with no results for their effort.

"I know... something about this place gives me a bad feeling," Minisc agreed.

Next, Lily walked over to another desk, where she picked up a stack of papers. She sifted through them before neatly putting them back where they'd come from. "Nothing but old discarded bank documents over here," she said.

Minisc did the same but with little results. They left the room and continued their path along the left wall heading to their next destination.

The exploration team of Yuri and Jules didn't fare much better on the second floor.

Jules flicked on light after light. Thankfully, they still had a bit of power left in the building. He wasted no time admiring his surroundings. The only thing he focused on was finding the escaped members of Luminosa.

"This is just a waste of time. Bex and Bronx aren't here. And after all that effort to get in too," Jules groaned.

"You're probably right, but we're already here now, we should at least do our due diligence. You never know what clues you might find that could be of use," Yuri advised.

Jules sighed. "I guess so." They were in the last room on the right side before hitting the stairs, but their search had come up empty on every front.

All the rooms looked relatively the same, a small set of furniture, a chair or couch, a desk, and a cabinet full of papers. Jules ripped open the final cabinet and in his haste, a pile of documents came tumbling out.

"Whoa," he said, jumping back from the scare.

Yuri spun around hearing his brother's yelp before seeing the mess created. "I know we're searching this place from head to toe, but try not to make a mess of things while we're here."

"Hold on," Jules said. He picked up the numerous folders and tried to stuff them back in the box but then noticed a strange insignia on the box. The letters EC were labelled on the side. "Why would paperwork from the EC be in here? Hey Yuri, I think you should take a look at this." He carried the box over to the desk where Yuri waited and dropped it in front of him.

Yuri scanned the papers, his expression changing with each page he flipped. First came shock, then frustration before he took a breath and regained his composure. Each folder of papers cited a profile of a person along with a name, residency, date of birth and a few other details.

"This can't be..." Yuri started taking a mental count of every abduction case he could recall as he flipped through the pages a second time. Then he landed on one name he could be sure of. Joy Peterson. The missing woman who worked in his old office. *Most of these names match those who've been abducted. But there are still a few dozen others here... what if those names are the next targets... but how could Luminosa have gotten their hands on this information, they would have needed someone on the...* Yuri came to the same conclusion Coro had earlier. Pascale.

He had no time to lament the traitor, though, instead, he turned to his brother and said "Jules, I need you to run a search on your phone for me."

"Uh, okay, what am I searching for?"

"All of the names on these documents."

Jules furrowed his brow at first but decided to forgo any other questions as Yuri began reading the names out one by one.

"Harry Stewart."

"Weird, the first thing to pop up is an article about his abduction. He was one of the ones taken by those monsters."

"That's what I thought… what about Veronica Wilson?"

"Same thing. She went missing last month." Jules' heart skipped a beat as an uneasy dread started to creep up, "Yuri, what's going on?"

"I think all of these files are records that were stolen from the EC. They also seem to be a perfect match for all the people who were abducted over the last few months."

"But why would they be in an old, abandoned bank?"

"It's hard to be sure, but what I do know is this isn't all that's around here. Check the rest of those names for me will you, I'm gonna take another look around."

Jules nodded, spreading the papers out to confirm each name. He rolled through the list until he came to an unnerving person.

"Yuri… can you come look at this?" Jules looked pale as his brother approached.

"What is it, are you okay?" He asked.

"Just… look at this…" Jules' hand shook as he handed the brown folder over to his brother. Yuri flipped it open, but once he did he understood his brother's reaction. "Martel, Caroline…" Yuri looked up at Jules, "Why does the name Martel sound familiar?"

"Because that's Lily's last name… I think this is her mother…"

"Lily's mother is Human?"

"Yeah, her mother is Human and her father is an Elementalist… but she never said anything about her mother disappearing. You don't think she's been keeping that from us, do you?"

Yuri shook his head, "No, Lily isn't one to hide such traumatic news. On top of that, I never heard her name come up in any news reports. When you search her name, what comes up?"

Jules typed the name into his phone but shook his head when he got the results.

"Nothing, no reports at all. So, what do you think this means then? Why would her name be in this pile?"

"If I had to guess, it means she and anyone else in this pile that has not been abducted would have been part of the next wave of victims. It's just a guess, but Luminosa must have needed this information so their monsters knew who to abduct. By shutting down the factory, we slowed them down, but we can't just assume they won't still go after these people again."

"But that means Lily's mom could be in serious danger. We need to warn her and the EC right away. Maybe we can cut Luminosa off before they try anything else."

Meanwhile, with Yuri and Jules' troubling discovery, Minisc and Lily reached a door that nestled into the side frame of the stairs. Minisc unhinged the latch and swung open the door, expecting it to be nothing more than a closet, but to his surprise, there was a staircase leading underground. A veil of darkness shrouded the path forward.

"Do we go?" Lily asked.

"I'll take a quick look. I'm sure it's nothing, but even so..." Minisc snapped his fingers to illuminate his path with a ball of light.

Lily watched him descend below, casting away the darkness but as he went further in the shadows reformed swallowing him up.

When she lost sight of her friend, she said, "Hold on Minisc, I'm coming with you." With a deep breath she bravely marched down the stairs until she reached Minisc.

"Be on your guard..." Minisc whispered as they continued down. Lily gripped his arm tightly refusing to let go as they walked.

"I don't like this. Maybe we should go back and get Yuri and Jules?" She fretted. But much to her surprise, Minisc said nothing, opting to continue. Each step he took was like he had become possessed by some instinct to lead him on his path. A dozen or so steps later and they hit the bottom floor of the building.

"We'll take one quick look around. If we find anything, we can let them know," Minisc finally said as he cast his ball of light into the center of the room. The rays revealed the size of the room to be unusually small. Minisc and Lily side by side could stretch out and touch the walls, and even walking forward would only be six steps at best.

"See, it's empty, now let's go back up. The sooner we get out of this place the better," Lily pleaded.

Without a doubt, they could both agree the room was empty. But that begged Minisc to ask another question, "Why would someone build a room this small and leave it empty? Something isn't right here." He gave the room a once-over, tapping on the walls, looking for any oddity that he could find. Much like when they were in the sewers, Minisc was sure a fake wall existed somewhere, but each time he tapped his knuckle, the test came back negative.

"What are you doing?" Lily said, tapping her foot impatiently in the middle of the room. Minisc froze, spinning around to look at his friend.

"Tap your foot again," Minisc said.

"What, why?" Hoping for an explanation, Lily tapped her foot three more times. A hollow clank echoed in unison with her steps.

Minisc raised his hand and a ball of light formed. "Stand back for a second."

Lily did as she was asked and stepped back into the doorway. Minisc took her place, getting on his hands and knees and feeling around the floor. Once he found his target, his hand gleamed bright gold and he punched the ground.

"It's official, you've lost it," Lily said, still confused as to what Minisc believed he had figured out.

"Look!" Minisc started to pull back the shattered concrete pieces on the floor.

"Is that a sewer grate?" Lily asked, "Why would a sewer grate be inside a basement?

"I don't know but I'm gonna take a look." Minisc lifted the lid, which was quite heavy, and shoved it over to the side wall before it landed with a thud. Free of any more barriers, he began climbing down, his ball of light following close behind him.

CHAPTER 16
DARK DISCOVERIES

RANCID ODOURS OF SEWER WATER HIT MINISC AS HE climbed down the ladder. Although a faint scent, Minisc would not soon forget its pungency with all his sewer adventures of late. Behind him, Lily followed, much less accepting of the putrid smell. Unlike the sewers, however, there was no running water around, or even stagnant water for that matter. They had made a return to the sewers, Minisc could be sure of that, but all other routes were cut off. The room appeared to be a one-way access point.

A few things stood out, the first of which Minisc noticed was the intricate piping that layered the ceiling. The second was a number of canisters big enough to hold slime monsters of their own. For a second, he wondered if he had somehow gone in a circle. After all, with every connected sewer stretching across multiple cities, big and small, travelling would be easiest below ground. Even if it meant dealing with such a rotten environment.

But his theory would be quickly debunked when Lily ran up to the nearest canister and said, "Look Minisc!"

He walked over to his friend who had her hands pressed up against the container. Inside sat a full-grown woman still wearing work attire, but floating in a greenish liquid, just as the monsters from before had. Minisc swallowed the lump in his throat as he stepped away checking the next closest canister.

There were about twenty-five in total, which was less than the fifty holding the slime monsters, but just like before, each one was filled with a person inside.

"No way..." Minisc muttered as he reached the end of the row of tanks. Men, women, even children were all stuck in a deep sleep, blissfully unaware of the fate that awaited them.

Lily held her hand over her mouth as a range of emotions passed through her. The sadness of seeing such innocent lives trapped. Anger at knowing the fate that would befall them, and regret for those they couldn't save. As she walked past a little boy no older than the age of four or five, a pain jolted her chest. It reminded her of Maya, and how she could have been subjected to such a fate.

"Are these... all of the people who were abducted...?" Lily asked.

Minisc turned to her and whispered, "The ones remaining anyways... remember President Osiris said those abducted first were being turned into the slime monsters..." They both understood what that meant for those who met such a terrible fate. "This must be where they've been storing those they abducted. If I had to guess, there is an easy route to the factory that my father destroyed the other day."

"This is disgusting... how could anyone do this? To rip the life away from so many innocent people... all to create a bunch of awful creatures to do your bidding for you. We can't let this go on."

Minisc nodded and started to investigate the tanks once again. There had to be a way to free the Humans from captivity, but all the buttons and panels were more complicated than he could comprehend. On top of that, he didn't want to cause an accidental reaction that could harm the Humans.

Finally, Lily said, "I think we should go back and tell Yuri about this place. He can get President Osiris to send over the police and probably some ambulances as well. They can take care of things in a safe way, I'm sure."

Deciding not to push his luck any further, Minisc agreed. The team prepared to retrace their steps when they heard a call from the hole above.

"Minisc! Lily! Are you two down there?" The voice belonged to Jules.

"Yeah, we're down here," Lily called back. She could hear the metal creak of the ladder as Jules and Yuri made their way down.

"Lily, we need to-" Jules started in a panic, but quickly lost his train of thought once he saw the room. "Whoa... what is this place?" He asked as he jumped off the second step of the ladder. Yuri followed close behind with a box of folders snug between his arm and his chest.

"We think this is where all the people abducted by Luminosa were being hidden," Minisc informed them.

Yuri started holding up pictures from the folder, matching them to the tanks. "You would be correct... all of these match the files we found upstairs." Yuri and Jules looked at a few of the tanks with the same array of emotions that hit Lily.

"We need to call President Osiris and get people down here to figure this out. It might not be Bex and Bronx, but this is just as important, right?" Lily asked. Everyone agreed. The chance to save dozens of lives could not be passed up.

"Indeed, I'll call Zale right away, but we have another pressing issue to attend to as well," Yuri added.

"Huh, what is it? Did someone spot Bex or Bronx?" Minisc asked.

Jules' mind snapped back to the reason he came searching for his friends in the first place. He stared directly at Lily and asked, "Lily, is your mother at home?"

"Yeah... why?" The last word had a tinge of fear in it.

"We think we found files for future abduction targets for Luminosa." Jules handed the only folder stashed under his arm to Lily. She flipped it open before letting out a sharp gasp.

"Please no..." She muttered.

Minisc looked over her shoulder with an equally horrified expression. Lily spun to face him, pain in her face and tears at the ready, "Minisc, we need to do something, please!" She begged.

"Don't worry, we won't let anything happen to your mother. I promise."

"Yeah, Minisc is right, as long as we're around, we won't let anyone take your mom, or anyone else on that list!" Jules said, doing his best to comfort Lily.

As per usual, before the brothers even found their friends, Yuri concocted a plan the second he learned Luminosa's plot. Granted he had not expected to find the missing Humans underground through an abandoned bank, but that would allow them a chance to save lives once thought to be all but lost. He spoke in a calm tone making sure to keep Lily at ease.

"First and foremost, Lily, we need you to take us to your house. Once we've confirmed your mother is safe, we'll be able to make our next move, but we need to act fast. We don't know how much time we have."

With a new destination set, the group returned above ground and Yuri made a few quick phone calls explaining the situation and how the search unfolded. In minutes, police, ambulances, and a half-dozen EC members close to the area arrived on the scene to handle the aftermath. They would be able to take care of the abducted Humans and ensure they were safely removed from stasis. That help would also free up Minisc and his friends to handle their new problem.

Once he finished speaking with other authorities Yuri asked, "Any luck reaching your parents?" As he approached his brother and Minisc. In the middle of the two, with a phone pressed to her ear, stood a visibly distraught Lily. She ground her foot into the dirt with her arm grabbing at her side. Once Yuri saw the look, he could piece together the answer to his question. But that wouldn't stop him from adding some comfort to her world.

Once Lily pulled the phone away, she slumped her shoulders and looked at Yuri.

"Nothing… they must be asleep."

"Alright, well Zale gave us permission to leave and check on your family. Once there, we'll wait for an EC transport van to arrive. The plan is to take all those whose names were in those folders, along with their families, and place them in a secure location for the time being. It's all going to be okay. This time we're one step ahead of Luminosa."

Minisc and Jules both threw their arms around the girl with cheerful smiles.

"Come on, we got this," Jules grinned.

"Yeah, we would never let anything happen to your parents. You know that. So let's get going," Minisc added.

Lily joined their smiles grabbing her friends tight and suffocating them in a hug.

"Thank you, guys, you're the best friends a girl could ask for."

Through the dead of night, Lily led the way down her home street with a speed backed by concern. From the business district in Scarborough, Lily's house would normally be a good 45-minute walk, but Lily got there in record time. Streetlights guided their path through the couple dozen homes that lined the small subdivision. In the dark, differentiating their look and design was difficult, but most of the houses were nothing more than small bungalows with flat roofs and tiny yards.

Once they arrived, they stopped in front of a modest looking yard with a small white fence boxing in the house. It had a chocolate brown roof, like most of the other houses, and a small, well-kept garden with flowers in full bloom around the front. There was one car in the single space driveway as well. It was everything one pictured of a small, suburban home.

Nothing looked out of sorts, which let Lily breathe a sigh of relief. While everyone behind her took in the quaint area Lily hurried up the steps to the door. She twisted the gold knob unaware she was holding her breath. The door creaked open much to her surprise and she tip-toed in. If her parents were indeed asleep, then she didn't want to scare them by busting in. She entered the front hall and flicked on a light before finally releasing the breath bottled up inside. With a confusing if not outright perplexing conversation ahead, she wanted to remain calm. After all, her parents were far from being experts in the Elemental world.

As a child, Lily faced many prejudices common to Elementalists for their strange powers. After her first year of school and the issues that arose, her parents more or less cut ties with most things elemental. However, in the past year and a half, their worries and desire for their daughter to fit into society became less of a demand and more of a wish. Especially when Lily expressed her desire to attend EA.

Lily called out as softly as she could, "Mom, Dad, are you guys awake?" After a moment, she heard a ruffle of footsteps before a light flickered on in the kitchen which was to the left of the front hall.

Everyone turned to see a man with round glasses and freshly cut black hair walking into the front hall. He dressed in checkered red and black pyjamas while also wearing a silver robe. Nothing about him came off as intimidating.

"Lily, you're finally home," the man said, fighting back a yawn.

"Dad, so you are up? I tried calling Mom's phone, but nobody answered."

"Her phone is probably upstairs and your mother is asleep. I decided to stay up until you got home. What's wrong? You seem worried. Did something happen?"

Lily exhaled in relief, "Phew, we made it in time." She dropped her shoulders releasing some of the pent-up stress, but the ordeal was far from over for her.

"In time for what? Lily, what is going on?" Her father asked. He sounded just like Lily when she was worried.

Yuri decided to help bring the group back on track so they could ensure a smooth process going forward.

"Lily, why don't you take Minisc and Jules and explain the situation. I'm going to call the EC and make sure everything is under control on their end."

Lily turned back and smiled at Yuri. "Okay." She then granted her attention back to her confused father, "Dad, can you go wake up Mom, it's sort of an emergency."

"Um, okay one sec." Despite lacking any understanding of his daughter's urgency, the man did as he was asked and headed up the stairs that were straight ahead from the front door. Yuri left to make his phone calls, and Lily brought Minisc and Jules, who had been awkwardly standing behind her, into the living room where they could all sit down.

A multitude of picture frames hung around the living room. Most of them were of Lily at various ages with her parents scattered throughout. Along with those were a set of all white chairs, a couch, and a coffee table.

After a moment, Lily's father returned with a woman who continued to rub the sleep out of her sea blue eyes. They matched Lily's perfectly. Regardless of an abrupt wake up call, she carried a semblance of positivity on her face. Her autumn brown hair had been tied up in a small bun with a few strands shaping her round face. She also wore a long white robe over her pyjamas that stretched down to the floor.

She fought back another yawn before taking a seat across from her daughter.

"Lily, what's going on? Your father said it's an emergency? Are you hurt? Did something happen?" She had a soft voice, but it was dripping with worry.

"No, it's not that. I'm fine." Lily tried to reassure her mother. However, once the woman noticed Minisc and Jules beside her, she went into house party mode.

"Oh Lily, you didn't mention you were bringing guests. I'll put on some tea for everyone."

"Mom, we don't have time for tea!" Lily snapped, catching everyone off guard. She paused, regretting her tone and changed her course of action, "Please, I have a lot of stuff to explain is all."

Everyone got comfortable and Lily proceeded to clarify the situation to her parents. She remained calm and focused, but that felt much harder when the crisis involved her own family.

Her father stared in thought, trying to gauge the situation.

"Well, this is quite the conundrum, isn't it? We certainly can't let these... what did you call them?"

"Slime creatures, Dad, and they're no joke. They've been kidnapping Humans all over the city, and we think Mom is next. We need to protect her."

"Who would have thought all of this was going on in our little neighbourhood," Lily's mother said. She took a sip of tea, showing almost no concern for the situation Lily conveyed to them.

"Mom, this is serious, you could be in danger. Why are you so calm?" Lily complained. She knew her parents were averse to the outside world, but this was another level.

Lily grew up in a simple house as an only child. Her father had been a moderately skilled earth Elementalist and her mother a Human. With Elemental and Human relations up in the air when Lily was young, her mother often worried that being an Elementalist could lead to issues so she decided to shelter her daughter, as any parent would. The family kept news in the house a rarity and anything Elementalist had been all but wiped out, even to the point that acknowledgment of The Hero of Light did not exist.

"Hun, there's no use getting all worked up about it. Nothing has happened yet."

Lily took a deep breath, "Yeah… I guess you're right, but that doesn't mean we can be careless. This is a real problem and dozens of people have been abducted already."

If Lily had learned one thing about her parents since she joined the EC, it was that in matters involving their daughter, the two were far more feverish. They would overreact, panic or worse, and yet when it came to anything involving them, they were far more subdued. Lily chalked it up to an act they were putting forward so she wouldn't worry about them, but she was not buying such a calm demeanour.

With Lily feeling no sense of urgency from her parents, Yuri walked back into the house, tossing her a lifeline.

"Well Lily, I have some good news."

"What is it?" She asked.

"Zale has a ride coming shortly to pick your family up. They've secured where everyone is going to stay for the next few days. So, there's no need to worry anymore, everyone will be taken care of."

Lily smiled as wide as she could. "Thank you, Yuri. Truly." She turned back to her parents and said, "Come on Mom, you and Dad need to pack. We should leave as soon as possible."

"Alright dear, if that's what you and your friends think is best, then I guess we have no choice."

"But what about you?" Her father asked, "I don't want you having to stay by yourself if things are this unsafe. What if these monsters come here and find you?"

Luckily Minisc already had a solution for such an occasion, "It's okay, Mr. Martel, Lily can stay with me and my father for the time being. We have a spare room and everything."

Lily spun around looking at Minisc, "That's really sweet, Minisc. Thank you." She grabbed and hugged him to suffocation. "Great, with that, decided we need to hurry, your ride will be here soon."

"Okay okay slow down Lily… I still need to go pack and so do you." While Lily rushed off pushing her parents to act with the same haste, Yuri reminded Minisc and Jules of the other issue they were to oversee.

"Come on guys, we need to get back to the bank and double check things are going smoothly. Lily has everything under control here."

The two nodded in agreement.

When the three finally arrived back in the business plaza of Scarborough, they were met with far more commotion than when they left. Multiple trucks were parked along the road and the entire bank had rolls of yellow tape wrapping around the lot that said *Keep Out* repeatedly in black. Media groups even started to form, not daring to miss their opportunity to break open a massive story.

"There you three are, took your sweet time coming back didn't you." They recognized the gruff and tough voice as they turned around to see Dwayne.

"Dwayne? What are you doing here?" Minisc asked.

"Yeah I thought you retired after the whole Dusk whooping your butt thing?" Jules said with a smirk.

"Easy there, kiddo, I'm pretty sure the only one who can claim they didn't get their clock cleaned by that monster here is Minisc." Dwayne laughed.

"Dwayne, good to see you," Yuri said, nodding more formally.

"So, what're you doing here?" Minisc asked.

"Well Jules was somewhat right. I did take some time off after everything that happened, but I got bored pretty quick. I guess you just can't replace the rush that comes with The Hero of Light constantly putting your life in imminent danger. So when Zale called me up and asked if I could come back for a bit, just while the EC was being built, I figured why not. But then all these abductions started happening and I knew I had to help in any way I could. Guess some people just aren't meant for retirement."

The four continued to catch up as men and women began wheeling out bodies on gurneys. Each abducted Human looked to be in moderate health, but all of them remained unconscious and dripping in the same green liquid that filled the tanks.

Dwayne led the team past the tape and back down underneath to where the bodies were first discovered. Almost all the victims had been removed, and the room had little left in it. Everything that could be taken for examination had been.

Dwayne put his hand on one of the last remaining canisters wiping off a drip of the green liquid.

"It's hard to say what sort of serum was in these tanks, but I think based on the condition of each abductee so far and how long they've been gone, it must be some sort of life-preservation liquid. I'd guess they weren't changing people into monsters overnight if they had to store and preserve bodies underground."

"Well, I'm glad tonight wasn't an entire waste, but we still haven't found Bex or Bronx." Minisc sighed.

"Not yet, but wherever those two are, they're making sure to stay low," Dwayne said.

"But now that we have their list of targets, we should be able to draw them out right?" Jules asked.

Dwayne agreed, "Yes, but we need to be careful. We must be ready on all fronts, or we'll risk being overwhelmed. But for now, at least, we remain one step ahead."

The rest of the night went on as predicted. The search for Bronx and Bex yielded a lack of results, but thanks to Jules and Yuri, they could predict the next striking point, which meant steps could be taken to ensure the safety of those in the line of fire. Those already captured were taken to hospitals for examination, while the families were contacted and informed of the safety of their loved ones. The EC also took the liberty of informing all those who had been part of the stolen EC files that they were to pack their bags and would be taken into a shelter to be kept safe for the time being. Although many were fearful and distraught at the upheaval, nobody could ignore the evidence presented over the last few days.

Those on the list were taken to an undisclosed hotel where only people of immediate importance were informed. On the outside, the hotel ran and operated like normal, but on the inside, on various floors, multiple families were now given rooms to live in for the next few days.

Lily stood in the hotel room doorway granted to her mother and father. She bowed to President Osiris, who was making the rounds ensuring everyone's accommodations were settled. "Thank you so much, I can't properly express how much this means to me. Truly."

"That's quite alright Lily. If it hadn't been for you guys finding that list and those victims, then we never would've been able to make sure everyone remained safe. And don't worry, this building will be monitored twenty-four seven. Unfortunately, your parents won't be allowed to leave for the next forty-eight hours at minimum, as we want to see if we can flush Luminosa out, but I promise I'll be in touch with everyone after that or if the situation changes. Your parents will be in good hands around here."

Lily smiled while taking another bow before closing the door to her parents' room. As far as hotel rooms went, they were in a rather nice one. The floors were filled with fresh carpet, they had a bathroom, kitchen, and a bedroom that was near the same size as they had at home. There was even a television hung on the wall, which they didn't have at home.

For a second, Lily thought maybe it would be nice to stay here with her parents, but she opted not to. She didn't want to risk going back and forth, with the potential to draw any sort of attention to the building. Besides, she liked Minisc's house and his father. Staying with them for a few days would be no issue at all.

She walked into the bedroom, where her mother continued to unpack the two small suitcases that were filled with whatever they could find in the dead of night.

"I know this isn't ideal, but it'll only be for a few days. Just until we can catch the bad guys who are causing all of this."

"Don't worry, honey, this place is just fine." The woman turned around and hugged her daughter. After a long and stressful night, the warmth of her mother's hug brought Lily some sense of ease. Yet, even in times of danger, her mother remained focused on her daughter. She looked into her daughter's eyes and said, "But you have to promise you won't do anything reckless, understand? Your father and I can't keep watching you get hurt so much…"

"Mom…"

"We know this is what you want to do. You want to help people. I know we've tried to shelter you from all things elemental, but it was only because we feared how you would be treated. But we've seen just how much you've grown since you started EA. This is who you are, and you make your father and me proud every day, but if we were to lose you then we would never forgive ourselves for letting you do this. So please, no matter what, come home safe. That's all we ask for." The words cut to Lily's core, her face starting to scrunch up. She could feel her mother run her fingers through her brunette locks. With a small sniffle, Lily buried her head in her mother's chest.

"I promise…" She whispered, "I'll be careful. I won't make you worry anymore."

Often Elementalists in the EC were more worried about protecting others, making sure they could help keep the city safe in whatever way required, but that made it easy to overlook the loved ones that suffered through watching their family members face such a fight. For Lily, hearing her mother's words put that in a new perspective. She, unlike Minisc or Jules, was not someone brought up in the world of the EC. Her father was not a hero, nor did she have a sibling who had been an elite Elementalist, so having parents unfamiliar with the stresses of her life choices was tough. For everyone. Although she wanted to help people, a small seed of doubt crept in on if the worry she caused her parents was worth it.

CHAPTER 17
OFF THE BEATEN PATH

ALMOST EVERY EC MEMBER AND VOLUNTEER ALIKE remained out all night looking for the escaped convict Elementalists Bronx and Bex. Only, one had not aided in the call to action. At least not in the traditional way.

Coro received the same alert and phone call that all others in his position had, but he paid it no mind. He also did not inform his partner and current boss Olivia, or President Osiris of his plans. That, of course, was by design. When it came to dealing with his father, he remained adamant he wanted to deal with the situation alone. Why so, he still was not entirely sure himself, but something in his heart continued to push the idea this mission was his and his alone.

He walked down the same dreary, smelly sewers that Minisc and his team had already explored. But he wanted to see the area for himself.

When Minisc informed him of all that was going on below the city structure, the notion of a multi-faceted factory being built stood out most to him. Even if damaged beyond repair, he believed he could pick out small clues that only someone related to his father would notice.

At night the sewers were even darker and colder than most would be willing to subject themselves to. Luckily for Coro as long as his arm remained lit with dancing flames he had nothing to worry about.

A trail of debris led Coro straight to the rooms Minisc told him about, but when he arrived, he couldn't believe his eyes. Just as

Minisc explained to him the night before, tanks upon tanks filled the room. Thankfully they were empty, but they also appeared to still be in working condition. Of course, without Human subjects they were no more than decorations at this point.

The room beside it, on the other hand, had met a far grimmer fate. When Coro stepped into the factory room almost all of it had been totaled. Sparks from loose wires, a bunch of broken metal and glass on the floor, and a fair bit of goop splashed everywhere. If not told beforehand what the room was used for, he never would have guessed.

However, that meant there was nothing left for him to investigate. He wouldn't even know where to begin in such a calamity. While standing in the room Coro clenched his fists. He turned and looked back at the other room and the red in his face started to boil.

"You caused this…" he muttered into the void of the room. Even if Luminosa abducted his father, even if he'd been forced to create such atrocities, he should have died before allowing those nightmares to exist. That would have been the noble thing to do, but then again Coro never knew his father to do anything noble.

Bursting with rage, Coro lifted his left hand to the glass jar filled with its green toxic water. A chilling wind enveloped his body and with a flash of light, he skewered the entire room with ice. The glass shattered and water spilled onto the floor from every which direction. Anything not destroyed by The Hero of Light would be demolished by Coro.

Now nobody will be able to make use of these damn things again.

With his quest unsuccessful, Coro started to head for the exit but came to a stop when he heard the patter of footsteps coming from down the sewer ways.

Who would be down here… he thought.

Because he ignored the EC phone call, he remained unaware Bronx or Bex were free from jail. Putting out the flame on his hand, he dimmed the source of light to stay shrouded in shadows. Unfortunately, he had not pulled off his camouflage tactic in time. He could hear Bronx speak.

"Hold on," the evil man said in a low whisper, "We're not alone…"

Coro held his breath trying to slow his pounding heart. He lingered in the shadows of the makeshift lab letting the darkness absorb him, but much to his surprise the tunnels began to grow even darker. Like a mist of fog taking over.

I've heard that voice before… but where… Coro wracked his brain on the voice but could not place a name on it, however, he did know it was trouble.

The hope for an escape route faded with darkness overtaking the sewers. In seconds, he could no longer see his hands. It was clearly not a natural caused shadow.

There were two options in his mind. Stay concealed and hope those who were lurking the sewers passed him by, or summon his flames and prepare for a potential confrontation.

Then he heard the voice of the other person he had caught a glimpse of from before the shadows.

"Who cares if we're not alone, Brooklyn said we can kill anyone we come across down here didn't he?"

That voice Coro would not soon forget. The squeaky child-like thirst for blood had tried to kill him, nearly erasing his element in the process.

If that's Bex… than the other voice must be Bronx… but how, they should be locked away…

The new information would be enough for Coro to cement his decision. He was not to engage in a fight against them. Not this time. It would be far safer for him to keep his distance and stay out of sight.

Except, just before he could seep deeper into the shadows of the room, he heard a chill whooshing sound. Sharp stabbing pains shot through his left shoulder. He dropped to the ground sprawled out in agony. Nerves chewed away at his pain tolerance as he reached for his impaled shoulder. Whatever hit him gave off a cold air, which sealed his suspicion. Bex impaled him with a sneak attack through the smoke that Bronx created.

Biting his lip to fight the pain, Coro's shoulder burst into flames, the light from his body expelling every ounce of darkness. His hope had been two-fold, though. With the insane heat generated from his body, the jagged icicle logged in his shoulder melted away, leaving a puddle of water and blood at his feet. The flames caught Bronx and Bex off guard, blinding them just long enough for Coro to get to his feet. He grabbed at the deep wound in his shoulder, wincing from even the air touching it.

"Well look who it is... I didn't think we'd be running into you here," Bronx said with a slow growing grin. He had no motive to attack though. That would be left to the tiny girl beside him who seethed with fire in her eyes at the sight of Coro.

"You..." She growled. "Well isn't this a joy. Out of jail only a few hours and just like that I get to kill the first person on my list... I'll make you pay for what you and that Premier kid did to me back in the rail yard," Bex said with a lip-smacking smile. She bent down with her hands glowing a frozen white once again.

Coro had one hand pinned to the wound on his shoulder, while the other remained limp. He was in no position to defend himself and both Luminosa members knew it. Even so, he had no intention of going down without a fight. He would just have to use his feet to defend himself.

Bex clutched her weapon made of ice and hurled it at Coro like a throwing knife. Acting on instinct, he jumped to his left, sending a roaring blaze of fire towards the two as he hit the ground. Even a small side jump once he landed sent shock waves through his shoulder. Along with that, the simple act of breathing stung his body. Toughness could help him drive the pain away to a degree, but at what point would it become too much to handle? He only had one way to find out. Fight. Fight until he had nothing left.

"How did you two escape?" He yelled as he stomped his foot. Ice soared out like pillars from the ground arching towards his opponents. Bronx and Bex both took the brunt of the impact being slammed into the concrete wall. They coughed as the breath shot out of them. Yet Coro knew the battle would be far from over. Just as he expected the two of them got to their feet, but Coro refused to let them acclimate.

"Tell me what you've done with my father!" He switched from ice to flames hoping to incinerate the two. He would kill them if required. Unlike Minisc, he knew he was fighting for his life, and any sort of soft-hearted weakness would spell his end.

Bex showed no signs of worry though. Her eyes slanted as her temper grew. Thrusting out her hands, swirls of wind jammed the fire to a halt, allowing Bronx to step in and fire off a shadow ball that crashed into Coro's other arm. The fire ceased and Bex's wind gripped him, tossing him into the air. He bounced off the concrete floor and rolled onto his stomach.

Damn it… I don't stand a chance if they can both match my elements. Maybe if I still had the use of my left arm, but not like this. Coro knew he was in trouble. He should have told someone, Zale, Olivia, even Minisc where he was heading… but regrets would do little to help now.

Bex looked at her prey. "After all this time you're still looking for that deranged scientist you call a father? So what, did you come here looking for clues? Or did you know we'd be down here and thought you could play hero? No that's not it. You thought coming down here you would actually find your father. Was that it? Either way it was stupid of you to come alone."

She walked forward without the usual hop in her step. A sure sign she was serious about killing Coro this time.

Come on, I have to think of something. Anything. I can't let these two get away like this. A strange feeling came over him. On his wounded shoulder, he swore he felt a touch followed by a soft yet familiar voice whisper to him, *Please Coro, look for your father, find him and bring him home. Let us all be a family again. Please, can you do that for me?*

A flash of the last conversation Coro ever had with his mother played in his mind. The warm touch on his shoulder drew all his pain away, if only long enough for him to push himself up. He had a tear ready to roll down his cheek and his body quivered from the jolt of adrenaline. One of the few displays of such emotion he ever had. His body burst into flames, his chest panting up and down. He could feel it, the same raw emotion that boiled over when he faced Minisc in the finals of the Tournament of Elements. Back then, he learned to let go of the unrelenting grudge he carried in his heart. The hatred for his father, the very man he was now fighting to find. But this time it was the lingering memories of his mother that broke the dam. An aura of blue burst around him sparks of energy ready to shoot off in all directions. Enough so that Bex stopped in her tracks.

"Bex look out, something's different about him," Bronx said.

"You… Luminosa… tore my family apart. Kidnapped my father, and if that wasn't enough, it's because of you that the one person in this world who showed me love and compassion is gone. You guys took her away from me, and I'll never forget that pain. Never. This time I'll make sure there's nothing left of you to put behind bars!"

Coro motioned both his hands forward, not caring one ounce about the pain in his shoulder. The bitterness in his heart trumped it tenfold. A flash of fire and ice exploded from his hands spiralling forward with all the hatred he could expel. Bronx and Bex were in trouble, and their faces registered that knowledge.

Bang.

Smoke from the explosion filled the sewers and probably beyond. The earth shook to its core, while Coro stood hunched over, ready to collapse. Yet, when he thought his job was done and his revenge exacted, what he saw through the smoke suggested this nightmare was far from over.

"You continue to be a pain in our asses, Coro…" Bronx huffed between breaths. The entire left side of his body had been drenched in blood. Beside him, Bex had met a similar fate. Her face had streaks of blood, and horrible burn marks across her body. But they both remained on their feet, far from defeated.

No… that was everything I had… how could they have survived that?

Coro shut his eyes, as the remaining strength in his body

evaporated. He had no will to respond. Like his spirit had left his body all he could do was fall backwards, like a husk.

I'm sorry mother… I couldn't do it… I couldn't bring him home… I'll see you soon…

CHAPTER 18
FAMILY AFFAIRS

CORO'S EYES FLUTTERED OPEN, BUT ALL HE COULD SEE were the blurry lights beaming down on him. He tilted his head squinting to dull the brightness. He sat in a wide-open room with nothing around him. The walls were made of wood, and the roof a good twenty feet high.

What... is this place... the last thing I remember was fighting Bronx and Bex in the sewers...

As his eyes adjusted to the light, he still struggled to examine his surroundings. He hung his head before noticing the wound in his left shoulder. Then as if something in his mind clicked, the pain started rushing back. His arm continued to throb and bleed.

He sat on a chair in the middle of the large room. A reactionary instinct to the pain caused him to try and move his hands to clutch the injury, but that's when he realized his hands were stuck. They were chained behind the chair. He tilted his head towards his feet, seeing they were met with the same fate. Hoping to break free, he did his best to concentrate heat in his legs. Perhaps he could melt the cuffs, but they seemed to resist any sort of heat he could muster.

After a futile effort, he heard a voice say, "Don't bother trying to break free. Those cuffs are designed to resist even the hottest flames you can produce."

Coro's eyes darted around the room, his mouth turning into a snarl and his limp and exhausted body no longer a thought. He recognized the voice, and that's what put him on high alert. The coldness, the matter-of-fact tone, and the arrogance that followed the man's words, could only belong to one person.

"You..." Coro growled. He remained still but on high alert.

More lights flickered on and as they did Coro could see a figure in the distance. He looked older than the boy remembered, and not only by three months, but by years. The man stepped towards Coro, letting his box-like face and oval glasses reflect the light. His hair had grayed significantly, and bags rested under his eyes that could only come from repeated days of not sleeping. Yet none of that could stop Coro from recognizing the man he carried such a hatred for.

"So boy... what were you doing snooping around my factory? Did you plan to burn it down to the ground the way you did my lab? You realize you could've killed Pascale with that power I granted you. If it hadn't been for the new form I was able to give her, her consciousness would have died with her body..."

"She had it coming..." Coro spat in return.

"Then perhaps you finally made the wise choice and came to realize your full potential as my most prized experiment... Have you come to your senses?"

The man stood only a meter away from Coro, who dropped his head again, his steel hair falling to block the rage in his eyes. He spoke calmly, but malice followed his every word.

"My potential... my senses... I've been trying to find you... I've been searching high and low looking for any clues to your whereabouts... Not so I can join you, but so I can finish you off once and for all." The life in Coro's voice picked up, "I know the truth... No matter how much I denied it, no matter how much I tried to believe in Mother's words, I always knew. She wanted to believe so badly that she was right. That you weren't the monster I believed you to be. That you actually cared about your family. But no. I knew she was blinded by a sense of loyalty to the man she once knew and loved. You're not that man though... the man who stands before me is nothing but a monster." Coro glanced back up. "You were never abducted by Luminosa, were you? They had nothing to do with your disappearance. You sought them out. After the Tournament of Elements, when I showed my true power, you were never given your proper due all because Luminosa stole the spotlight from you and your experiment of a son. I know you. That would've infuriated you. All you care about is your fame, about your legacy as this scientific genius... about creating that perfect weapon. So, you decided to get some new test subjects. You joined up with Luminosa, granting them power, and in return, you would finally be able to create the perfect fighting warrior you always dreamed of me being, and not for a second did you care who would be sacrificed along the way. Even if it cost the lives of your own family!"

Dr. Jarrad loomed over his son from a foot away. He gave a look of disgust, but Coro dropped his head down refusing to look the man in the eye.

"Even after all this time you still remain an ungrateful, spoiled child. You could never see the bigger picture. Humans, Elementalists, it doesn't matter, this world was built on science. It was built through constant testing and experimentation, always pushing the boundaries of what the common man could comprehend. That is the only way one can push the world forward in its development. The Elemental Council as it's constructed now only works to stifle the progress of science. An Elementalist's power has the potential to be unrivaled in this world by man or machine. That kind of power can fix this world that has been created, but the only way to continue is to rid society of the laws that serve to disrupt such progress. If they allowed me to continue my work, then I would've been able to make an army of Elementalists the likes of which the world has never seen. They would have been the perfect fighting machines, with the depths of their power stretching universes. War would cease, hunger, famine, plagues, all of it could have been rid to create a utopia. Luminosa will now help me achieve that goal."

"You disgust me... this power you seek, this world Luminosa

seeks... it's nothing more than a façade. A utopia built by the likes of you would only ever serve to benefit yourself. Nobody else wants that and you know it. Or else you never would've had to go through all the trouble of abducting Humans and turning them into those things... was this world you dreamed of a utopia for them? Was it a utopia for the thousands of lives that were sacrificed along the way? Of course not, because you don't care about any of them. They were just blank faces to you. Disposable assets to the greater evil. That's exactly what everyone is to you... the people of this city... me... even your own wife... who died because of these monsters, and you don't so much as bat an eye..."

Coro could feel the fight in his body coming back, his words were filling him with the conviction needed to stand up to his father. When he set out, he always knew this outcome would be inevitable. The sole reason he avoided asking Minisc for help came from this belief. Because all along he knew the truth. His father had caused so much pain to those around him and without an ounce of remorse in his body. In the end, he was too ashamed of the man to ask for help.

"Insolent boy!" Dr. Jarrad held out his hand letting it glow bright gold. Gold like The Hero of Light's aura.

"You made yourself an Elementalist... how...?"

"Boy haven't you learned yet? There is nothing I can't do in this world."

Coro could see it in his father's eyes. The last shred of humanity prepping to be cleansed from his soul as he struck his son down in cold blood. But Coro refused to give the man any satisfaction. After all these years, how could he start now? He wouldn't. He would stare down the man who ruined his life in every conceivable way. Any fear, any remorse, he would bury it until he was dead.

The potent brightness of the light shrunk slightly, and the mad doctor gave his son one final chance, "Join me," he said. "Become the weapon I created you to be. Become the perfect Elementalists I always dreamed you would be, and I'll spare your life."

"What, now you need me because The Hero of Light destroyed your little creations... surely your big brain can whip up new ones."

"Those monsters were nothing more than a simple test, to see how the Human body would react to being force fed Elemental cells. Unfortunately, their bodies were so destroyed that the only way to keep them going was to wipe their consciousness and then reprogram them in the form they took. I dare say they were a big success, but next time they will be even better."

"There won't be a next time if I have anything to say about it..."

"Fine then, let this place be your grave..."

Coro pretended to mull the words over. Of course, he would never be swayed even in death. He refused to be the coward his old man proved to be. But he needed to buy as much time as he could to think of a strategy. An escape route, a way to fight. Anything.

"..."

He came up empty, and his time was up... he would die at the hands of his father... the worst possible way to die.

Dr. Jarrad walked away from his son, almost pretending to toy with him. Once he was a safe distance back, he turned around, staring daggers at his own flesh and blood. The humanity in his eyes was replaced with the hollowed, empty malice that could only be matched by the slime monster creations of his.

"Good riddance to you... boy." He fired off the ball of light.

For the first time, as reality dawned on him, Coro squeezed his eyes shut. But instead of feeling the potent blast crash into his body, he heard a voice scream out.

"Coro!"

The glass windows around the roof came crashing down as a woman landed with a vicious shock wave in front of the boy. She redirected the blast into the air, crashing through the ceiling causing most of it to tumble in while letting the moonlight shine in on the single space torture chamber.

Coro's eyes sprung open in disbelief. In front of him like a mirage stood Olivia, her long platinum blonde hair waving back and forth from the ripples of the blast. He wanted to rub his eyes to make sure he was not dreaming but of course, he couldn't move. So instead, he said, "Olivia, what are you doing here?"

"No time, talk later."

In a display of what happens when talent and hard work come together, Olivia spun around and fired off a perfect blast of dark energy that broke Coro's leg cuffs. While that was going on she had not forgotten about Dr. Jarrad.

"Watch out!" Coro yelled but Olivia remained one step ahead. Even with her back turned to the disgraced father and scientist she had a shadow crawling along the ground.

Olivia personified everything about the elite in the EC. Her talents, hard work and determination drove her to surpass close to everyone in the EC despite her age. But it was not only that.

Her smarts and strategic mind proved more than most threats could handle, Dr. Jarrad being no different. Her signature move, Sneak Shadow, was a combination of her quiet and reserved persona, and her powerful relentless desire to stop those who commit wrongdoings.

Before Dr. Jarrad could enact any sort of revenge, he was gripped by the ground. But it wasn't the ground. It was shadows pooled below his feet and rising up from the shadows were whip-like straps that latched on to the doctor's arms and legs. He tried to fight his way loose, but Olivia walked up to him ready to land a deciding blow.

Before she could land a hit though Coro yelled, "Duck!" She followed the instructions as blades sliced over her head nicking her hair. She leapt back next to Coro, who still had his hands locked, but could run if need be.

"Sorry to jump in on the family reunion, but this was only supposed to be between the kid and the doc." The voice came from a plain looking boy with messy hair. His protruding claws steeped in shadows were stuck in the ground before he ripped them out.

"... I should have known you would never face me alone, you coward," Coro yelled towards his father.

"Hey, don't forget about us!" Bex slithered forward her blue pigtails bouncing around. Bronx, with a scar over his eye stood beside her. They were watching in the shadows, knowing Coro often had something tricky up his sleeve.

That being said, Brooklyn and Bex focused their worry on the wrong person. Olivia flashed in front of Bex with a shadow ball in hand. She stuffed it into the girl's chest and with a boom, Bex sailed back into Bronx, knocking them both to the ground. Shadows morphed up from the ground grabbing at the two Luminosa members attempting to hold them in place. For Olivia, a potential four on one fight was far from fair, but her strategy was never to win. Only to rescue Coro. After that, they could regroup with a better, more thought out plan.

The woman moved so naturally like an Olympic athlete that she bore down on Brooklyn before he could react. However, as she tried to engage, an icicle whizzed past her cheek narrowly missing her.

Damn, I spread my shadows too thin to hold them down. Although Olivia could capably use her element to lock down foes, using the technique multiple times in different areas severely weakened it. Choices were limited, so she took a chance, but the risk did not pay off.

Olivia turned her attention back to Bex, but Bronx joined in, sending a shadow ball of his own her way. Even so, she ducked the attack doing everything to hold the three Luminosa members at bay.

Stuck in the chair, doing his best to free himself, Coro couldn't help but be swept up by Olivia's fighting tactics. Not because they were so special, but because they were so familiar.

I knew she felt strong, but her instincts are incredible, and her movements look so familiar, but I can't place it.

Olivia continued to stay on the defensive, always keeping Coro's safety at the top of her mind, but for the time being, nobody appeared to care about him. Despite Bex and Bronx's best efforts, they couldn't come close to touching her.

Wait, now I know where I've seen that style before. But that can't be, it wouldn't make sense. Coro continued to watch the woman's moves as she dismantled her opponents with ease. It was an eye-opening display of skill the likes of which Coro had seen only a few times in his life. *She mimics The Hero of Light to a tee...*

Olivia continued her assault, refusing to give a moment for her opponent to think. A strategy that had Bex fuming at the mad doctor. "Hey old man, what's going on here? Your stupid experiments aren't helping us in the slightest here." She crossed her arms in the shape of an X taking the blasts to her forearms. The sharp fangs of her teeth bit into her pale lips as she endured the hit.

"You really think a bunch of faulty experiments would let you keep up with me? I've worked tirelessly, putting in gruelling hours day after day, week after week for years to master my element. You guys might have power, but you have no clue how to truly use it!"

Bex slid back next to Bronx and Brooklyn. They glared collectively at Olivia, debating what their next move would be. The battlefield was slanted in their favour four to two, or more accurately four to one and a half, but still, those odds did not bode well for them.

"My name is Olivia Middleton, first officer of the Elemental Council. The four of you are hereby under arrest for crimes against Humanity."

Brooklyn groaned and put his head in his hand, "Crimes against Humanity? All I've ever done is work to improve Humanity and this is the thanks I get."

"You're nothing more than a cold-blooded murderer looking for power," Coro shouted back.

Brooklyn took his eyes off Olivia and glared at the boy, "You know, you're really starting to piss me off kid… your dear old father tried to lobby for you to join us, but so far you've done nothing but stand in my way. I think it'd just be easier to kill you now."

Coro knew he was in no position to fight, except for his legs, with which he could send a tsunami of ice if needed, but that would only get him so far. Yet when he shifted his eyes to his partner and saviour, he could see a plan forming. That's when behind Brooklyn along the wall he could see a faint shadow moving. It squirmed across the wood before hands sprung out and grabbed at the three other members of Luminosa. They latched on with a tighter grip than before and that left everyone restrained.

"Damn it, not again with the garbage," Bex whined as she squirmed like a wild animal.

"Surrender now or I'll take you back in body bags," Olivia ordered.

Coro wondered if the woman was bluffing, or if she really believed she could wipe out the entirety of Luminosa in one fell swoop, but either way what he did realize was President Osiris had not exaggerated her skills one ounce.

"Body bags… and here I thought the EC was supposed to be the civil group of the two…" Brooklyn seethed, "I've already seen this trick, you can't keep all of us restrained at the same time, it's far too much on your element. Which means breaking free is no challenge."

He ripped his arms free of the shadows and launched forward, "If it's blood you want, I'd be more than happy to spill yours."

Olivia moved quickly, but Brooklyn matched her. Despite her dodge, the shadowy claws nicked her left arm leaving three thin cuts through her navy-blue jacket.

He's faster than he let on… Olivia thought.

Brooklyn refused to let up slashing at Olivia, keeping her on the defence. Finally, he got in close thrusting at her chest, but that gave Coro the opening he needed. He was ready to return the favour of being saved. A tidal wave of ice shot from his feet and swam towards Brooklyn like an avalanche.

"I thought sneak attacks were for cowards!" Brooklyn yelled. He spun around and slashed clean through the ice, the moonlight flashing bright off the remains.

Through the shards of ice falling to the ground, Olivia felt a pain in her chest. *I'm out of time…* She felt the grips on her shadows loosening. She had stretched her powers too far and because of that, they needed an escape plan. She would've enjoyed taking down Luminosa in one clean sweep, but coming alone she knew backup would not be arriving. However only she knew that, not Luminosa.

"Face it, Brooklyn, the EC will be here any minute," she said.

Brooklyn glared at his opponents, his three alleys managed to break captivity, so he debated a full-on assault or to live and fight another day. He chose the latter. If he or any of his followers were to be placed in Penatang successfully, he would've failed Dusk's ultimate goal. He would fail to achieve his dominance as a leader of a new race.

"You cheated..." He muttered, before saying, "We're done here, I've had enough people time for one day..." He shot Bronx a look and the man nodded, holding his hand out to create a wall of black fog.

The three core members of Luminosa entered first with Dr. Jarrad close behind, but before he could make his escape Coro yelled, "I won't let you get away with this you coward. Mark my words, I'll stop you!"

And just like that Coro and Olivia were alone in the middle of nowhere with only the howls of wind and soft moonlight peering in on them.

Olivia turned to Coro, her face glistening from sweat. In one clean hit, she broke the handcuffs that hampered him before asking, "Can you walk?" Her voice returned to the cold, stoic tone she was known for.

Coro gave her a look, expecting her to have a few questions, but as he had learned many times, Olivia played everything close to the vest. So instead, he nodded and said, "Yeah I'm fine." But that was a lie as they would soon find out. He took two steps towards the doorway and collapsed in the middle of the room.

CHAPTER 19
ACCEPTING HELP

FOR THE SECOND TIME IN AS MANY HOURS, CORO WOKE up feeling groggy and disoriented. Only this time a warmth covered his body. Also, he was laying down on something soft. A bed. Far more pleasant than being tied to a chair, to say the least. Even the stabbing pain in his shoulder from Bex's attack subsided slightly. He ran his fingers along the wound realizing the damage had bandages on it. He still wore his ragged clothes from the night before, bloodstains and all, but clearly, someone had wrapped him up.

Once he managed to sit up in the bed, he looked around. Something about the room remained off-putting to him. It was small, and the walls were a dusty red, but that was all to be expected. What really threw him through a loop was the paraphernalia hung all around. Different articles, multiple posters, and even a couple of souvenir ordainments, and each one all showed the same heroic man that almost every Elementalist revered. The Hero of Light.

"Where am I... and who did this? It looks like some sort of Hero of Light stalker's room..." As he settled down to assess the situation he thought back to the evening before, "The last thing I remember was... him." Coro clenched his fist before sucking in a deep breath and exhaling. He had a chance to end things. To stop his father in his tracks, to take down the man he hated more than anyone on earth. The man who abandoned his family while simultaneously destroying hundreds more.

The inadvertent adventure of the night started to play in his mind, the awful memories slowly coming back into clarity.

Wait… what happened to Olivia? The sudden worry that crept into his mind spurred his attempt to stand up, but as he leaned on his injured arm, the hot, dagger-like pain drilled into his shoulder blade with vengeance. Letting out a wince he gritted his teeth biting through his lip to draw the agony to another part of his body. Tears wanted to form in his eyes, but he refused the weakness. With all his might and as much effort as he could muster, he managed to sit straight up with his back against the wooden backboard. He could move no further. Then he heard a doorknob twist from the front left end of the room, and he attempted to raise his arms in defence. But once he saw who stepped through, he exhaled and lowered his still-functional arm again. A good thing too, because he had no clue how much, if any, energy he had left to protect himself. His tank was empty.

"Olivia?" He said before pausing and thinking again. The logical conclusion would have been to suggest she took him to safety after saving him from Luminosa, but of course in a state of panic logic rarely prevails.

"Good, you're awake. I was getting worried." Even her most concerning words came off with a drip of monotone disinterest. She walked over to the end table and placed two ceramic cups with piping hot tea on the table. The aroma of different herbs gave it a sweet morning garden scent. She handed one to Coro before taking one for herself. "Drink this. The herbs should help you get back some of your energy. It won't help with the injury to your shoulder though."

Coro wrapped his none injured hand around the mug letting the warmth fill his fingers. He took a small sip, looking like a sick child in bed.

"Where are we?" He finally asked.

"My apartment. It was the only place I could think to take you at the time. Your injuries were bad but not life-threatening, and I was concerned if I took you to a hospital, Luminosa might attempt to finish you off. So I bandaged you up and took you back here to get some rest."

Coro nodded, "Thank you…" then he took another sip of his tea, "But how did you know where I was?"

Olivia reached into the drawer beside the bed and pulled out a small black device that Coro recognized as his phone. Not his original phone though, but the one Zale gave him when he started volunteering at the EC.

Olivia explained, "All of the EC's new phones have a tracking capability on them in case of danger ever arising and nobody is around to back you up." She took a sip of her tea and continued, "Once you discovered how those monsters were being created, I could see a look in your eye. You were putting all the pieces together. The more information we gathered, the closer we got to finding your father the more I could see your emotions starting to rise. Then when you failed to arrive at the emergency meeting tonight I had a bad feeling you were going to do something stupid. It wasn't long after that your beacon started going off and I could tell you were being taken into a forest way outside the city. None of it added up, so I came looking for you. As it turns out, that led me straight to Bex and Bronx as well."

"I thought they were supposed to be locked up?"

"If you had shown up to the meeting instead of going off gallivanting on your own you would've known someone broke them out last night. We were hunting them all night and the one person who wasn't even aware of it is the one person who finds them…" Olivia paused, her tone becoming the slightest bit more motherly than before. "You know if you hadn't fallen onto your phone and had it go off, I never would have found you." She glared at Coro. "What the hell were you thinking?" Before Coro could give an answer, she continued, "Did you honestly think you could just take down Luminosa by yourself? Or was your plan the whole time to get yourself killed by your father? Because I can't for the life of me figure out another reason for you to be dragged from the sewers to a forest and left for dead."

Coro lowered his head, staring at the purple sheets covering his legs.

"I know it was dumb, but to answer your question, none of those things were my intention. All I wanted to do was look at the factory my father supposedly created in the sewers and dig up some information. Obviously, I had no clue Bronx or Bex would be there."

Olivia softened her tone, deciding the answer was somewhat acceptable. But not entirely.

"If that was all you wanted, then why would you not at least tell me where you were going. President Osiris entrusted your safety to me. He knew Luminosa would likely have a bounty on your head, and that's why he chose me to make sure you remained safe on your mission. But I can't do that if you're gonna go running off without a word."

Coro stayed silent while he tried to formulate the right words. "I didn't tell you... because I knew the truth. Ever since my father disappeared and I saw the powers he granted Bex, I understood the choice he made. That bastard joined Luminosa of his own free will. Nobody abducted him or made him work for them. He chose it all. I thought if I stopped him, if I was the one to take him down, then I could still preserve his legacy I guess. I hate the man, I always have, but my mother of all people believed in him until her dying breath. Where it stood right now, he had been left a no-name scientist that was taken by Luminosa. I wanted to keep that façade in place instead of letting the world know of his true self. I didn't want to be known as the one created by such a monster. One who he experimented on over and over again to be his so-called perfect weapon. I didn't want to be seen as the monster he created."

Olivia's glare faded and she did her best to talk to Coro as a partner, not a child. Not her strong suit, but yelling at Coro would serve no more purpose.

"I understand you wish to stop your father; we all do. The irreversible damage he's caused by creating those monsters cannot be minimized. But now you've seen the strength he and Luminosa are building up. Fighting them alone would be nothing more than a suicide mission. Anyone else stuck fighting the way you were would have been left in a pool of their own blood. Luminosa is now at full strength, we know that to be fact. And they're only going to be stronger from here on out. A solo effort will not be enough. It's time to put aside the desire to stop your father and let the rest of us help aid in this mission of yours." Olivia took a sip of her tea before staring at Coro with her piercing eyes. "I get how personal this is. It's between you and your father, so I haven't told Zale of the events that took place yet. I'll leave that up to you. The decision is yours; you can continue to go it alone until you either succeed or fail, or you can let the rest of us who are trying our best to keep this city safe, help."

Coro reluctantly nodded. He hated the fact he needed help, a trait developed on the sole premise of self-preservation, but if his father was willing to hide behind the monsters of Luminosa to do his bidding, then he would have to keep the playing field even.

"Besides, as long as we have The Hero of Light, we still have a fighting chance," Olivia added.

Hearing about The Hero of Light triggered another question in Coro's mind. He looked at the four walls of the room again before saying, "That reminds me, what's with all these Hero of Light posters? Also, your fighting style last night, it mirrored him perfectly. I've only seen him fight a few times but I would never forget it."

"That's because he used to be my idol. From the age of ten, when he saved me from a group of bandits. They were capturing and selling Elementalists for profit and I happened to fit the bill. From that day on, I wanted to join the EC. I would fight alongside the Hero himself and make the world a better place. Not an uncommon thought by most my age at the time. If you were an Elementalist, The Hero of Light was and still is the pinnacle. See neither of my parents were Elementalists, so they could never show me the true potential I knew I had, but The Hero of Light could. His strength, his dedication, his discipline to bettering himself to help those around him. What nobler thing could you ask to become in life.

Although times were more peaceful than they have been of late, I trained day and night pushing myself to be the best I could. I patterned everything after the way he fought. With Dark and Light elements being so similar, I could use him as the perfect model."

The Hero of Light's influence on Elementalist society was not new to Coro; he just struggled to imagine such a stoic and emotionless warrior mimicking the Hero. More than his incredible skills and lifesaving heroics what made him an icon was the way he spoke. How when he arrived on scene a calm came about everyone. He was a leader through and through and people would follow him to the ends of the earth. People like himself and Olivia were not those types of people, but it showed him he could still make a difference in the world even if he was not at the forefront of it. Something his mother told him long ago.

Olivia stood up, done sharing the sentiments of her life. As she did, she said, "I'd take a few hours and try to get some more rest. You're in no condition to be moving around as it is. Most of the EC is still on the lookout anyways. I'm off to go meet with President Osiris, there is food in the fridge if you need it." And with that, she left. For such a distant person, she provided quite hospitable care for Coro. He couldn't help but smile slightly.

After Olivia left Coro passed out for another few hours. His mind might have been continually rushing with thoughts but even that couldn't compete with the weariness of his body. Once awake, he gingerly got to his feet. His arm remained limp, but his legs could carry him around the apartment at least.

The rest of Olivia's apartment was far more modern than his own. Large windows provided a beautiful landscape view of the city, and much more sunshine beamed into her living room than Coro's place. All the woods were chestnut and the furniture all white.

He took a brief look around to see if Olivia returned but saw no sign of the woman.

Since he was alone, he figured now would be the best time to make his phone call. He needed to talk to Mr. Osiris and first apologize but second let him know all the information discovered on his inadvertent adventure. However, before he could do that, he needed to talk to someone else first. He sat down on the couch and began dialling.

CHAPTER 20
AN AFTERNOON OF BLISS

WITH THE WIDE-SCALE SEARCH FOR BRONX AND BEX unsuccessful, those who were on the hunt all night were relieved of their duties. For Minisc, Lily, Jules, and Yuri that meant they would head home for some long-overdue rest. While Jules left with his brother, Minisc and Lily were escorted back to Lily's home to pick up her suitcases before heading off to the Premier household.

"Thank you so much for letting me stay with you guys for the next few days," Lily said, giving Don a bright smile as she dropped off a small duffle bag onto the freshly made bed.

Minisc walked in behind her, huffing and puffing as he dropped the last suitcase onto the floor with a heavy thud. "You know, you probably didn't need to bring this much for only a few days. If I didn't know any better, I'd say you were moving in with us."

Lily sat on the bed next to her clothes and said, "Well I wasn't sure how long my parents would be staying in their hotel, so I wanted to be prepared. It's possible we won't find Bronx or Bex anytime soon." Then she paused before frowning as she popped open the suitcase. "I know we can't keep my parents under supervision forever, but what if we don't find them, and they have to go back to living at home. I get President Osiris is taking care of things, but still..." She knew negative thoughts would only serve to make things worse, but how could she not think of all the possible scenarios. It felt like her only way to stay prepared.

Minisc sat down beside his friend, "Don't worry, we'll find them. They can't hide from us forever."

"Minisc is right. Zale and I are doing everything we can to put an end to all this madness. Not only for your family but for everyone who has been affected. As long as I'm around, Luminosa won't have their way." Don displayed glowing confidence when he spoke. Such strength in his words filled Lily with a courage only the Hero of Light could provide. "Besides, you two have done more than your fair share in this battle. Now it's time to rest. Both of you must be exhausted."

"I might be a little sleepy," Lily said, pushing the words out through a wide-open yawn. After all the events that continually kept her awake and alert, now with things slowing down, her body started to call the shots.

"Come on, Minisc, let's let Lily get some sleep."

Minisc smiled and gave his friend a soft hug, "Try to relax. Everything is just fine. Your parents are safe and so are you."

"Okay," Lily yawned again. As Minisc and Don readied to leave the room, Lily curled up on the bed and gave in to the beautiful lust for sleep. Before Minisc closed the door entirely, he walked back in and put a blanket over her body.

When Minisc left the room, he could feel his body caving to the same sleep deprivation that defeated Lily. He too had been warding off his desire to crawl into bed all night to help in the search. However, before he did that, some lingering questions still needed to be addressed.

Making his way to the kitchen, he found his father sitting drinking a glass of water. The man endured the same wear and tear as the kids, but he appeared to be handling it quite well. Now whether that was a façade or not Minisc remained unsure, but either way, he took a seat beside him.

"Thanks for letting Lily stay here. I know I should've asked beforehand, but we were desperate."

Don looked at his son with a warm encouraging smile, "You know Lily is welcome as long as she wants. Besides, I'm sure last night must have been hard on her, knowing her mother is deemed a potential target for Luminosa. That would put anyone in distress."

Don took a swig of water while Minisc let his thoughts develop. Finally, after a long silence, he asked the million-dollar question that everyone wanted to know, "Do you think we can actually stop them this time?" Minisc's voice was low, and the concern could not be hidden. "I mean we beat Dusk, but even that didn't seem to stop Luminosa. And now Bronx and Bex are back on the loose and if your power is fading..." Minisc sighed, "I don't know maybe I'm just tired is all."

Don put his hand on his son's shoulder. "You can't let doubt seep in. Once it does, getting rid of it is very hard. No matter what, when the time comes, we'll always rise and triumph over Luminosa. Whether that someone is me, you, or a hero we've never met, someone will always be ready to take up the mantle and fight. I can promise that." Don looked at his son more sympathetically. "I know it feels like things have been piling up lately, like every time we think we've stopped Luminosa, they find a new way to fight back, but you can't forget about all the good that's been done along the way. Thanks to you guys, we found the abducted victims before Luminosa could change them into those monsters. Also, you were able to warn the EC about potential targets for the future. With those files, we can make sure even with Luminosa at full power, we can prevent their plans from coming true. I know at points it feels like we're spinning our wheels, but sometimes when it looks the darkest, it means you are only a step away from the light. But for the time being, I think the best thing you can do is be there for Lily and help take her mind off the situation for a bit."

Minisc agreed, "Yeah, she's been through a lot."

"That being said, the first thing you need to do is get some sleep. You were supposed to be in bed recovering before this all started up. Leave everything else to Zale and the EC, he knows what he's doing."

Minisc ran his hand through his dishevelled hair and fought off a yawn. "Yeah, I guess you're right. There isn't much to be done right now anyway." He stood up and took a look out the back door. The sun was only beginning to peak over the tops of the trees. "It's so early though, I'm not sure I'm gonna be able to fall asleep."

Don stared at his son before chuckling, "Since when have you ever had trouble sleeping through the morning?"

"That's true..." Minisc said rubbing his eye. He fought back a second yawn before saying, "I guess I could take a nap for a few hours."

Those few hours flew by and Minisc rolled around in the irresistible warmth of his blankets. His desire for more sleep challenged his willpower, but he made a painstaking effort to sit up in his bed. He stretched his arms to the ceiling letting out a far more satisfying yawn. Although refreshed, there was no doubt if he surrendered himself back to his bed he would be out for another few hours. However, when he looked at his clock, he realized that would not be wise.

"1:07... huh, guess I slept longer than I thought." Once he began to wake, he started to remember he had a guest in his home. "I wonder if Lily's awake yet?"

He got out of bed and headed down the hall where he could hear the sweet, soft laugh of his friend. The angelic chime always brought a smile to his face and this time was no different. *Sounds like she's in good spirits at least.*

Minisc stepped into the kitchen where his father and Lily were currently sitting around the table. They both were smiling, but Lily in particular looked to be quite rejuvenated. She nibbled on a piece of toast before taking notice of Minisc.

"Look who finally decided to wake up. I thought you were gonna sleep all day," she giggled.

"Yeah... guess I was more tired than I thought. When did you wake up?"

"Only maybe an hour ago. Your father was just telling me stories about you as a kid." She smirked, making Minisc's cheeks turn flush. He could only imagine the tales his father had of him. "I had no idea you were so scared of roller coasters that you made your mother take you on the little trains all day instead." She had the sweetest smile, but underneath, Minisc could feel the mockery in her voice.

"So... I liked trains..."

Lily laughed, "At least now I know why you always refused to go on any roller coasters when you Jules and I went to the amusement park."

"They're a walking death trap and I've had enough close calls for a lifetime..."

Don smirked as well before interjecting to save his son, "I made some breakfast for you as well, Minisc." He walked over to the counter grabbing a plate. "Take a seat."

Minisc obliged, trading places with his father to sit across from Lily. That's when he noticed several pictures on the counter. They were old enough that Minisc couldn't pinpoint the memories associated with them until he noticed the same one of him and his mother that resided in his room. They stood in front of an amusement park when he was at best five years old.

"So no school and no volunteering at the EC. What do you two plan on doing with a rare day off?" Don asked.

"Oh, that's right. I didn't even think of that. We were all so preoccupied with the search last night, I completely forgot President Osiris gave us the week off," Lily said.

"Well, we were supposed to be in recovery after all. But to be honest I feel pretty good. That sleep did wonders for me."

"Me too," Lily chimed, "So then what do you wanna do?"

Minisc stared blankly back at his friend with no answers coming to mind. It felt like an eternity since he had a day with no obligations. No rehab, no training, not chasing down Luminosa. He shrugged his shoulders, so Don decided to pipe up with an idea.

"Lily, have you ever gone to see the cherry blossoms in High Park? They should be in full bloom right about now. I'm sure Minisc would love to take you to see them."

Lily looked at Don and clapped her hands together, "Oh, I've always wanted to see the cherry blossoms." Her eyes lit up as she spun back to look at Minisc with the sweetest most convincing smile she could muster, "Can we go, please, please, please?"

Minisc was taken aback by the reaction but when he saw the glimmer in her eyes, he remembered his father's words, *I think the best thing you can do for the time being is help Lily take her mind off the situation for a bit.* This would be a perfect opportunity to act on that vow. Besides, he could never shut down such excitement from his friend.

"Yeah, of course we can." He smiled back though it paled in comparison to the girl across from him.

Lily sprung from her chair with contagious enthusiasm. In a lot of ways, it reminded Minisc of when they first arrived at Scotia Coliseum for the Tournament of Elements. The rambunctious activity, the number of events and sights to see along with the electric energy of the crowd filled Lily with excitement for that whole week. Since then neither of them was granted a similar excitement and Minisc was more than pleased to see that side of Lily once again.

In record time, Lily flew out of the room to get herself ready, while Minisc couldn't help but turn to his father and raise an eyebrow.

"So... how'd you come up with that idea so quick?" He asked, "I never took The Hero of Light as the flower enthusiast type."

Don chuckled in return, "Very funny, I took your mother there on our first date. So, I figured now would be a good time for you two to go." Don's grin turned into a devilish smirk once he saw the scarlet shade of red cross his son's cheeks.

Before Minisc could put up any sort of rebuttal, Lily returned bringing along her glowing excitement. She wore what looked like a new white and blue sundress.

"Are you ready to go, Minisc?" She asked, bouncing up and down on the balls of her feet.

"Yeah, if we hurry, we can catch the next train."

"This place is beautiful!" Lily cooed as she spun around, looking at all the pink petals that lined the path from start to finish. Each tree was in full bloom blending into each other looking like a pristine painting. Even Minisc couldn't help but be sucked in by the elegance of the petals dancing through the air as they walked.

The weather for taking in a scenic nature walk was as perfect as they could have hoped for. A warm summer afternoon, with a light breeze that spun the petals around as if it were putting on a show. A sight fitting of High Park, which was considered one of the most popular areas in Toronto. Not only did it give a home to the cherry blossoms every summer, but it also provided many different events year-round such as sports, a zoo, as well as other nature exhibits.

Being one of the most beautiful and romantic attractions the city could offer, Minisc and Lily were far from the only ones on the trail. Many couples came from all over the world to admire the sights at this time of year. Everywhere Minisc looked, he could see happy couples smiling and cooing as they snapped countless pictures to commemorate the occasion. The whole vibe created a sense of awkwardness for him to say the least. But as long as Lily enjoyed herself, he could accept a little bit of embarrassment. Besides, he had no time to worry about such things, he could barely keep up with the childlike awe of Lily as she wandered around, mesmerized by the pink cotton candy like trees and bushes of flowers. He felt a hand grab his arm pulling him out of his thoughts.

"Isn't this place beautiful? I'm so glad you took me here; I absolutely love it." She pulled out her phone in preparation to take some pictures.

"I must admit they are stunning," Minisc said.

Click click click.

Lily snapped multiple photos until a new idea popped into her head. "Oh, we should get somebody to take a picture of us!" She called out to an elderly couple who happened to be walking nearby.

"Excuse me, could you take a picture of us in front of the cherry blossoms?" She asked.

The woman gave a warm, grandmotherly smile, "Of course dear."

Lily surrendered her phone to the woman, before grabbing Minisc by the arm and dragging him into the perfect position.

"Ready, smile."

Lily cozied herself up to Minisc making sure the two were tightly in the frame together."

Click

The woman took one look at the screen and then showed it to her husband behind her. With their stamp of approval, Lily and Minisc walked back up to the woman.

"How's it look?"

"You two make a beautiful couple." The woman smiled. Minisc and Lily both had blushes paint their cheeks while Minisc tried to set the record straight.

"Oh umm yeah… we're actually not together," he stuttered.

Lily remained hushed.

The woman let out a wholesome grandmotherly laugh, "Oh that's too bad. You two would look great together." The woman wrapped her arm around her husband as the two started to walk along the path once again.

Tranquillity and enchanting walks captured the afternoon until the sun began to arch low for the evening. Minisc and Lily sat on the edge of a small pond in the middle of the park. Most people left for the night giving the two some time to enjoy the calming sounds of the water. Minisc leaned back staring up into the sky while Lily sat looking into the water. No words needed to be said. It had been the perfect afternoon that was sorely overdue.

Lily pulled her attention away from the crystal-clear pond and laid down on her back looking up at the sky next to Minisc. She sighed contently, "I'm really glad you brought me here. Everything about this place is magical. It's exactly what I needed."

The thought of Lily's parents being cooped up in a hotel room while she enjoyed the privilege of seeing the beauties her city had to offer ate at her, but she knew the guilt would not change the outcome. She needed to enjoy it. That's what they would've wanted most.

"I'm glad you liked it," Minisc said.

The two continued to rest peacefully on the soft grass watching orange streaks of light meld into the blue sky.

"I wish we could stay like this forever," Lily said softly. There was a small hint of sadness in her voice that Minisc picked up on.

"What do you mean?"

"I just... today... walking around High Park, everyone seemed so happy, so stress-free. Nobody was worried about being abducted or fighting monsters, or if Luminosa would attack..." She sat up, wrapping her arms around her knees, "I guess sometimes I just wish life wasn't like this. I chose EA to learn more about myself as an Elementalist, something I always wanted to do, but it feels like ever since school started, we've been stuck in a never ending fight, worrying about what fates stood around the corner. I don't know, sometimes it's just tough. Worrying about what could happen, worrying if my family will be okay, will I be okay, or Jules and you. I just wish we could live our lives in peace... everyone... as equals. No more hate, and no more Luminosa..." Lily trailed off in silence leaving Minisc at a loss for words. Then she decided to speak up again realizing how her words sounded, "Don't get me wrong, I loved working at the shelter, and I want to help people, I really do, but even seeing everyone misplaced because of something that we as Elementalists caused. It's tough... I don't know, maybe I'm just not cut out to work for the EC."

"Lily..."

"I know Jules has always dreamed about joining them, and I'm so glad he keeps pushing for his goals even if I worry about him getting hurt, but if this is the life that being in the EC is like, I just don't know... I don't know if it's for me." She sat up and looked Minisc directly in the eyes, "How do you do it? You've been through so much over the last year, but you just keep going. I never see you blink in the face of danger, and whenever someone needs to be rescued you're the first one to act. How do you do it?"

Minisc pondered the question, not sure what he could say to make his friend feel better. There were so many different answers he could give.

"Honestly, I don't know. I've never felt that strong. Not the way my father is. How he has always been the symbol for this world to look up to for so long is beyond me. Always at a moment's notice ready to fight, to sacrifice himself for a single life. I never realized how tough it must have been for him, and I never really understood how or why he did it. At least, until I met you."

Lily looked at her friend, puzzled.

"The reason I wanted to go to EA was to help make my mother's wish a reality, to help Humans and Elementalists live together in peace. But after I met you, after the fear I felt when Luminosa first attacked me you and Jules, I knew I wasn't strong enough to make that wish come true, not while Luminosa was forming. My father wanted to be a symbol for everyone, but me... I just want to be able to protect the people I care about most. If I can help create the world my mother envisioned, then I know I would be strong enough to protect those I love as well. Sometimes it's hard to keep fighting, but I guess... I just know if I stopped, if I gave up, then all we've been through, all we've had to deal with, was any of it really worth it? The only way I can give you that world of peace is to keep fighting. I have to do everything I can alongside the EC and my father to stop Luminosa. So we can live happily."

Lily shifted her body, so her head rested on Minisc's shoulder.

"I'm so glad I met you, Minisc..."

CHAPTER 21
A TALE OF TWO

WHEN MINISC AND LILY RETURNED HOME FOR THE evening, they marvelled in their adventure. It acted as a much-needed break for the two who were dying for some peace. But reality would soon set in again. While Lily went to clean up for the night, Minisc's phone began to ring. Surprised at the ID on screen he quickly picked up.

"Coro? I didn't think I'd be hearing from you anytime soon after I didn't see you at the EC meeting last night."

"Yeah I know… but I have stuff you're gonna want to hear." Minisc took a seat on the couch and listened as Coro explained his story. Minisc was well aware of Coro's disdain for his father, but he struggled to believe the man would openly join Luminosa.

When Coro finished explaining, Minisc said, "I wish you would've told me your plan… we could've helped…" he trailed off for a moment, "…But still, I'm glad you're okay. Enough people have been hurt throughout this whole ordeal."

"I know, but actually, that's not why I called you…"

"Huh? Then why'd you call?"

"Well, everyone we know of in Luminosa was there last night… all but one person… Ignis…"

Minisc sucked in deep, feeling his chest tighten at the mention of the name.

"What do you suppose that means? I can't imagine he just left them? He hates me too much for that."

"I don't know. That Brooklyn character, he indicated that he along with Bex, Bronx, and my father were the only ones part of the group."

Minisc began to debate the logic he knew was infallible.

Is it possible Ignis had a change of heart, there's no way... the Ignis I fought in the park that night... that Ignis would never change his mind. He wanted me and Father dead. Nothing would sway him from that.

Realizing he had left Coro hanging in silence he said, "Okay, thanks for letting me know. You should call President Osiris and inform him of everything you've learned. With the information we found last night as well, we should be able to cut Luminosa off and bring your father down. We will stop him."

"We will."

Minisc hung up the phone with lingering thoughts. Not sure what to do, he decided to sit down with Lily and his father to explain the situation. The obvious frustration they felt by Coro's actions was at least washed away with the sentiments that he survived. On top of that, they now knew the truth involving the boy's lost father and could make the necessary preparations for a counterattack. Each obstacle blocking their path from missing Humans to slime monsters, to Bronx and Bex escaping custody, was finally being solved with methodical precision. However, Minisc had left out one small detail, a nugget he felt was of no use to the battle, and really only important to him. He excused Ignis' lack of an appearance, deciding to keep that to himself.

Once he learned Ignis might not be with Luminosa any longer, a ray of light filled his heart. He knew it was wrong. To believe Ignis was anything but evil would be foolish. His father and Lily both would surely reiterate that point. But Minisc still didn't want to hear such talk. His desire to bring his childhood friend to the light could not be extinguished.

The three had dinner and Lily called her parents after to check on them. Don had a meeting with Zale to discuss all the information presented by Coro, as well as their plan moving forward. Minisc also gave Jules and Yuri a rundown of the information.

With everyone on the same page and the end of a long day around the corner, Minisc readied for bed.

But after a couple hours lying in the dead of night, Minisc tossed and turned in frustration. Wide awake, he walked over to his window, hoping the crisp nighttime air might help alleviate his insomnia. The forest behind his house was shroud in darkness while the moon hid behind the glowing clouds above. He couldn't stop thinking about the conversation he and Lily had at the cherry blossom festival.

I just wish we could live our lives in peace... everyone... as equals. No more hate, and no more Luminosa...

Those words, her desires, were engraved in his mind playing on repeat. He wanted to give her that world, that life where she would no longer have to worry about those she loved being taken away or injured. As he often did when feeling unsure Minisc began to wonder what his late mother would do. Would she deem fighting a necessity to bringing equality, or would she have found another way?

"Maybe I just need to go for a walk... I haven't visited Mother's grave in a while."

He tiptoed down the hall trying to avoid disturbing Lily or his father.

It only took a few minutes to reach his mother's grave and once he did, he sat cross-legged staring at the elegant tombstone as he'd done so many times before. Whenever he felt lost or needed to think out loud, he liked to visit the burial site and speak to his mother. It helped create a connection and give him a way to feel like she was still with him. He began to speak indirectly to the woman in the form of out loud thinking.

"I know we can't just give up. Luminosa has to be defeated. It's the only way we can ever truly bring some form of peace back to everyone's lives. As long as they're around then nobody Human or Elementalist can really feel safe. And I know right now everyone still feels safe with The Hero of Light around, but with Father's power fading, once it's gone there will be no one left with the strength to win. Not against monsters like them." Minisc stuck his hand in the dirt picking up a clump before letting it sift through his fingers. "If only I could convince Ignis to join us. If what Coro said is true then maybe there is hope for him after all, if he were here, we could take down Luminosa once and for all. I know it. But if Coro's wrong... then it will be me vs him... and I know he won't stop fighting 'til he has nothing left. That's just how he is. I've tried not to think about the outcome. I guess I still believe he can be saved; I know he can. He hates me, he hates The Hero of Light, but what does that even matter, he can hate us all he wants, but I've seen the good in him. He still has a heart. He must."

Speaking to his mother's grave felt liberating in ways human interaction could not provide. He was free to say anything without repercussion or judgment, and yet when he did, in his soul he could feel his mother's presence. Even through the silence of the air, she managed to lift the fog clouding his mind time and time again.

Formulating his next thought Minisc heard a branch snap violently in the distance. He tensed up while getting to his feet.

"Lily...?" he called out hoping it was his friend coming to check on him. He cautiously turned around attempting not to make any hasty moves in the process. But when a cold chill climbed his spine, he knew it was not the presence of his friend. Or any friend.

A void of darkness stood in front of him, and yet with each step forward through the shadows he had a feeling he knew who decided to make an appearance. Finally coming into a small beam of light there stood the boy he used to call his friend. The black cloak that he dawned to work with Luminosa cast to the abyss.

Such an act should have given Minisc hope, but instead, it brought on more fear. Something was amiss.

"What are you doing here? Shouldn't you be hiding with your new leader?" Minisc goaded. The question would give him an answer on Ignis' allegiance right away. From there he could predict what steps to take next. At least, he hoped.

Ignis shot him a look of annoyance, "Those idiots are nothing more than a bunch of cowards if you ask me. Wasting time with them is beneath me. They talk about killing the Hero of Light, about how he has finally grown weak enough to be defeated, and yet still they simply wait in hiding. It's pathetic."

"If that's what you think, then why join them? Why kill all those innocent people? What purpose did that serve in the end if you didn't even want to be a part of Luminosa?"

"Simple. I joined them so I could gain information. To learn how they would kill your father. And now that I know The Hero of Light is at his weakest, it's time to leave him gravelling at my feet. I don't care about eliminating Humans, that's a waste of time. Humans, Elementalists, they're all the same, and as long as they feel protected, they will continue to act as they want. I'll take that protection away from this world. Then they can realize the pain they cause each other."

It didn't take long for Minisc to realize negotiations were going to fall on deaf ears. His hopes for Ignis leaving Luminosa disappeared into the night and all that remained was the rising tension in his body.

"You know I won't let you do that, Ignis. I don't care if you feel like my father failed you. That the world failed you after your parents died. I refuse to let you continue this idea of hate. I won't let you lay a finger on my father."

Ignis scoffed at the thought. "You know what I hate most about you, Minisc? You're everything I ever wanted in life. Here you are, saving the city from Luminosa, living up to your father's legacy, working alongside him. It was everything I ever dreamed of. And the worst part is, even as kids you never wanted it. You never wanted any of this. Yet here you are. It's disgusting."

Hearing those words cut Minisc. In that sense, Ignis had a point. He was living out the dreams of his former friend, but Ignis was missing one large point on the matter.

"Maybe you're right, Ignis, things should have worked out differently and you should be in my position... but you know what? Even so, that doesn't give you the right to kill whoever you want out of revenge. After your parents died, you could've worked to cement their legacy as heroes. You could've kept their memories alive and lived on in their name, fighting alongside us to stop Luminosa, the way you know they would've. But you didn't! You chose this path instead. My father had nothing to do with that, and neither did I. You made those choices all on your own."

Minisc spilled his heart in a feeble attempt to open Ignis' eyes, not necessarily in hopes of him joining the team. No, that seemed unlikely. But in hopes of preventing a fight. Mentally, let alone physically, he was not prepared to face an opponent with the tenacity of Ignis. And not to the death. He couldn't handle the emotional toll.

On the other hand, he might not have a choice in the matter. Ignis' balled his hands into fists as they burst into flames. His nostrils flared and his chest puffed out as he raised his fists.

"I'll make you pay for those words!" Ignis thrust his hand forward, expelling a blistering wave of fire in Minisc's direction.

The blond-haired boy remained agile, hopping out of the way, but it was not without consequences. Since they were surrounded by forested trees, and with Ignis being a fire Elementalist, the terrain would be as much an issue as the fight itself.

He refused to peel his eyes away from Ignis, but the smell of burning bark gradually started to waft its way through the forest while sizzling crackles sprang from tree to tree.

Ignis continued to light the forest in a fiery blaze while Minisc remained on the defensive. Before long, smoke lined the sky, while orange flames lit up the battlefield.

At this rate he's gonna burn the whole forest down... and with me in it. If Minisc could hold out long enough perhaps his father, or even Lily, a water Elementalist would arrive to help, but finding them in such a large forest not to mention through the flames seemed unlikely. He needed to fight back, no matter how much he wished for another solution.

Minisc held his hands out and fired a series of Lum Bombs. However, Ignis deflected each blast into the treetops, shaking the forest around them. Branches started to fall while bushes continued to catch fire. The scorching temperatures began to take a toll on Minisc, who glistened in sweat.

Ignis saw his opening and roared, "Now you can meet the same fate as your father soon will! Hell flames!" An explosion of fire drawn up from the deepest hatred in Ignis' heart burst out in all directions.

Left with no other option, Minisc created a barrier of light, but even the defensive maneuver couldn't withstand Ignis' relentless flames.

He's got me trapped. Minisc could feel the shield tighten around him. The claustrophobic feeling of the flames attempting to reach his skin seared fear in his mind.

The ferocious fires continued to spread, but even worse than that, he knew it would soon burn a path to his house. He had no way of stopping it, and with Lily and his father asleep, they would lose precious time to react. Lily might have been able to hold off some of the flames herself, but as the fires grew, Minisc knew she would be overwhelmed.

Sliding backwards, Minisc felt a rock buried in the ground hit his foot. Only it wasn't a rock. It was a tombstone. The last remaining connection between mother and son. He could hear the maniacal laughter of Ignis on the other side of the smoke.

I can't hold this any longer…

He needed to make a move. In an act of desperation, he dove away from the attack. The forest erupted in red light like a volcano. The tree's once beautiful weaving branches were smoke and ash while bushes were casting off flames six feet tall. No doubt any animals around were long gone, hopefully escaping to some sort of freedom. For Minisc, the left side of his body endured an incalculable amount of damage from the blast. He lay rolled over behind his mother's grave. The elegant tomb cracked and shattered with only a third of the rock remaining.

As the fiery boy often did, Ignis let rage fuel his attacks, and because of that, he burned through his supply of energy in short order. The growing aches in his arms indicated he could not take The Hero of Light in his current state, the way he hoped, but his message had been sent regardless. Leaving Minisc clinging to within an inch of his life would bring more than enough pain to the man Ignis despised most.

While trying to catch his breath, Ignis heard the cries of a girl along with the Hero of Light. Knowing he couldn't continue his death match under the circumstances, he faded into the smoke-filled night, returning from whence he came. He would let the flames of the forest finish Minisc off and would soon return for The Hero of Light.

Meanwhile, Minisc could hear the voices of his father and friend. He wanted to call out to them, but nothing but gasps for air came out. The walls of fire began to close in on him only adding to the already incomparable pain running through the left side of his body.

"Minisc, if you can hear me, raise your energy as high as you can."

Minisc recognized his father's voice fraught with fear. He knew if he could raise his energy, the light emitted off his body would be able to guide his father to him, but such a task felt impossible in his current state. He lay flat on his stomach, paralyzed. His eyes remained closed, but the uncomfortable warmth of his surroundings continued to scorch his already beat red skin. With nothing left he could feel the energy begin to burst outward. He had no idea if it was helping, or if he was only imagining it, but he forced it out. Life draining from his eyes he faded into a sleep saying his prayers. He prepared to see his mother for the first time since childhood.

"Please wake up, Minisc. I can't lose you." Lily sat on her knees with her head buried at Minisc's bedside. She fought back the pools of water that continued to flow as she held his hand. She was at a loss, and thanks to a feeling of helplessness, all she could compel herself to do was keep her head down and pray. The left side of Minisc's arm had severe burns which would leave lingering scars for the rest of his life. The damage sustained would be irreversible, but any long-term effects could not be projected.

Along his body were numerous soaked towels that were being used to bring down his body temperature.

Once Lily composed herself, she pulled the white towel off Minisc's forehead and dunked it in a bucket of water before returning it to its home.

The last gasp of Minisc's energy had been faint, but just enough for Lily and Don to find him. Lily had already assumed he would be close to his mother's grave, and that knowledge proved to be the deciding factor between life and death. She did her best to heal his excruciating injuries, but even then, she could only do so much. Even worse, the fires had spread so rapidly that while Lily and Don searched for Minisc, the rest of the flames soon overtook their home. Nothing remained. Not that anyone cared about such trivial belongings. They would sacrifice it all again to ensure Minisc would survive, but the loss of their home still stung.

Once they found Minisc, he was rushed to the hospital to be treated. Then once he was stable, they moved him to the same hotel that the Humans under threat resided in. Because there was so much ambiguity about Minisc's attacker, they needed to keep him in a place where he would be safe and secure. Doctors were around as well to keep watch if things were to grow worse. Thankfully his permanent injuries mostly extended to his left arm only, but the rest of his body remained in silent anguish.

Lily opted to stay with Minisc and help tend to his wounds while the doctors were not around, but Don had other issues to deal with. Focusing on the task at hand knowing his son's current state would be tough, but many questions remained from the incident and those answers were sorely needed. Not only for the city, but to ensure they would not return for his son.

Nestled under Minisc's chin sat the only thing that miraculously survived the fires: his familiar stuffed donkey that he had held so dear since birth. But even that failed to escape harm's way. The purplish grey animal that made Lily laugh when she first saw it suffered the same fate as Minisc. Irreversible damage for sure, with burn marks all over its once-soft fur changing the colour to a charred grey and black.

The rest of the house was gone, all other possessions wiped clean, and nothing but smoke and ash remained from the forest. Lily did her best as a water Elementalist, but even the most skilled of her kind would be no match for such uncontrollable fires.

Behind Lily, the doorknob shook, and she spun around to see Jules standing in the doorway. He didn't step in, or even take his hand off the handle. He looked past Lily like she was a ghost. Shock overtook him as he saw only a part of Minisc's face and arm, which were still wrapped with soaking towels. His legs started to tremble, realizing the severity of the injuries. Jules knew it had been bad. He could gather that from the incoherent crying of Lily over the phone, but when he saw the damage in person, reality began to set in.

Both had seen Minisc in rough shape before, fighting in battles he himself would admit he had no business being in, let alone winning, but this time the injuries felt different. For Jules, dark and buried memories of Yuri in the hospital forced their way up. He tried to hide his anger, ignoring his lust for revenge, instead choosing to focus on Lily.

"Lily... what happened..." He tried to choke out. The words barely made it past his lips in a whisper.

"We don't know..." she replied, her voice weak. "Don woke up last night and said Minisc was missing. I figured he went to visit his mother's grave to clear his mind after speaking with Coro, but when we got outside the forest erupted into flames. It spread so quickly. I couldn't stop it." Lily began to tremble as she forced herself to continue. "Don and I ran in to find him, but the fires were impossible to get through. He must have used the last of his strength to make his body glow so Don could find him." Her lip quivered as tears began to roll again.

Unlike when Yuri had been ravished by injuries, Jules knew this time he needed to be a pillar of support. The anger that led him down such a dark path before could not be an option this time. Not for him, and not for Lily either.

Jules finally walked into the room and hugged his friend tight, the way Minisc always would when they needed it most. "Just breathe... he's going to be okay... we know Minisc, he can't die like this. He's the son of The Hero of Light, he stopped Dusk... and most importantly he's our best friend. He's going to wake up. I know he will."

Jules poured his heart as best he could, not sure if he believed his own words. But he had no choice. He had to believe. The thought of losing his best friend would break him. It would break both of them.

"Thank you," Lily sniffled. She took three deep breaths exhaling slowly to calm herself. She had to believe. They had to believe.

Jules took one more look at Minisc, before trying to choke out the question that plagued his mind.

"Do we know what caused the fires?"

Lily shook her head and sighed, "No. When we found him, he was alone, I can't imagine if anyone else had been in the forest they would have survived."

Jules contorted his mouth, staying silent for a second before whispering, "I can think of one person who could survive it, and he would also have a bone to pick with Minisc and his father..."

"You don't mean..."

Jules nodded, "Think about it, the only people who would try something like this are Luminosa... and the only fire Elementalists that we know of in that group is Ignis. He would also be the only one willing to attack Minisc or his father directly, thinking he could win. If Luminosa thought they could have succeeded in doing so they would have done it already. This has to be his doing."

"But to be beat this badly? With these injuries...? Ignis couldn't be that strong."

"Strength doesn't matter when it comes to Ignis and Minisc. At least not physically. Minisc might be stronger, but when it comes to fighting Ignis, he simply can't bring himself to do it. His heart still wants to believe the childhood Ignis he knew is still alive. That somehow he can be brought back to our side. I don't understand it, but until Minisc can escape the guilt he feels, he won't ever be able to beat Ignis."

They looked at each other, remaining silent. They were lost. Lily looked back over to Minisc, the marks on his face tearing at her heart. She watched as he winced in his sleep, almost like he was having a nightmare.

In her heart, she understood why fighting Ignis was so hard for Minisc. Although whenever she asked him about the situation, he would say little; she and Don had spoken about it once. The man explained most of the situation in painful detail, but only now could she truly see the ramifications of their falling out.

Minisc had a rather lonesome childhood, of that everyone knew. And with Ignis being his only real friend at the time, it caused him to overlook so much harm his friend had done. In one way it was admirable to hold such faith. Yet now it was proving detrimental.

Lily said, "I know he's scared. Deep down there are still fears of being left alone. Worries that eventually he will lose everyone he ever cared about. First his mother, then Ignis..." She placed her hand on Minisc's. "But he'll never be alone. He has us and he always will. As soon as he realizes that, he can see he doesn't need Ignis. That it's okay to let go of some things in life. No matter how hard."

Jules nodded. It's not that he thought Minisc took him for granted, far from it. But lingering trauma continued to eat away at his friend, and Jules simply wished he had a solution. But only time would ease that childhood pain.

Finally, Jules asked, "Where's Don?"

"He's with President Osiris. They're going over the situation. I've never seen him so scared. I can't get the image out of my head." Lily began to shake again, trying to keep her composure.

Jules sighed, rubbing her arm, "I can only imagine."

After a few more tense seconds, Jules glanced at Lily again. This time he looked like he had something to say but was fearful of backlash.

Lily met his look and said, "What is it?"

Jules somberly shook his head, "I know you're gonna fight me on this, but just hear me out okay."

Lily stared at her friend wordlessly beckoning him to continue.

"Let me watch over Minisc for a bit. You need to get some sleep. We don't know how long Minisc will be out, and you've barely slept in two days now."

"No... I can't... what if-"

"He'll be okay. I swear, I'll keep watch and make sure he's safe. You can trust me. And if he wakes up, I'll come get you immediately."

At first, Lily thought he was only relieving her of her duty for her sake, but staring into the broken eyes of her friends she could see that Jules required the same alone time to grieve that she had been granted. No doubt he felt some guilt that he could not be there to protect his friend. All he wanted to do was feel useful. Like he had some control over helping his friends feel better.

"Okay," Lily nodded. She knew Jules would take good care of their friend, even if she wanted to remain. But just to be sure she grabbed the bucket which only had a quarter of water left and stuck her hand inside until it filled to the top. "Make sure to keep a fresh towel on his burns at all times. I suggest switching them out every twenty minutes or so. The bathroom has a stack of towels you can use, but if you run out, I'm sure you can call the front desk and tell them you're with the EC. They'll get you more quickly."

"Alright, now you go try and sleep even if it's only for an hour," Jules said, attempting to direct Lily into the adjacent room while she continued to give him instructions. He knew her heart meant well, but all the stress and worry from her parents to Minisc would break even the strongest person mentally. She needed to rest.

Jules pulled off the corners of the bedspread as Lily crawled in.

"I promise I'll wake you if anything new develops."

A content sigh left Lily's lips as her head hit the pillow.

Finally, with his friend in bed, Jules left, closing the door quietly behind him before making his way back into the other room.

He felt the towels on Minisc's head with the back of his knuckle and decided they needed to be re-soaked. He dunked the towel and replaced it before looking over his friend's body.

"I know you're scared of losing people. You've always been worried about being alone in the world, no matter who is around you or for how long. But one day you have to accept Ignis can't be saved. He's gone. And that's alright, because you have me, and Lily, and your father. You're not alone anymore. We will always be with you."

Jules rested the towel on Minisc's head, a drop of water rolling down past his friend's eye as he spoke. It looked like a tear was being shed.

CHAPTER 22
TIME IS UP

WORD SPREAD FAST, AS DID ANYTHING INVOLVING THE Hero of Light. Waves of shock spread through the city as they caught wind of the violent attack on his home. Zale and company did their best to divert the news away from any injuries, but soon reports of the Hero's son being involved surfaced. Before long, theories were flying around on what took place that night in the forest. All of those could be dealt with over time though, at the moment they had to deal with the threat of Luminosa. The group they all deemed to be behind the act.

Outside of The Hero of Light, Luminosa and Brooklyn deemed two others major threats to their mission. The first being Coro, the dual Elementalist, and fighting weapon created by his father. The second would be the offspring of The Hero of Light. But both of them were now out of commission and with Don growing steadily weaker every day, they were free to move in and finish their third target.

Journalists were lining up en masse to document the historic attack on the world's hero and his family, but thanks to the EC they were only granted so much access. Ignis might have forfeited his privilege to be in Luminosa, but their goals aligned enough so that by taking out Minisc he handed the enemy a decisive victory, a fact that was not lost on Don, Zale or anyone else who found themselves in the middle of such a catastrophe.

Even if journalists were lining up in waves to document the damage, Don and Zale had done what they could to downplay the events, not mentioning a word of Luminosa or any other threat that could send the city into chaos. After all, if the public found out their multi-time saviour was no longer feared by those who tried to inflict chaos, how could they feel safe? It was for the best.

Aside from that, they also tried to keep Minisc's name as far from the headlines as possible. The reasons for this were two-fold. Even talking about Minisc's injuries sent Don into a state of shock and anguish. He couldn't possibly remain the symbol everyone expected him to be when thinking about his son fighting for his life. On top of that, Minisc had been taken to the same hotel that acted as a shelter for the Humans on Luminosa's hit list.

A hospital would have been more ideal, but Don knew the dangers that came with that. Someone had gone after Minisc specifically, someone who had power that even Don needed to be fearful of. A hospital would be too public, putting not only his son but everyone around him in danger as well. Instead, they placed him in the locked down hotel and brought help to him.

Don, Zale, and Dwayne - who came as soon as he heard the news - all stood on the ashes of what remained in the once-luscious forest. It took half the night to contain the blaze, but now it was safe for Don to return.

They walked through the forest, the range of destruction to such a serene place nauseating. It looked more like a ghostly forest where the trees were baron and the ground covered in burnt wood and ashy dirt.

They stopped at the scene of the crime. The area where Don found his son nearly engulfed by flames. Don had already witnessed the damage once, but staring at his late wife's shattered grave was a second gut wrenching experience.

Zale and Dwayne stood behind him, neither knowing what to say. There was nothing that could be said.

"Zale... your plan..." Don turned to the man who was left in confusion for a moment.

"Don..." He started, "We don't need to talk about that this second. You need some time to think, we need to see how Minisc is doing, we need to make sure we're prepared. Nobody is in any condition for the plan right now."

Don's voice became a little sterner, "That doesn't matter anymore. We're out of time."

Neither Zale nor Dwayne understood what the long-time guardian meant. The Humans were safe, and without the slime monsters on the loose, they outnumbered the core Luminosa members by the hundreds. Even if only a select few were on par with Minisc and Coro, in sheer numbers they should be able to win.

Zale shot the man a puzzled look, "What do you mean we're out of time? Look I know how personal this is for you, Don, but we've managed to cut Luminosa off at every corner. We have them pinned."

Zale had a point. After he talked to Coro and the two had a tough conversation about his health, the whereabouts of his father, and his mistakes, Olivia had arrived in his office. Not only did she manage to save Coro from Luminosa that night, but she also used her Sneak Shadow to place a tracker on Brooklyn. When Zale said they had Luminosa pinned, he meant it literally. They knew the group's exact whereabouts and were preparing a counterattack. Don knew this information as well.

Don could have chosen to get angry, to lash out wanting a personal vendetta to bring down those who targeted his son, who burned down his home, but he didn't. It wasn't his style. Cooler heads would always prevail and so Don spoke with a clear and honest message.

"Dwayne, do you remember when this all started... the night you showed up at my door and asked me to return as The Hero of Light? To join the EC once more to help stomp out Luminosa for good, and I hesitated? My strength was fading, and I could feel it. Howland made that clear when he taught me how to master Celestial Light. When I fought Dusk, I thought that was the end of my strength for good, but thanks to Minisc I managed to rekindle it for a little while longer... but no more. And Luminosa knows this. Dusk suffered the same decay, and I have no doubt he's informed his apprentice of my vulnerability. They don't fear me. That's why they attacked. I always knew this day would come, the day I would no longer be able to protect the world anymore. When I stepped away after Erika's death, I guess in part it was so I could prolong my ability to continue acting as The Hero of Light when it was needed most. But once Minisc started school and Luminosa rose from the ashes, I made a decision. I would use every last ounce of my strength to make sure my son and his friends lived in the world they deserved, and not like the one we grew up in."

"So what does that mean? You're going to sacrifice the last of your strength to beat Luminosa yourself?" Dwayne asked.

Don looked at his friends and colleagues with a sombre smile. He had come to terms with the decision long before they or anyone else even thought about it. Negotiations were out of the question. This was the way it was meant to be.

Even so, Dwayne wanted to put up an argument, while Zale stayed quiet.

"We can't put this all on you again, Don. This is nothing more than a death wish. You can't win alone, and you know it. Think about your son. He has grown into an incredible Elementalist with your blood flowing through him, and if Luminosa did do this then they had no issues nearly killing him. What am I supposed to tell him when he wakes up? That his father went on a suicide mission and died trying to protect his son? He's already lost his mother, don't leave the poor kid without a father as well…"

"I'm not going to die, Dwayne. I'll win. Exactly for the reason you just said. For Minisc. So that I can continue to watch him grow up as the son I am so proud of. I know the strength Minisc has within him. He will surpass me one day, I know that as fact, but it's my job as his father to protect him."

Dwayne shot Zale a look begging him to speak some sense into the man, but for once Zale ignored the request.

"Fine, you win. It will take five days, but I'll set up our defence forces around the city to make sure we don't have a repeat of three months ago. Just remember, Don, we won't get a second chance at this, so you better be prepared."

Zale turned away grabbing Dwayne as he left Don at the crime scene.

Don bent down on one knee, picking up a small chunk of rock that was chipped off the remaining grave of his wife. From a glance, recognizing it to be a tombstone would be impossible. The damage was well beyond repair. However, it served its purpose in the end. He looked at the wreckage and then to the sky.

"I know you're out there Erika. Thank you, for keeping our son safe. For watching over him... You saved him... and now it's my turn. I promise I won't let your efforts go to waste. I love you..."

CHAPTER 23
A FIERY REVENGE

BROOKLYN SAT WITH HIS FEET UP ON THE TABLE LEANING back in his chair. He gripped a newspaper with glee, the front picture showing remains of the Premier household. His lips grinned with delight at the sight.

"This is too perfect. With the Premier kid done in by Ignis, and the doctor's kid out of the picture, all that remains is The Hero of Light. And once he's gone, nobody will stand between me and my new kingdom."

On the table in front of him sat a little black device which Bex picked up and examined.

"Get your grubby hands off of that Bex." Brooklyn glared. The girl pouted, placing it back on the table before reaching for a rotten apple and taking an enormous bite.

"What makes you so confident The Hero of Light is gonna show up?" Bronx asked.

"It's simple. He knows his power is waning. With his son left for dead, he doesn't have any choice but to try and stop us before his clock runs out. The Doctor confirmed this little device is a tracking signal, which means they know exactly where we are, and I plan to use that to our advantage."

"What if they bring more backup?" Bex asked.

"That won't be our problem. Because we won't be here for them to find us."

Bex and Bronx both looked at their leader, raising eyebrows.

"That brat Ignis wants the Hero dead, right? And so do I. So why should I have to get my hands dirty if someone else is willing to do the work for me? I say we sit back and watch the fireworks display ensue."

"But how do you know Ignis is going to go after The Hero of Light, or even when for that matter?" Bex asked.

"I think we can arrange that..."

Nearly five days passed and Minisc showed no signs of waking up. Lily and Jules continued to keep a close eye on him along with doctors that Zale brought in, and all results were positive, if not minimal. His body was recovering well, but the way he squirmed in his sleep told a different story.

Coro as well, although awake and alert, had his own critical damage and remained unaware of the situation unfolding. He wanted to find and stop his father, however both Olivia and President Osiris agreed if he were told about the plan, they could not trust him to avoid doing something reckless.

The EC had the location of Brooklyn, which appeared to be in a small area off the outskirts of town entirely covered in forestry.

In an ideal world, Don would have the backup of not only his son, but Coro as well. Despite their age, there were no arguments they were two of the strongest Elementalists available and also had the experience in life-or-death battles to comprehend the dangers. However, both were out of commission.

Unfortunately, the EC, although filled to the brim with talented Elementalists, was not equipped for a life and death battle. Almost none of them even dabbled in the sort of battles that Don or those around the man endured in his years. They would be overwhelmed in seconds, and that meant needless lives would be lost due to nothing more than arrogance. If they were going to do this, they would do this right. Taking the days they had, monitoring that Luminosa remained put, Zale set up his personal at different points in the city making sure no attacks or rampages could erupt again. With them in place, the day of reckoning came, and Don marched his way to the signal of Luminosa's location.

In the untouched forests a few miles off the city outskirts, Don continued through the woods. The overcast clouds suggested a foreboding fight ahead, but there was no turning back now.

Since the day Don started training his son, he could see an incredible power stored away. A power that would be able to overwhelm any threat this world could offer. But even then, he worried about putting such pressure on the boy. It wasn't by choice that his son faced so many difficult battles, but each time the boy survived through strength and determination, traits Don would need to display now if he were to succeed in giving his son the world they both wanted.

His body began to shake. Was he nervous? Was it his body trying to tell him he wasn't ready? Or worse, telling him the last of his strength was no more? This was new to him. The Hero of Light, scared of a fight.

He stepped into a clearing much like his own makeshift battle arena, only this one was far from cultivated. In the middle sat a small black device half buried in the dirt. At first, Don couldn't tell what it was, but as he stepped closer, he began to recognize the shape of the device. An uncomfortable chill added to his suspicion and slowly it dawned on him they were set up.

The one to step out from behind the trees shocked him more than he could fathom.

"So you were actually arrogant enough to show up... I shouldn't be surprised, playing a pretend hero all these years has gone to your head, I'm sure." Out from the trees walked Ignis. He wore a long red coat with a single button in the middle tying it together. The hair covering his eyes couldn't hide his menacing look. He marched into the arena showing no fear of the Hero. He had no reason to be afraid.

On the other hand, when Don saw Ignis, the pieces fell into place. Everything about Minisc's injuries, the engulfing flames of the forest, all of it added up. Rage made his blood curdle and he gripped his fists. He needed to stay calm to bring out what remained of his power, but the unbearable fury of seeing his son's attacker face to face proved a tough task. He knew of Ignis' hatred towards him, it was hard not to be aware. He could recall his wife having to console their son for days if not weeks after Ignis announced his hatred for their family.

For a long time, the loathing appeared to be nothing more than a petty grudge from a young, misunderstood boy. Sure, he picked on Minisc, and Don always wished he could put an end to his son's torment, but for years Minisc remained adamant for him not to get involved. They both believed it to be a coping mechanism and eventually the grudge would subside.

Unfortunately, after Dusk attempted to resurrect his reign of power, Minisc informed his father of Ignis' betrayal. At that point, even with Dusk defeated they knew things would steadily grow worse. Still, in Don's mind, the biggest threat was not Ignis. Brooklyn as the chosen heir apparent for Dusk needed to be stopped above all else so Ignis could not be his biggest priority. Minisc did not necessarily agree with those views, but he knew his father had a point. On top of that, it meant he still had hope in his heart. A belief that Ignis could change given time and realize the errors he'd made.

Although Minisc didn't have the heart to fight, Don lacked any such compassion. Not after seeing his son's condition.

"It was you, wasn't it, Ignis?" He growled, "You were the one who ambushed Minisc, the one who burned everything to a crisp and left my son within an inch of his life."

Ignis glared at the man and spat, "That was his own fault. You were my target. He just got in my way. But that doesn't matter because you're here now and it's just the two of us. So now I'll prove you're a fake once and for all by killing The Hero of Light."

An interesting part of Ignis' sentence caught Don's attention. His eyes had been shifting from tree to tree looking for other members of Luminosa, expecting an ambush, but Ignis implied otherwise.

"What do you mean we're alone? You expect me to believe you don't have the likes of Luminosa around with you? That's laughable."

"The only laughable thing is you thinking I would ever need the likes of those pathetic Elementalists to kill you. They're long gone from here. Probably hiding somewhere, knowing them. This fight is mine and mine alone. I don't give a damn about their stupid Elemental Kingdom; the only thing I want is to expose the world to the fraud that you are."

Normally Don would never be goaded by such words. He might have been beloved by most, but there were always some who believed him to be a phony. It came with the territory, but the anger that spawned from his son who remained in a secretive hotel being tended to still linger. Rational thought was not something he could use right now.

He clenched his fist feeling light begin to glow off it, "Fine, if it's a fight you're looking for, then it's a fight I'll give you. But I warn you, unlike Minisc I won't be holding back. I'll put an end to this once and for all." Perhaps Luminosa had escaped to live another day, and he would not last long enough to bring them down. Their true plan had backfired. However, he could still protect his son from the monster who harmed him. That would be a worthy last use of his power.

The wind around them rippled as the two wasted no time unleashing their full power. Don knew the young Elementalist was strong, his display of willpower and feisty tenacity at the Tournament of Elements showcased those traits to the world, but that level of skill would never come close to handling The Hero of Light. Strength fading or not. But due to Minisc's lack of will when fighting Ignis, Don had no way of gauging the boy's power. He would have to go all out and leave nothing to chance.

"This is it, Ignis. My full power." The ground below them started to shake with rocks dancing in the air as they rose. Waves cut through the air slicing nearby trees clean in half as Don pushed his body as far as it could go. "Celestial Light 100%!"

Ignis' eyes became cross, "You can't fool me. What you call 100% power is nothing compared to me. Now prepare to die!"

"We'll see about that!" Don roared.

With the two ready, Ignis dashed forward, his fists bursting into flames the way Don had seen countless times before. He coated himself in a thin barrier of light while also dodging the incoming punch. The speed of Ignis caught Don by surprise. Just like Minisc, it appeared he'd been training hard. Don narrowly dodged before stretching his hand out and firing a ball of light at Ignis. His attack would be punched away with ease though, and the two skidded past each other to a stop.

Don typically always fought with a smile on his face. Not because he enjoyed the thrill of a bout, but because he knew the most intimidating weapon in his arsenal was to show his opponent no fear. To show them his unwavering confidence. In this fight he had no smile, no heroic demeanour. He fought with fire and anger that consumed his strength far faster than anyone could have anticipated. He charged at Ignis with sparks shooting off his body as he moved, the famous gold aura around him dancing like a fire in the wind. He could barely control it, but he failed to notice. His desire to stop Ignis placed blinders on the feelings in his body.

He threw everything he had at Ignis, with balls of light flying all over the battlefield. His golden fist cut through the air sending shockwaves with each punch, but with nothing to show for it.

"This is pathetic, even your lousy son put up a better fight than this," Ignis snarled.

He fired off a series of fireballs into the sky, each one spitting out smaller flames that Don had to dance around. As they did, the forest around them quickly became engulfed in flames. Don was finding himself in the exact scenario Minisc found himself in the night prior.

Is he really this strong... no it can't be that... it's me...? I've lost all remains of my power. Just as Howland told me I would...

Don lost focus at his sad realization and one of the balls of fire struck his knee. He dropped down, gritting his teeth as he reached for the wound. He looked up seeing Ignis march towards him. Not a shred of decency or compassion in his eyes. Only hate.

"Everything that's happened in my life. The dreams that were stolen away from me. The family I lost. All of the years of suffering I endured because of you. All so you could be praised as a hero. I'm the only one that knew. The only one who saw the truth. You let my parents die so you could live. They sacrificed everything and for what? For you to march around and take all the glory. I've dreamed of this day for so long, Hero of Light. Now say goodbye." Ignis raised his hand to his wounded and exhausted counterpart. A swirl of flames began to spin in his hand as he created fires from the depths of hell. With one final attack, he would finally extinguish the Hero of Light once and for all.

"You're right, Ignis, I did fail you. I failed you and I failed your parents. I wanted to save them. More than anything I tried to keep them alive. But they chose to lay down their lives so everyone else could go on living. You're right, they're the real heroes, not me. I know for a child to hear his parents died such a noble death brings no solace but killing me or anyone else will never be the answer. They fought to protect others, to make sure the world they left behind for you was better than the one we as Elementalists inherited."

Don could feel the emotions of that dark day starting to boil inside him. He may have lived but that didn't mean he left unscathed by the memory. The anger he felt towards Ignis vanished, if only for a second, replaced by regret. Since that day he knew he failed. He failed to protect them, and because of that, he found himself at Ignis' feet. In a way, all of this was caused by him.

However, unlike his son, he couldn't let emotions get in his way. He wished Ignis chose another path, but he didn't. He chose to kill those not only uninvolved with the situation altogether but in an act to help Luminosa as well. And of course, he could not forget the condition of his own son. His time as The Hero of Light was not over yet, not while he continued to draw breath.

As Ignis prepared his final strike, Don raised his hand, meeting the blaze with a burst of light. He winced in agony, feeling the jolt run through his arms, but he held on. The blast grew bigger and bigger, separating them further, but as it did, the energy within the attacks grew. Both were holding on for dear life now. If one attack overtook the other, mortal damage would likely be inflicted.

Unfortunately, the stalemate confirmed the information they both already knew.

"So those losers weren't bluffing, your power really is gone. Or do you refuse to fight me like your son? Is it because you know you deserve to die?" Ignis started to push the man back with the same overwhelming flames that defeated Minisc.

I need to push further... for Minisc... for Erika... for this world... Sparks shot off Don as he forced his way forward. "This path you've chosen, Ignis, it's not what your parents would've wanted. They loved you so much and they wanted you to make this world a better place. To continue living for what they died for. But you're throwing it all away for nothing."

"I am making this world better. Without you!"

Even with Don pushing himself to the limit, his element was like a match now burning from both ends. The feeling of mortality washed over him as he could see the inevitable around the corner. The rage spurring Ignis on proved too much for him to handle. He could feel the power slipping and as he did the flames inched closer to him. Glistening sweat dripped down his face as heat from the front and back burned inches from his face.

"Any last words, Hero of Light?" Ignis growled.

I'm sorry Minisc... please forgive me... I'll see you soon Erika.

"Block it!"

"Don we're here!"

Before Don's defences shattered, Jules and Lily shot through the forest onto the battlefield. Water and wind blocked the flames before an eruption of mist followed. Ignis flew back, skidding to a halt, while Lily waved as much water around her body as possible, casting it off in every direction to douse the flames.

The ground began to crack as Dwayne roared onto the scene with Yuri close behind.

"What are you guys doing? You shouldn't be here. It's too dangerous." Don said, looking around at those who arrived in the nick of time.

"You didn't think we'd actually let you march to your own death, did you?" Dwayne smirked. He walked up to his friend and stuck his hand out.

"But why is only Ignis here? Where are the others?" Yuri asked.

"Luminosa fled. They left Ignis to kill me," Don said. Dwayne threw his arm around the man's shoulder and started to limp to the back of the field. Yuri joined in before they all turned to the boy at the other end of the battlefield.

Ignis seethed, gnawing his teeth as small sparks of fire erupted from his hands. He glared at Don's rescue party before turning his attention back to the only one he truly cared about killing.

"You coward!" He yelled. "You had backup this whole time..."

Before Ignis could launch an attack a swirl of wind trapped him. He struggled, squirming in an attempt to break free as Jules narrowed his eyes.

"What's wrong, Ignis? Don't like when someone sneaks up on you? The way you snuck up on Minisc? Well too bad. Unlike him I don't have any pity for you. You're nothing more than a monster who's been a pain in our sides for far too long." There was a different tone to Jules' words as he spoke. Unlike the rage plaguing him when fighting Bex, this time the hate was subtle. He was in control of his emotions.

As Ignis tried to break free of his imprisonment, a blast of water crashed into his chest sending him smashing into a tree. Lily huffed as she lowered her hands, the same calm anger that Jules displayed followed in her words.

"For all the pain you've caused people, the lives you've needlessly taken, Minisc still tried to save you. He wanted to believe in you so badly, and you've been so blind with hate that you could never see him constantly reaching out. You're alone in this world because you chose to be and for no other reason. Not your parent's death, not because of The Hero of Light, it's all because of you!"

Don got a safe distance away before dropping to one knee again. He winced before looking up at Dwayne and Yuri. "You need to get everyone out of here. Ignis is stronger than he looks. Lily and Jules aren't prepared for this. We need a new plan."

The ground beneath them shook and even the temperature in the steaming misty forest rose.

Yuri looked back at his brother and Lily before saying, "I don't think that's gonna be an option. Once this fight starts, the only way to end it will be by beating Ignis."

"Damn it, I thought my power would last longer than it did. I didn't expect things to fail so quickly..."

Dwayne stood to his full height. "Well we don't have time for guilt now, come on Yuri we need to help the kids."

"Right." Yuri nodded.

Back on the dampened battlefield, Ignis should have been at a distinct disadvantage thanks to the moist surroundings, but as he picked himself up and hunched over the sparks in his hands only became more intense. Small popping sounds rung out as he glared at Jules first then Lily.

"Minisc got what he deserved. Every dream I had he stole from me. He lived the life I should have been living. But now I can show him just what it's like to have everything taken from him. And once I'm done with you two, I'll finish that damn Hero off as well."

Jules, Lily, and even Dwayne were all good matches for the hot headed fire Elementalist with elements that could be used at a distance. But they quickly learned why Don struggled so much. Ignis began launching fiery attacks at his opponents with relentless vigour. Lily and Jules did their best to hold off the incoming waves while Dwayne and Yuri went in for quick hits but with little success.

Ignis moved too fast and used the flames to wall off any help as he did. Lily would put the fires out as fast as she could, but by the time she did, Ignis would start his new attack. He would lay everything down to win this fight.

Ignis dodged swiftly, and then landed a punch into Dwayne's stomach before tossing him into Yuri. Next, as Jules trapped him in a vortex, the wind turned into a flaming tornado before evaporating into nothing.

The battle only lasted minutes, but Ignis quickly disposed of

Jules as well, burning his leg and arm with a fireball causing the boy to yell in agony.

"Jules!" Lily yelled, directing her water on Ignis to draw him away. Except he would not take the bait. He had Jules, Dwayne, Yuri, and Don all in his sights and with the four unable to escape, his entire body began to shimmer in a crimson red.

"Now say goodbye!" He roared, thrusting his hands forward. He unleashed volcanic fires the likes of which only a few could produce.

Everyone shut their eyes raising their arms in protection although they knew it would do nothing to help.

"No! I won't let you hurt them!" Lily cried out as she slid in front of her friends. A wall of water formed from her body, absorbing the hell flames turning her shield into a hot spring.

"Lily?" Jules whispered. Everyone watched in shock as they observed the girl standing in front of them expelling whatever strength remained in her body to protect them.

"I won't let you hurt any more of my friends Ignis. I refuse!" She cried out. Her legs clattered and her arms felt like they were being ripped apart, not to mention the growing heat boiling her water made her body glisten in sweat. She could feel her feet digging into the brittle dirt as she inched backward.

But none of that mattered. Lily thought back to the day she first fought Ignis in training. She and Minisc came up with a plan to use her water shield and absorb Ignis' reckless but intense flames. It was at that point she first realized her weakness, and how that caused Minisc to sacrifice himself to save her. Since then, she never wanted to be seen as a burden again. A person who caused her friends to get hurt due to her weakness. She might not have been strong enough back then, but this time she had no choice. She couldn't give in and let the flames through.

Lily dug her heels deeper into the dirt refusing to budge, but everyone could tell she couldn't withstand the raw power, and with nobody able to join her they all knew it was only a matter of time.

"Face it, you can't win! You'll meet the same fate as that stupid friend of yours!" Ignis roared.

"That stupid friend believed in you to a fault. He refused to give up on you no matter the situation, so if that makes him stupid then I'll take a stupid Minisc over a selfish monster like you any day." Lily cried out pushing her hands forward. But no matter the desire in her heart she couldn't maintain protecting everyone.

I can feel it slipping, I can't hold him off any longer, Lily squeezed her eyes shut. She began to fall backwards as the shield of water imploded granting access to Ignis' flames.

"..."

Suddenly, a blinding light came crashing from out of nowhere, sending shocks through the battlefield. A cloud of dust formed causing everyone to begin coughing and attempting to find the cause. Once the flash of light disappeared, those who lay on the ground finally caught a glimpse of the source.

"It can't be..." Jules whispered.

"I should've known..." Dwayne smirked before resting his head back on the dirt.

Lily's eyes fluttered open as her body felt weightless. She was staring up at the sky but with a shadow peering over her. Her body began to shake uncontrollably as tears sparkled in her eyes.

"You're okay..." She whispered. Holding her in a bridal carry was Minisc.

"I told you I would always be there for you, didn't I? Now it's my turn." He wore that warm comforting smile that always put Lily at ease. He gently placed her on the ground next to Jules before saying, "Thank you, Jules. When I was unconscious, I could still hear what you said. I could feel it... what you said was true; I was still scared of being alone. I was scared to accept the Ignis I knew was gone. But you're right. I'm not alone. I have you and Lily and my father, and so many more."

Minisc turned and shot Ignis an intimidating glare. He stepped forward with confidence he had rarely displayed. Even Don picked up on his son's change in demeanour.

For Ignis, his face turned pale white like he'd seen a ghost. He pointed his finger at Minisc and said, "You... but I left you to burn in that forest. There's no way you could've possibly survived that."

Minisc lifted his glowing gold arm examining the still bubbling and scared skin. "I owe a lot of people for that one. It seems you're not as good at killing me as you think."

Minisc continued walking further from his friends and closer to Ignis. Yet as he approached the battlefield, Don and company could feel the sense of despair washing away. For Don especially. Seeing his son bathed in the same incredible aura often associated with The Hero of Light was surreal. No concerns about the world, or fear for his son's safety. At that moment he had seen the outcome before it happened. Like it was a foretold prophecy. For the first time in his life, he knew what it was like to be on the other side. The wounded staring up at a hero who would save the day. His own son, a true hero.

Dwayne lifted Don to his feet and when the two looked at each other, he asked, "This is it, isn't it? He's tapped into that hidden potential of his?"

Don nodded. The magical glimmer, the fluidness in his movements, there was no mistaking it. Minisc indeed was fighting free of the burdens he carried. He was ready for the next steps.

Minisc stood firm in front of his friends and said, "Lily, Jules, can you guys get everyone as far away from here as possible? I don't want anyone else getting hurt because of me."

Normally the two friends would never dare let Minisc go one on one with Ignis, and especially not after the injuries he'd already sustained a few days ago, but they could sense something different this time. The same innate feeling Don witnessed. Minisc was no longer holding back. He was prepared to stop Ignis in his tracks no matter the cost.

"Okay," Jules nodded.

"Make him pay Minisc!" Lily yelled.

Lily and Jules could feel their muscles cramping up, but they forced their way over to the others. Lily helped Dwayne first so that he could help Don up while Jules helped Yuri. In reality, there were no safe places to escape to, but the further away from Minisc they got, the easier his life would be. The less he had to split the focus between his friends and Ignis, the more capable he would be to draw on his full power.

Minisc focused his attention back on the boy, who remained in shock. "I told you, Ignis, I won't let you hurt anyone else, least of all the people most important to me. I'm stopping you right here, once and for all."

Ignis spat at the dirt and then cracked his knuckles before glaring at Minisc. "Fine have it your way, I'll kill you all!"

Minisc braced himself for the fight of his life. The one battle he refused to accept despite the common sense tied to his brain. Holding on to the hope Ignis' heart could somehow reawaken from the depths of darkness that consumed him. But now Minisc understood the real reason why he held onto that naive belief for so long. It had nothing to do with Ignis.

It all stemmed from the feeling of being alone. The fear of being left by those he cherished most. It blinded him to the truth of the matter. He was not alone, he had Lily, Jules, his father and so much more to be grateful for. People who would never leave him the way Ignis did. And he refused to lose that at the cost of Ignis. With that fueling his inner strength, he tapped into the power he would use to put Ignis down once and for all.

Ignis charged forward, throwing haymaker punches with flames gripped in his palms. "You should've stayed down while you had the chance. You could've run away and lived that pitiful waste of life you wanted. But you can never help yourself. You just have to try and save people. And now you're willing to sacrifice your own life in your father's battle. Fine then! Prepare to meet your end. Minisc, this time you won't come back!"

Minisc exploded forward with rays of light shooting off his body as he moved. Before anyone could blink, Ignis let out a gasp as the air from his lungs shot out like a puff of smoke.

"You always talked about being a hero when we were kids, Ignis, you wanted to be the strongest. But you never understood why people idolized my father, and I guess in a sense I didn't either.

It's not because of his power. It's how he protects people, how he brings calm to those who are scared. How he would never leave someone in need of help. You might have power, but you don't have the heart he has. I can see that now. So I'm done holding back. No more hoping you will change your ways. No desire for things to go back to the way they were. Not anymore."

Minisc started his frontal assault of Ignis. Each punch he threw, each blast of light he unleashed had an incredible shine to it. Ignis tried to dodge, but the gleaming light enveloping Minisc's fists flashed with each staggering hit he landed. Rays of light burst through the air with each attack. Ignis had never seen such power, such tenacity in his life. And never from Minisc. It was as if the boy had undergone an entire personality change. The kind-hearted, peace-loving boy who wanted nothing but to help his friends had washed away, and left in the aftermath was an entity pushed past his wit's end. He refused to sacrifice the world all to give in to a grudge that one person held.

Each punch Minisc landed sent stinging shocks through Ignis' body. Either his eyes were playing tricks on him or Minisc was moving so fast he could only see the remnants of faded images.

"I get it now. The only way to truly free you from your pain is to stop you," Minisc said.

If Ignis' acts were what sprung Minisc to a new level of power, then Minisc's words were starting to do the same to Ignis. Hearing the heroic speeches of someone he hated only made the fire in his body burn hotter and with more hatred.

Minisc fired a Lum Bomb towards Ignis, but he deflected it away and dashed forward. This time it was Minisc's turn to feel the gut-wrenching pain of wind being forced out of his body. He flew through the air from the hit.

"You have no chance!" Ignis launched a stream of fire towards his opponent but with unwavering determination, Minisc managed to maneuver his way around the blast with a well-timed shield of light. He slid to the ground, getting to his feet with no signs of slowing down. Neither were willing to give an inch, let alone concede defeat.

"You have no right to lecture me about what it's like to be a Hero. You and your father are nothing more than fakes and I'll wipe you from the face of the earth to prove it!" Ignis thrust his hands forward, spitting out a fireball towards Minisc, this one big enough to consume his entire body.

Minisc remained resolute, cocking his arm as the hurling ball of fire came rushing at him and with one golden punch, he evaporated the ball into nothing.

Too bad for Minisc that fell right into Ignis' trap. The enraged boy burst through the smoke striking Minisc clean in the cheek. Minisc once again flew through the air before hitting the ground, creating a dust cloud that blocked all vision.

Ignis growled, "I've waited so long for this moment. The last person I'll ever let ruin it is you!" While marching forward.

"He's down!" Yuri yelled.

He couldn't see Minisc through the dust clouds, but it looked like a horrific hit.

Dwayne sighed, "He never stood a chance against Ignis. Not with the injuries still lingering. This fight was over the second Ignis ambushed him in the forest." He and Yuri both stood side by side with the rest of the group. They wanted to fight, they wanted to save Minisc, but they knew they would only get in the way at this point.

"You're wrong, Dwayne. I know Minisc, this is far from over," Jules said, refusing to give in.

"Yeah, Minisc still has a lot of fight left in him. He might be hurt but he won't give up. He'll win. He has to." Lily clapped her hands together praying to the sky.

"The kids are right. Look." Don weakly gestured to the settling dust cloud where a hazy shadow could be made out. The silhouette began to stand up although hunched over. Then with a surge of energy that rippled through the air, the dust cloud cleared and revealed Minisc.

"Okay, that one hurt," Minisc muttered to himself. He tried to catch his breath. The surging power burned through his energy supplies at a rapid rate. But even with his body covered in streaks of blood and unquestionable injuries lingering, he still carried the look of hope in his eyes.

"You still don't get it, Minisc. I never joined Luminosa because I wanted to be like them. Wiping Humans off the face of the earth is pointless. It won't change a thing as long as The Hero of Light lives. No, I joined for one reason and one reason only. Power. When I saw the power Coro displayed in the Tournament of Elements, I knew I couldn't win. No matter how hard I trained, his power far surpassed mine. And that meant so did yours. It wasn't just his dual elements. Two elements instead of one is only useful if done right. But when I finally learned how Coro became that strong, I pursued it. That's when I realized the path I chose would be dictated by Luminosa. All so that I could be granted the power I would now use to destroy you and your family. Thanks to Dr. Jarrad I'm now stronger than you could possibly imagine, and that makes me invincible."

Minisc burst forward throwing a punch, but Ignis blocked it with ease. Before Minisc could react, Ignis landed three hits on him sending him backwards.

Minisc grabbed his left arm wincing. The pain stemming from his previous burns started to seep back in.

"Once I kill you, I'll eliminate Luminosa myself. Then I'll show the world what a true hero is. One with the power to defeat anyone who stands in his way."

"No Ignis, whatever power you have came at the cost of your own humanity. Through the lives you stole, and the pain you caused. So don't kid yourself. You're no hero. You're nothing more than a child who refused to let go of his pain. You might have more power, but it'll never make you a hero to the families you ripped apart without a shred of regret. The only fraud here is you. You will never be a hero, never!"

Ignis grew more infuriated listening to Minisc's words. Even the sound of his patronizing, heroic voice was enough to make the boys blood boil.

"That doesn't matter, I'll destroy anyone who can't see the favour I'm doing for them. Starting with you."

Ignis clapped his hands together and started spraying fireballs one after another. They bore down on Minisc in seconds and even those that missed headed straight for the group behind him in the distance. Minisc dodged the blasts before realizing his friends were also in danger. He turned around, but to his relief, Lily created a wall that doused the flames with ease.

"You're gonna have to do a lot better than that if you wanna kill me Ignis," Minisc goaded.

"You dare to mock me. I'll summon fires from the deepest parts of hell and burn you into oblivion," Ignis roared.

He jumped high into the air and before Minisc could even process the threat, flames began to spew from Ignis' body like a volcano. He tried to brace himself but Ignis sent out an unfathomable blaze that quickly absorbed him into the ground ready to explode through the core of the Earth.

"Minisc no!" Jules yelled.

Everyone else gasped in shock as the flames continued to crash into the ground.

All hope looked lost until Lily noticed a faint shadow still glowing in the flames.

"Wait no, he's still alive in there, but how?"

"Come on Minisc, fight it! You can win this, I know you can," Jules cheered. Everyone started to join in trying to encourage Minisc. He might have been alone in battle, but he was not alone in life. As long as those that stood beside him through thick and thin remained, he was never truly alone. A feeling that filled him with life.

Don whispered to himself, "I'm sorry, Minisc... I know I should be alongside you fighting this battle. This is never what you wanted, but now our hopes rest with you. I know you have the power within you. It doesn't matter how strong Ignis is, remember all the lives he's taken, all the pain he has caused. You can do this. I trust in you."

Minisc's friends were not the only ones that noticed him withstanding the flames. Ignis could see the faint glimpse of light peering out from the spiral as well, and it infuriated him.

"You think you can keep this up, fine, let's turn up the heat!" A second wave of fire ripped towards the ground causing the volcanic stream to grow twice in diameter. It pushed Minisc back down to one knee, fighting for his life.

The barrier of light kept him alive, but he could only hold on for so long, and with the unrelenting death bearing down on him if he faltered, there would be no coming back this time.

The heat sweltered with flashbacks of his night in the forest. But that was a different boy. One scared of losing something he never had. Not anymore though.

If my shield breaks, I won't be able to survive this time. Focus, you can do this. Not a single nerve in his body could keep from screaming. Yet those screams were not what he could hear through the unrelenting roars of the flames. What he could hear were the calls of his friends. Of his father.

"You can do this, Minisc, we believe in you," Dwayne called.

"Make him pay!" Yuri yelled.

"You're my best friend Minisc! I'll always be with you!" Lily added.

Hearing the encouragement, the racing in Minisc's mind began to slow. The heat closing in weakened and he started to raise his left arm, which was currently the only thing continuing to repel the flames around him, much to the shock of Ignis.

As his mind calmed, the pain faded into the background, and the strength of his friends began to flow through him. At that moment, he could feel nothing but the hopes of his friends, of his father, of the world. When he finally reached his full height a beam of light shot out, ripping through the volcanic flames striking Ignis out of the sky.

Ignis crashed to the ground in a heap. His body remained beat red from the raw taxation of his attacks, and he lay crumpled. He got to one knee, wiping the blood from his face as he fixed his gaze on Minisc. The boy was walking towards him, the energy radiating off him potent enough to taste.

"It was never supposed to turn out this way. I know what you've been through, Ignis. I know the loss you felt, the pain ingrained in you. In some ways, I guess it's my fault. I should've never let you push me away so easily, but we were children. I didn't know how to handle death any better than you did. I wasn't a good enough friend and I let you walk this path. I wish things could've been different, and I've learned my lesson from those days. But when you try to hurt my friends, my father, that's your own choice. I can't forgive that. I won't forgive that."

Minisc walked with unbridled conviction. When he stepped, Ignis flinched, perhaps for the first time in his life. He showed fear. Fear of the ones he hated. He showed fear of The Hero of Light.

"Why you, what is this... where do you keep getting this strength?"

"You know, I'm not really sure, but I guess this is what happens when you fight for those you love, rather than fighting to kill. I can feel it. The hope of everyone flowing through me, pushing me forward. It's a pretty special feeling. Too bad you'll never know."

"Even with all of them, you can't win!" Ignis thrust forward, flailing at Minisc, but with little effect. The bill for using so much energy was coming due, and now he could see trouble on the horizon.

"So here we are at the end, and nobody's coming to help you. Face it Ignis, this is one fight you can't win."

"I will finish you!" Ignis roared.

Minisc hopped back giving himself enough distance to brace for Ignis' last stand. He looked calm in the face of danger, his mind coming to grips with what had to be done. No more doubts plagued his heart, and finally the time for him to face up to the ending he so desperately wanted to avoid came to roost.

"You're wrong, Ignis, you're the one who's finished." Minisc blocked the incoming punch before cocking his arm back. He waited for the precise moment when his fist started shining like the sun, and with an emphatic roar Minisc yelled from the depths of his heart, "Solar Impact!" He thrust his hand forward and a beam of light exploded through Ignis' chest blinding the entire forest and beyond.

The monster who used to be Minisc's friend let out an agonizing cry of pain that cut to his core. When the light faded, Minisc stood in a giant crater. In front of him buried in the ground unconscious lay Ignis. The fight was over.

He dropped to his knees ready to collapse further but he held on, panting hard.

"I truly am sorry, Ignis, I wish things could have been different."

Once everyone realized the outcome of the battle, Lily and Jules were the first to run up to Minisc. They practically toppled over each other in excitement landing beside him and hugging him to near death.

"We did it! You did it. I'm so proud of you Minisc," Lily said through joyous tears.

"I never doubted you for a second." Jules grinned.

Yuri and Dwayne helped Don to his feet again. Amazingly the man looked in worse shape than his son. When Minisc got to his feet he walked over to his father, his emotions about to spill over as well. All he could do was wordlessly hug his father.

CHAPTER 24
A NEW ERA

THE AFTERMATH OF THE BATTLE WAS A WHIRLWIND. Just as Dusk before him, Ignis was taken to Penatang likely for the rest of his days. Even with that Minisc still could not look at the boy without welling up inside. He left that task to the EC and his father.

Although the history books would never know about what took place between Ignis and Minisc that day, those who bore witness to the epic clash would not soon forget.

Just like all the families affected by Ignis' selfish actions Minisc and his father had a few changes upon the horizon as well. For starters, they would need to rebuild their home. Thankfully, the EC was more than willing to chip in labour for their efforts. Second and far more concerning to the public was The Hero of Light's retirement. Some knew of his declining power, and rumours could always be found, but for most, they would be blindsided by the loss.

Along with that somewhere out in the world Luminosa still stood, but for another day they were safe.

Beautiful blue skies with not a cloud in sight stretched all across the city.

Once the smoke cleared and everyone was given a few days to relax and recover, the moment Don always knew was around the corner finally arrived. He stood in the doorway of the EC entrance wearing a black and grey suit with a small orange tie. The mass of cameras positioned below the marble steps could not see him, instead choosing to focus on the podium in which he would soon speak.

The crowd of reporters along with a large group of the public stood waiting for the announcement. Don knew they would be shocked and no doubt a little frightened for the time being, but he also knew they needed to begin moving forward. After his fight with Ignis, he had to accept that his time as The Hero of Light was done. He could no longer be the beacon of hope for those in fear. Yet that was okay because he knew the future was in good hands. In his son's hands, and in his friend's hands, they would handle whatever came their way, just as they had before.

Flashbulbs continued to go off as Zale's voice boomed out from the podium, but Don lacked any focus on the man's words. For the first time in his life, he grew nervous about speaking publicly. A natural born leader with charisma that drew so many to him, he spoke in public far more naturally than his son, yet this time he could feel the butterflies in his stomach. No matter how many times he went over his words, they slipped his mind just as quick.

Before he had too much time to think, he saw Zale turn and look at him. The man nodded and Don's heart jumped. But just as one would expect from The Hero of Light, he would face his next challenge straight on. He walked up to the wide wooden podium and took a seat next to Zale. He stared out, ignoring the cameras and dazzling lights to see his son in the front row. Beside him stood Lily Jules and Yuri. They were all smiling and encouraging Don with their looks.

Don opened his mouth to speak, but nothing came out. His voice caught in his throat and he froze. The words refused to leave. Unsure, he locked eyes with his son. Once he did, everyone ceased to exist. It was only him and Minisc speaking, letting his son know the world would be safe.

"This will come as shock to most here, and it comes with great sadness, but as of today, The Hero of Light is officially retired," Don started. The crowd gasped, sucking the energy out of the city.

"I am no longer capable of being your beacon of hope. The one that can always be relied on to stomp out evil when it arises..." He looked down for a moment before looking back up, "...but that's okay. Because no matter what happens moving forward, when evil tries to thrive, I know that someone will always rise up to match it. Elementalists or Humans, we are all fighting on the side of peace. It is not dependent on one of us to uphold justice, but the responsibility of us all. As a society, we need to come together and show those who try to tear us apart that we will not be beaten so easily. Together we can continue to show this world that our light will never die."

Minisc listened to his father speak and several emotions came over him. Ever since childhood, he had a precarious relationship with his father's fame. It took his father away from him many times as a child, it created havoc on his childhood growing up and on several occasions, it nearly got him killed. Yet the respect he gained for his father grew immensely after Luminosa returned. He never understood the burden the man had taken on for the city, always being there when danger called. But watching him give his retirement speech for good this time, Minisc had a new vision of him. An image of someone he looked up to, someone who he was proud of. And most importantly, someone he could call his father.

After the press conference ended, everyone returned to the sight of the new Premier household. It would be built on the same foundation as their old home, but this time with a few modern upgrades. Don and Minisc were both adamant they wanted to continue living in the same place, despite the lingering memories that came with it.

The house had not been entirely finished yet, but with the help of their friends, it would not take long. The new home, although more modern, mirrored the original quite well. The layout remained the same, only this time instead of old and dusty articles of The Hero of Light hanging up on the wall, there were newer, more crisp pictures. Pictures of Minisc and Lily, Don and Dwayne, and a group photo of everyone from the housewarming party.

Even Coro managed to arrive, despite his dislike of social interactions. His father, the man he hated, still remained in the shadows, but at least now he knew the truth. As far as he was concerned, his father was dead, replaced by whoever was there that night in the warehouse. He may have been left with no parents, but he found a new partner in Olivia who treated him like family. She might have been cold and unrelenting to the naked eye, but when push came to shove, she helped him with his demons and saved his life far more than his father ever had.

It had been 15 months or so since Minisc, Lily, and Jules first encountered Luminosa. From that time forward, their lives were forever changed. And even though uncertainty remained for them, the future looked bright. As long as they had each other the world would be their oyster.

With the celebrations gradually wrapping up for the night, Minisc had one more item to check off his to do list. He returned to the scene of the crime. Alone. The place where he could have been left for dead. The forest would take decades to grow back but just like himself, the forest he loved so much as a child proved resilient.

In the middle of all the stumps and charred remains, Minisc took a seat in front of a tombstone. It, much like the house, matched the design of the previous tombstone that had been destroyed by Ignis. Minisc looked at the elegant carvings of his mother's name on the slab of rock before smiling.

"Thank you, Mother," he started, "You saved me. I don't know what divine power you used to do it, but you saved me. I know you were beside me when I fought Ignis. The way you always have been. I love you. Thank you for everything."

When Minisc finished his speech, he heard powerful footsteps coming for him. This time he could relax though as he knew exactly who they belonged to.

"I figured I'd find you out here," Don said.

"Yeah, just wanted to talk to Mother for a bit," Minisc said sheepishly. Even if it was his own father, Minisc still felt embarrassed at times admitting his habit.

Don smiled warmly before wrapping his arm around his son's shoulder.

"I have no doubt she's listening to every word, watching over us both and keeping us safe as she always has. And you know what she wants to tell you?"

Minisc looked up at his father, "What?"

"She wants to tell you how incredibly proud she is of you. Of everything you've accomplished in your life but even more of the person you've become. I know it hasn't always been easy for you. From the day you were born, it's been a roller coaster, but every challenge you faced you gave it your all and put your heart into it until you succeeded. You never gave up no matter how bad you wanted to, and at the cost of yourself, you fought to protect everyone. We both could not be prouder of you."

Minisc hugged his father back, both of them taking a second to stare at the grave. Even in spirit, they felt like a family.

A content sigh escaped them.

Minisc did not know what the future would hold, and without his father being the Hero of Light, life was about to change. But for the time being, he had no interest in worrying about the future. For now, what he wanted more than anything was to crawl into his comfy bed and sleep away the night knowing he and his friends were safe once again.

ELEMENTS:
A TIME TO RISE (PREVIEW)

"NO MORE, I DON'T WANT ANYONE TO GET HURT." ROBIN whispered. In a split second Minisc thought he saw the boy glow white, and as he closed his eyes ready to absorb the pain he felt his body freeze. Robin placed his hand on the spike stopping it in place for fractions of a second but it was long enough for him to escape Minisc's arms as the older boy sailed off the cliff.

The spike flew over their heads, but only because Minisc was now weightlessly falling from over the cliffs and into the lake below.

"Robin!" Minisc yelled, holding his hand up to the sky. In an act of either desperation or fear Robin held his hand out towards Minisc as well, almost like he was waving goodbye. There were tears in his eyes. Then he disappeared, likely into the arms of Dominos. In that instant Minisc felt his heart rip in two.

Even as he fell, splashing into the water, something he vigorously hated, all he could do was try to hopelessly call out "Robin!" But it was no use. It was over. He started to sink into the water, much like his own despair. He knew in his mind he was falling deeper to his death, but he couldn't force his body to move. It was like the will had been drained from him. Everything went black.

AFTERWORD

HELLO AGAIN, THIS IS WILLIAM RICHARDS, AUTHOR OF *Elements Volume 3: Burning Hopes*. As I have made a habit of doing at the end of my books I wanted to take a moment to talk to you guys, not though a story but as a person.

First, thank you so much for taking the time to read Burning Hopes. This book especially meant a lot to me because for a moment I never thought it would see daylight. It was a challenge to try and piece all of my ideas together, and I worried so much that certain things were going to far out on a limb that they would betray the world I was trying to build. But in the end, I'm still happy with it, because it's something I put my heart into.

For those curious, the logic behind the title Burning Hopes was to signify both for Minisc, and for Coro, their need to give up hope. Hope for events to be different, hope they could change the people they wished to change. For them to move forward those hopes, those ideals, needed to be burned.

When I first started writing this series, I promised myself I would write three books. That was my goal, I would not quit until I managed to release three books and wrap up my series. I can say I have finally achieved that goal... however as you can plainly tell, Minisc's journey is far from over. There are many more adventures to be had, and more trials to face as we move further into a new era, and I hope you will continue to join in on the journey. I'd also like to thank StalkingP for once again doing the wonderful artwork for third book in a row. She's a joy to work with and her professionalism saves me a lot of headaches! So thank you for that! Along with that, thanks to my editor for helping to make sure I put out the best work possible. Also to my friends and family for working to keep my sanity as I question everything I do in life. So, with that, I will say thank you once again for the support, and I hope you will join me for the next installment of Elements. If you enjoyed this book, please consider writing a review on Amazon. com or Kobo.com. It would mean a lot to me and I make sure to read them all!

www.ingramcontent.com/pod-product-compliance
Lightning Source LLC
Chambersburg PA
CBHW030809210726
48290CB00002B/501